TWO TOMORROWS

A Novel

P.F. TORGERSEN

NORSETORG PRESS

Published by Norsetorg Press, Winchester, Virginia

Two Tomorrows: A Novel

ISBN 979-8-218-93803-1 (paperback)
Also available in eBook edition

Publication managed by AuthorImprints.com

For Lynn

For us there will always be a tomorrow

1

What are the odds we'll find what we're looking for . . . ?

BRIAN SLOWLY PUSHED his chair back away from the table. Sitting across from him was his wife, who was currently engaged in a discussion with the estate agent sitting to her right. On the table in front of them was another property portfolio, complete with additional pictures and a list of amenities. Brian glanced at his watch. It was now nine thirty in the morning, local Irish time, or four thirty in the morning in New Jersey, from where they had earlier taken an Aer Lingus flight. Brian tried to smother a yawn, not very successfully.

This must be property number four, he thought. Clare, his wife, had politely indicated that they were not interested in the other three properties they had reviewed, with comments about the individual properties either being "a tad too small," "a bit too cozy," or "not quite what we're looking for." Upon reflection, Brian had to agree. The estate agent had previously sent them material on the properties, but the included pictures must have been taken from very favorable angles. The additional pictures they were now looking at revealed a very different, less spacious story about each of the properties.

Brian did give Daniel, the estate agent, credit. The young man was not deterred by Clare's lack of enthusiasm for the properties. Brian figured that Daniel McGuire had to be in his early thirties. Athletic-looking, slightly shorter than Brian's six-foot, three-inch height, with a full head of brown hair, Daniel had an endearing smile. Earlier during introductions, Brian had noticed the man was smartly dressed in dark pleated pants and a blue button-down dress shirt with a very nice-looking plaid sportscoat, which was now draped across the back of his chair.

Brian gazed past Clare and into the interior of the nearly empty pub, where they had agreed to meet Daniel. *Too early for tourists or regulars.* A dozen or so empty tables over on the left-hand side of the pub waited patiently for the noontime patrons. The bar area was on the right, with beer taps standing at attention. On the wall behind the bar were bottles of different types of liquor neatly arranged in rows on glass shelves. There was that woman again, striding purposefully toward the bar with a tray full of clean pint glasses. Earlier, he had seen the same woman making repeated trips to the bar with trays piled high with silverware neatly bundled in cloth napkins.

"No Daniel, I'm afraid this house is—well—the house doesn't check all of the boxes," Clare said. She looked to her husband across the table. "Wouldn't you agree, Brian?"

"Yes, yes, you're right, definitely doesn't check all the boxes," Brian said, as he nodded his head in a display of spousal solidarity. Brian suspected his wife only drew him into the conversation to bring him back from wherever he had mentally disappeared to. She knew him too well.

He leaned back in his chair and regarded his dejected-looking wife as he reflected on the fact that they had struck out on all four properties they'd reviewed, and they were no closer to realizing their dream of owning a second home in Doolin, Ireland. On a previous trip to Ireland, they had stayed in this quaint village and had explored the immediate surrounding area. A short distance away were the towering Cliffs of Mohr, which provided an incredible view out into the vast Atlantic Ocean and the distant rugged Aran Islands. He and Clare thought this location would serve as a good base for future trips around Ireland and to other European countries. The proximity of Shannon Airport also factored into their decision to search for a house in this location.

As Daniel was placing the four property portfolios in his briefcase, Clare stood up and moved away from the table. She gazed around the pub with a somber expression. Brian smiled sadly as he looked at his wife. She couldn't hide her disappointment.

He marveled at how the woman he had married looked like she might be turning forty, but certainly not fifty. Tall, slender, with shoulder-length brunette hair and sparkling blue eyes. Even after six hours on the plane and another hour-plus in a car, she looked like she had just walked out of a boutique clothing store. Pleated black slacks, a light-blue blouse, and a flowered scarf draped across her right shoulder; she looked spectacular. *Too good for me. Well, let's not go that far*. He shook his head slightly.

Ever since receiving the very substantial inheritance and making their decision to look for a second house in Ireland, Clare had been over the moon with excitement, already planning out the interior furnishings for a house across the Atlantic. *Maybe something will turn up down the road.* Brian hoped so.

Truth be told, he was also extremely disappointed.

2

BOTH NOW STANDING, Brian and Clare patiently looked at the still-seated Daniel, who was intently focused on his phone and what appeared to be a text message. They wanted to thank Daniel for his time and effort and then see if they could possibly check in early to their room in the local bed-and-breakfast, so they could freshen up.

Daniel looked up from his phone and smiled. Clare and Brian glanced at each other, puzzled.

"Mr. and Mrs. Hansen, I just got confirmation of another house that'll be going on the market in the next couple of days. Something that I think will be much more to your liking!" Daniel said, with much enthusiasm. "Marketing hasn't been put together yet for the property, so I don't have any printed material to show you right now. However, the owners just texted me and they have agreed to let me give you a tour of the property. They're out of town, so we won't be inconveniencing them. Would you like to see the property?" Daniel asked hopefully, looking back and forth at the two individuals standing in front of him.

Brian and Clare looked at each other again. Both trying to hide their previous disappointment, they turned back to Daniel and gave a halfhearted nod.

"We've come all this way; we might as well see what the house looks like," Clare answered.

"Good. We'll take my car. The house is a very short distance away. I don't think you'll be disappointed," Daniel said, as he put on his blazer and grabbed his briefcase before ushering Clare and Brian through the pub's door and up the road to where his car was parked.

* * *

The car trip took less than five minutes from the parking area to their destination. They had traveled up the narrow lane that separated cozy cottages on one side from the shops and pub on the other side, before the lane turned sharply to the right. Further up on their right was the charming B and B where they had previously stayed and were scheduled to stay again for the next two nights. Just before the driveway for the B and B, the lane made a sharp left turn, which Daniel smoothly navigated, before the lane narrowed and transitioned from asphalt to gravel. To their immediate left was a large sweeping field of golden wheat, which sloped gently downward into the distance, where it was met by vivid blue ocean waters. To their right was another attractive B and B with a No Vacancies sign out front. After the B and B on their right, there was a small field where a half dozen or so seagulls were searching the recently upturned soil for a meal of grubs or worms. Another house appeared with a tall barnlike structure situated to the rear. On the far side of the house, open green pastures swept out into the distant horizon where sheep were grazing.

Brian figured they had traveled maybe about a mile, if not less, when they neared a house standing by itself up on the left-hand side of the road. The property was bordered by a low lichen-covered gray drystone wall. It seemed to Brian that all houses in Ireland were bordered by stone walls. This particular wall was interrupted by a driveway directly in front of the house. Daniel turned the car from the lane into the entrance to the property, the car vibrating as the tires crossed over a cattle grid. Once across the grid, the tires crunched on a pebble surface. Daniel brought the car to a stop in the driveway. Or was it the front yard? The entire area in front of the house, except for narrow garden beds up against the building and along the stone walls on the perimeter, was covered with a layer of small yellowish pebbles. *Low maintenance*, Brian thought. All three got out of the car and stood facing the front of the house.

There was no comparison between the structure that stood before them and the one-story houses in the photographs they'd viewed back in the pub. This was a rather large two-story building. The exterior walls were constructed of irregular field stone, and the roof was a dark-gray faux slate. Two large white garage doors, one on the far right of the building and another on the far left, bookended the house. Above both garages was a second story that extended across the entire front of the house. Three framed windows, one above each garage and one in the center of building, provided a break in the upper stonework. In between garage doors was a large bright-red door; a small concrete pad marked the entranceway. To the left of the front door was a large picture window with partially opened interior curtains.

Tilting his head to one side, Brian surveyed the house. Having the garages on either side of the house was a bit odd to him. He would have painted the front door a different color—a dark blue or maybe a dark green. He liked the fieldstone exterior. It brought back fond memories of his uncle's farmhouse back home, where he had spent many a summer as a boy.

Daniel led them across the pebbled driveway to the front door. They stepped inside to a small foyer and found themselves facing an interior door. Clare opened it to reveal a closet containing a couple of coats and empty coat hangers hanging from a wooden rod. While still in the foyer, they turned to their left and looked out onto an expansive open-plan area that extended from the front of the house all the way to the rear. The area was divided into two large sections, divided by the furniture arrangement. The front section presented a generous sitting area. Two dark-blue upholstered high-back armchairs were located by the very front of the house on either side of the picture window. A glass coffee table and a large red leather couch with end tables on either side were directly across from the armchairs. A roughly ten-foot-high white ceiling extended from the front and ended just beyond the couch, which provided the demarcation between the front and back sections of the open-plan layout. The walls in this area were a cream color.

The back half of the house was awash in sunlight, thanks to a series of eight-feet-wide by eight-feet-high glass window panels. Each panel was framed by two-feet-wide vertical wood columns and stainless-steel cross pieces. The wood columns rose upward two stories to a white vaulted ceiling that provided an atrium-like effect.

Brian and Clare moved toward the wall of glass panels and slowly turned around to survey the surrounding area. They tilted their heads back until they were able to see the ceiling, which had a slowly rotating ceiling fan as a focal point, and which was open to a partial second story above the sitting area in the front of the house, with a balcony that overlooked this back part of the house.

Impressive, Brian thought. *Incredibly impressive.* He would rely on Clare with her architectural background to pass judgment on the design of the house, but he already felt a sense of belonging. He liked the way the sunlight filtered into the house, providing a warm welcome. The expansive glass across the back invited the scenic outdoors into the living area.

The first-floor layout in this section was anchored by a large oak dining table with seating for twelve people, which served as a centerpiece for the area. Butting up against the back of the couch that divided the two areas was a long oak sideboard with inlay details that matched the dining room table, and which featured various items of china on display on top. The same polished wood flooring in the front section continued throughout this space to the rear wall.

They followed Daniel to the right rear side of the house and through an opening into the kitchen area. A large commercial stainless-steel refrigerator was located on the right, and a commercial stove with a gas stovetop range was to the immediate left of the entrance. A granite counter ran from the range across the back wall to a sink and then continued beyond the sink to a far wall. A wide, curtainless window above the sink provided a generous view out back. Maple cabinets were located both below the counter and above it on either side of the window. The kitchen floor was tiled. Brian noticed Clare nod her approval as she surveyed the area. On the right side from where they entered was a cozy area with a small kitchen table with seating for four. There was a single door beyond that. Brian opened the door, which revealed one of the two garages, crowded with moving boxes.

They retraced their steps out through the kitchen then across through the dining area, and Daniel opened a door to an area behind the other garage. Like the kitchen, the flooring was also tiled. On the left, another door opened to an uncluttered garage. Inside the area, along the wall backing up against the garage, was a wash sink, a commercial washing machine, and a commercial clothes dryer. The opposite wall had floor-to-ceiling storage cabinets.

"Let's go back to the dining area. I want to point out something to you both," Daniel said, as he ushered them out into the dining area and turned to face the front of the house. "Notice the set of stairs on either side."

Clare and Brian both looked from one set of carpeted stairs to the other, puzzled. As if on cue, they both asked the same question. "Why?"

"The people who built this house thought they might want to get into the B and B business on a limited basis," Daniel responded. Pointing to the set of stairs to the right, closest to the laundry area, he continued, "Those stairs lead up to what would have been the bedrooms for paying guests. There are two separate bedrooms, each with en suite bathrooms. There's also a large closet between the bedrooms where clean sheets, pillowcases and towels, cleaning supplies, and bathroom necessities can be stored."

"Did they?" Clare asked.

"Did they what?" Daniel politely asked.

"Did they ever have a B and B business?"

"I don't believe they did. That would have been the first owners of the property. The people who are selling the property now, the second owners, never did get into that business. Shall we take a tour of the upstairs?" Daniel asked, pointing to the stairs on the right.

Climbing the stairs toward the B and B side, Brian looked back down over the dining area. Once on the landing, he paused and looked out through the exterior glass wall in the back of the house. He took in the outdoor patio area, the field of wheat beyond, and finally the rugged cliffs to the left, and the vast blue ocean to the right in the far-off distance. He thought—

"Magnificent view," Daniel said, as if reading his mind. "You may notice there isn't any artwork on the walls. The current owners felt this view was their masterpiece. Shall we continue?"

Brian and Clare followed Daniel toward the back of the house and entered one of the bedrooms. The walls were painted robin's-egg blue. *Your basic B and B bedroom,* Brian thought. A made-up queen-size bed with fluffy pillows was on the right side of the room. Next to the bed on the far side was a nightstand with a lamp. On the near side of the bed was a small, cushioned chair. A small dresser was on the left side of the room. Next to the dresser was a rather narrow wooden wardrobe. No closet. There was a curtained window on the center of the wall opposite the door, and in the wall to the right of the bed was another window, with curtains drawn to either side, which revealed the sights out of the back of the house. A single overhead light and fan in the middle of the ceiling provided the main source of lighting. Another door next to the dresser on the left opened to a bathroom. In the bathroom, there was a toilet, a single-sink vanity with mirror, and a glass shower stall. A towel rack and a small waste basket was located on the near wall by the entrance to the bathroom. The bathroom floor was tiled, whereas the bedroom floor was wood with an area rug.

They left the room and returned to the landing and moved to the bedroom at the front of the house. The setup was basically a mirror image of the other room, reversed. This room was painted a soft yellow. The window to the left of the bed provided a view of the pebble driveway in the front of the house.

Once again on the landing, Daniel pointed out the door to the storage closet between the two bedrooms before moving on to galleried area in the front of the house, which served as a balcony looking over the first floor. The area was covered with a tan carpet. A small coffee table surrounded by three comfortable-looking armchairs provided a central focal point. Four-foot-high railings with decorative white wooden spindles bordered the entire landing. Daniel flicked on some light switches, which showed the recessed lighting that provided ample light all along the gallery. Floor-to-ceiling cabinets lined the wall, interrupted only by a large window in the center, which allowed a fair amount of light into this area.

Daniel opened the first door they came to diagonally across from where they started their upstairs tour. Once again, a relatively compact bedroom area and a separate bathroom. Moving along, Daniel pointed out that there wasn't a door for a storage closet on this side of the second level. He continued toward the back of the house and opened another door. This bedroom was obviously larger than the others. A king-size bed, with end tables and lamps on either side of the bed, was positioned to the right. The left wall had a waist-high dresser about six feet long. Directly above it, a window almost the same length as the dresser provided a panoramic view of the outside behind the house. A door next to the near side of the bed led to the bathroom. This bathroom was larger than the other bathrooms they'd seen. Similar set up, except there was room for a separate bathtub/jacuzzi. The walk-in shower was also larger than the other showers, and there was a double vanity with a large mirror. The lack of hallway closet on this side of the house allowed for the larger bedroom and bathroom.

Brian noted Clare's slight frown as she finished surveying the bedroom and the bathroom. He looked around and couldn't see anything wrong. Compared to the other bedrooms and bathrooms, he thought this area provided a very comfortable space. It wasn't enormous by any means, but who needed enormous? He was about to ask Clare what was wrong when she turned to Daniel and started to ask, "Where is—"

"I know what you're going to ask," Daniel interrupted. "You're wondering what happened to the closet space. Rather than take up valuable space in this bedroom, the initial design called for using the upright cabinets on the front landing for the storage of clothing. A little bit inconvenient, but a practical solution to maximize floor space for the primary bedroom." Brian looked around the room again—*no closets*. Brian could see that Clare was considering Daniel's explanation. If it was a dealbreaker, she would let them know. "Of course," Daniel said, "you could always turn the bedroom next door into a walk-in wardrobe." Brian imagined Clare would find that much more palatable.

Having concluded their visit upstairs, the three of them proceeded down to the dining room, using the opposite set of stairs from which they had ascended to the upper level.

"Well, what do you think?" Daniel asked, as he looked from Clare to Brian.

Clare deflected the estate agent's question with a question of her own. "Why are the people moving?" Brian remained silent, surveying the vast interior space.

"I'm told that either his parents or her parents, I can't remember which, are up there in age and are not doing well, health-wise. The parents, whichever ones, live in a suburb of Dublin and need more support. The owners put in a bid on a large house in that area and will have the older folks move in with them. When it comes to family, you do what you must," Daniel finished, nodding his head.

Clare looked at Brian and said, "We understand. We've been in that situation ourselves."

"Look, it's a nice day outside. Why don't you two go on out back and look around. I have to make a couple of phone calls." Daniel crossed the floor and opened one of the double doors to the outside.

"I should point out that this property includes three acres of land. The house and the immediate area, marked by the drystone walls, are approximately one acre. The rest of the property extends out back beyond the patio where those fields are. The current property owner allows a local farmer to farm the land and doesn't charge him rent. Believe me, that good will goes a long way in a small village like this. I mention it because if you do purchase the property, you might want to carry on that tradition."

Once outside, another perspective of the sheer scope of the glass facade along the rear of the house was evident. The bright blue sky and the few fluffy white clouds floating along could be seen in a reflection on the exterior glass surface. The immediate back area featured a fairly large slate patio, open to the sky. A teak table with benches took up a position in the center of the patio, and a large collapsed umbrella rose from the center of the table. Off to one side of the table was a wooden bench with back support, facing out toward the fields. Another low drystone wall, with an opening to the fields beyond, bordered the patio area. Between the wall and the patio were nice garden beds full of vibrant shrubs, white azaleas and purple rhododendrons, which provided a backdrop for the flowers planted in the front of the beds.

Brian tapped Clare on the shoulder and pointed to the left. "Look."

Clare turned and saw a series of seven-foot wooden posts with wooden cross members on the top. The posts were positioned about thirty feet apart. Open hooks were spaced along each cross member for the clothesline.

"Someone else hangs their laundry outside," Brian commented.

He turned away from the house and stared across the field behind the property, where tall stalks of golden wheat gently swayed back and forth in the light breeze. For a moment, Brian was mesmerized by the waving grain, which seemed to beckon him to come closer. Somewhere in the distance, the mechanical drone of a farm tractor brought him back to the business at hand. The house was perfect. *Absolutely perfect! The price, well, we'll soon find that out,* he thought. One thing kept nagging at him. And it was something that he had only briefly thought about when they had first started to seriously talk about purchasing a house in Ireland.

"Well. What do you think?" Clare asked, as she joined him by the back of the patio. "A bit unusual with the way the bedrooms are set up, but maybe that's a good thing if we have visitors, or our children and grandchildren come over to visit during the summer. The location is ideal. Close but not too close to the village." Clare could see something was bothering her husband. "You're deep in thought again. What's on your mind?"

Turning to look at the house, Brian sighed. "Forgetting about the price for the moment, the place ticks all my boxes. As quirky as the bedrooms setup is, I like it."

"There's a *but* coming. I know you."

"Yes. There is a *but*," Brian said, as he turned to look at his wife. "We're not going to be living here on a full-time basis. The house will be empty at times. No one to keep an eye on it. Sure, we could pay someone to stop by occasionally, but it's not the same as someone living here. That's my main concern. What happens if a water pipe breaks or there's a leaking faucet or running toilet? I'd been so focused on the type of house and location that I thought we could address this issue later. Well, later is now."

"That's not like you, Mr. Organized," Clare said, with a knowing smile.

Running his hand through his hair, he said, "Let me think about it some more. Should we go inside and see what the price is? It may be so unreasonable that my concern may become a non-issue."

They went back inside and were ushered to chairs at one end of the dining room table by Daniel, who had just put his phone away.

"I was just speaking with the owners, who are in the process of closing on a house right outside of Dublin. Apparently, that whole process is going very smoothly for them. They are, however, rather anxious to close on this house. Housing is more expensive there, and whatever they receive for this house can be applied to reduce the amount of their new mortgage." Daniel paused and then looked from Clare to Brian. "So, without further ado, here is what they are willing to sell the house for." Daniel had written a number on a lined sheet of paper from his pad, which he placed in front of Brian and Clare.

After looking at the sheet of paper, Brian lifted his head and stared at Daniel, tapping a finger on the paper.

After what felt to Daniel like a rather long time, with the only reaction being the stare from the man sitting across from him, Daniel shifted uncomfortably in his chair, looked from Clare to Brian, and finally said, "Is there something wrong? Too high? I can assure you, for the size of the house and in this location, the price is *very* reasonable."

"No, no." Brian broke his stare and focused his attention back to the sheet of paper. "I am trying to make the euro to dollars conversion in my head and I'm drawing a blank."

"Oh, I see. Wait a minute." Daniel reached into his coat pocket and pulled out his phone and started tapping away.

Finished, he placed the phone down, rotated it, and slid it across the table in front of Brian.

Looking at the phone, Brian took a pen out from his shirt pocket and noted the information down on the sheet of paper Daniel had placed in front of him. He then slid the paper over in front of Clare. Looking at Clare, he said one word: "Reasonable."

Daniel eagerly nodded his agreement and looked at Clare expectantly. Clare then nodded her agreement.

Sliding the sheet of paper back in front of her husband, Clare looked at Daniel and voiced what had now become both Brian's and her concern. "The house is lovely. I believe you said there are three acres. The location and scenery are, well, perfect. And the price seems reasonable. The one thing that Brian and I are trying to come to grips with is the fact that the house will be vacant for periods of time, and that's a big concern. To be honest, it's something that neither my husband nor I had given a lot of thought to until you showed us this property. I think it's fair to say that the idea that the house will be unoccupied for periods of time is making us reconsider our plans, whether it be this property or another one elsewhere," Clare said, apologetically.

Tapping his fingers on the table, Daniel appeared deep in thought, then nodded. "Look, it's lunch time. Why don't we go back to the pub? I've ordered some sandwiches, and perhaps we might be able to come up with a solution. I think I understand your concern."

As they followed Daniel across the floor toward the front door, Brian paused for a minute to once again take in the surrounding interior area. *This is* the *house*, he thought. He smiled sadly as he slowly shook his head in disappointment, and an audible sigh escaped his lips as he turned and headed toward the front door.

3

SINCE THEIR VISIT earlier this morning, the pub had come alive, with lunch now being served. The relative quiet of earlier was now replaced with the noise of conversations at nearby tables, the clinking of silverware on plates, and the bustling of people back and forth to the bar. Daniel had led them to a reserved table off to the side, away from the bar. Brian and Clare took seats against the wall, allowing them to take in their surroundings. Daniel had gone to the bar and ordered drinks. Diet Coke for the gentleman and himself and a half pint of lager for the lady. Brian had asked for the soda, knowing that after the long trip on the plane, the lack of sleep, and the drive over from Shannon Airport, one beer, even a half pint, would put him asleep. He hoped the caffeine in the Diet Coke would act as a stimulant.

While Daniel had previously called in the sandwich order, traditionally at an Irish pub you ordered your food at the bar at the same time you ordered your drinks, paying for both up front. Each table had a unique number embedded on its surface, which you mentioned to the bartender when you placed your order. Though the pub was not completely full, a good number of tables were occupied for the noontime meal. In front of the bar, there were probably a half a dozen or more people either standing or sitting on the stools, sipping their beers and engaged in conversation. *From the looks of them, probably tourists,* Brian thought.

The woman he had seen this morning was busy moving in and out through the door at the rear of the pub. Holding a tray in both hands with plates of food, she used her backside to push open the door as she entered the dining area from the kitchen, then moved swiftly across the floor toward a particular table and the people waiting to be served. Once she set the plates down, she was off with the empty tray to the kitchen area for the next food delivery. The aroma of food was enticing. In response, Brian's stomach made an audible growl. Clare looked over to him, smiled, and then shook her head.

While waiting for their food, Daniel decided to make some small talk. He turned to Brian and asked, "Hansen? Is that Swedish?"

"No. Norwegian," Brian responded.

He turned and looked at Clare. "Are you also—"

"No," Clare interrupted, and then continued, "Irish. Higgins and McCarthy."

Before any further discussion could take place, the same woman Brian had seen that morning, and again a few minutes ago hurrying back and forth, arrived at their table with a rather large serving tray in both hands. Standing at the open end of the table, she rested part of the tray on the edge. She reached down with one hand and took a stack of three empty plates and placed them on the table. She then took from the tray a large platter, which contained a variety of sandwiches, and placed it on the table before them.

"Daniel. How are you?" the woman asked.

"Moira. Fine, and yourself?"

"Fine."

"And how is your daughter? Still has her head buried in those schoolbooks?" Daniel asked, as he moved the empty plates over to the center of the table.

"Yes. She does very well in school, I'm glad to say."

"That's good. Please say hello to Maureen for me."

"I will. And your family? Everyone doing well?"

"Yes, thank you," Daniel said and nodded.

With empty tray now by her side, Moira glanced at Clare and Brian, then said to Daniel, "If you need anything else, just let me know."

"This is grand. I think we'll be fine," Daniel responded.

"Thank you," Clare and Brian said in unison, smiling at the woman.

Throughout the conversation, Brian had been taking note of the woman. A little bit shorter than his Clare and not quite as slender, he thought. Reddish hair that reached just below her shoulders, with a couple of gray strands, held together by a clip in the back. An attractive face, but one that looked like it had seen tough times. Very little to no makeup. Green eyes, of course. Crow's feet beginning to show on either side of them. When she had bent over to place the plates on the table, Brian had noticed her long-sleeved light-green blouse starting to show the beginnings of perspiration marks under her arms. *No surprise,* he thought, the way she had been back and forth all over the dining area serving meals. Looking down below her dark-gray knee-length skirt, he noticed she had athletic shoes on her feet. While they didn't seem to go with the rest of her outfit, *good choice in footwear,* he thought, given her back-and-forth from the kitchen to the dining area. Age, hard to tell, maybe . . . late thirties . . . forties.

"The lady is your friend?" Clare asked Daniel, after Moira had departed.

Ah, here we go, Brian thought. A natural-born interrogator. Clare missed her calling: she should have been in the CIA. Clare could dig out minute details from even the most closed-mouthed person, wielding her questions with the precision of a surgeon using a scalpel.

"Who?" Daniel looked up from the clean empty plates he was distributing. "Oh. Moira is my cousin," Daniel responded. "Her mom was my father's sister." Rotating in his seat and pointing over his left shoulder toward the bar, he said, "See the older gentleman behind the bar, with the gray hair and beard? That's Moira's and my uncle. We have another uncle and another aunt, and then there's my father. Three brothers and two sisters, a typical large Irish-Catholic family."

"You said *was,* about your cousin's mother," Clare prompted.

"Yes, Moira's mom passed away about ten years ago. Very nice lady, hard life. Her husband had passed away when Moira was just a wee one. Here, please, help yourselves to the sandwiches." Daniel nudged the sandwich platter closer to his guests.

Brian spotted an open-face sandwich with smoked salmon and scooped it up. Clare took a beef sandwich and Daniel picked up another beef sandwich. As they ate in silence, Brian noticed people occasionally walking up to the bar with empty pint glasses and returning with full pints to their respective tables.

"Moira. Hm. Moira. I wonder if that would work?" Daniel said out loud to himself. He appeared to be in a trance, staring at the half-empty platter of sandwiches with his partially eaten sandwich suspended in midair between his mouth and his plate.

Both Clare and Brian paused, about to take another bite into their sandwiches, and looked at each other, then at Daniel.

"Are you alright?" Clare asked, putting her sandwich down on her plate.

"I was just thinking about what you had mentioned before about a house being left unoccupied." He looked at Clare and then at Brian. "I have an idea. Don't know if it will work, but it might be worth a try."

"Let's hear it," Brian said, reluctantly putting his half-eaten sandwich on his plate.

"Well, bear with me. And I would like what I'm about to tell you to be kept in strict confidence." Daniel paused, the pair of heads across from him nodding in agreement. "You just met my cousin Moira. She has a daughter. A teenager. Maureen is her name. When Moira was quite young, she had a boyfriend who took off when he found out that Moira was—"

"With child," Clare interjected.

"Yes," Daniel said, appearing not the least annoyed at being interrupted. He continued, "The—well—let's just call him ex-boyfriend, although he has been called many other things, was never heard from nor seen again. Which is probably just as well, because I hate to think what would have happened if my father and my uncles had got a hold of him." Daniel paused, shaking his head before continuing. "So, Moira and her child, Maureen, lived with Moira's mother, and together they barely made a go of it. My aunt was very proud and would take no handouts. She and Moira both worked hard to make ends meet, while caring for the little one. When Moira's mother passed away, Moira simply could not afford to stay in her mother's house, which was mortgaged to the hilt, so I am told.

"My uncle, the gentleman behind the bar, took Moira and her daughter in, providing them with a place to stay. My uncle, Padraig is his name, owns this pub and, as you can see, gave Moira a job. Moira and her daughter Maureen share a bedroom upstairs over the pub. There's also a separate bathroom that they both use. My father and uncles have repeatedly offered to find Moira her own apartment or even a small cottage, but she is like her mother, too proud to take what she perceives to be a handout. In fact, Moira insisted that her uncle take money out of her wages to pay for their room and board. My uncle would not hear of it. I think you know where I'm going with this in terms of the house you just looked at and your desire to have someone occupy it on a full-time basis."

"A mother and a teenage daughter sharing a bedroom. I can't even imagine," Clare said, shaking her head. Seeing how Daniel was about to object, Clare held up her hand to forestall an argument. "I'm not making a judgment. I'm just saying I could never have shared a room with our daughter when she was a teenager." Pointing to Brian she added, "He's bad enough." Brian, about to take a bite out of his sandwich, put it down on the plate again and looked at his wife with a "Who? Me?" expression, before smiling.

Brian stroked his chin with his left hand as he stared off in the direction of the bar. The two others at the table were silent, deep in their own thought processes. Brian—the deliberating Brian—was weighing the pluses and minuses of what Daniel was proposing. First, this woman, Moira, would have to agree with the arrangement. If she said no, end of discussion. No property purchase. If she said yes, she and her daughter could have the B and B side of the house with the two bedrooms, and there would be enough privacy for everyone. There would be someone in the house to keep an eye on everything. Those rooms would be unavailable to guests, but that might not be bad thing. *We'd still have a spare bedroom.* Worst-case scenario, any overflow visitors could be put up in a local B and B. *However, what if she said yes and later backed out, after we purchased the property?* That would be a problem. *However, if she works here, the location of the property so close to the pub should prove ideal for her.* Not having to share a room with her daughter should be an incentive to move into the house. But what if something happens to her? *Oh, hell, I could get hit by a truck and then it wouldn't matter anymore, at least to me. What if. What if. Time to forget all the what ifs and just roll the dice. Worst-case scenario, we sell the house.*

"Let me ask you a question, and, please, don't take offense," Brian said, now looking at Daniel across the table from him. "Are Moira and her daughter both . . ."

"Trustworthy? you were going to ask," Daniel said with a smile.

"Yes," responded Brian.

"Absolutely. My father and I as well as my uncles and aunt can vouch for them both. I can understand how you might be concerned about having a teenager in the house. Let me allay your concerns. Maureen, the daughter, is an excellent student. While others her age might like to raise hell every so often, not that I did when I was her age," Daniel paused, arching his eyebrows and smiling before continuing, "Maureen's idea of fun is reading books. And, quite frankly, given what Moira's experience had been when she was not that much older than her daughter, well, Moira keeps a very close eye on things. Moira, herself, is devoted to her daughter. She would never do anything that might hurt her daughter or bring shame on the family."

Satisfied with the answer, Brian turned and looked at Clare and asked, "What do you think?"

"I think this might be the solution we are both looking for, and while you and I may agree that it's a good fit, it's up to Moira at this point. Let's ask her."

"If I may make a suggestion," Daniel said, leaning forward in his chair. "Padraig, her uncle, has also been her . . . guardian, so to speak. Moira is the daughter he never had, and Maureen is the granddaughter he never had. Padraig doesn't have any children. His wife died very young during childbirth, and the infant did not survive either. I'm told that my uncle took the loss of his wife and child very hard, as you may well imagine. My uncle never remarried. When his sister passed away, Moira's mother, Padraig became very protective of Moira and her daughter. So, before there's any discussion with Moira, you—we—really need to have a discussion with Padraig. To get his blessing.

"Quite frankly, I doubt that Moira would agree to anything without first seeking his advice. I'm going to play the devil's advocate for a minute. What happens if you decide to sell the house in three or four years? What then happens to Moira and Maureen? Where do they go? If Padraig didn't give his blessing in the first place, it's going to create an extremely awkward situation for all of those you left behind."

"That's a very valid point," Clare answered. Brian nodded his agreement.

"Do you think we can talk to your uncle today?" Clare asked.

"Why don't we finish our meal first," Daniel responded. "By then, the lunch crowd should have died down and my uncle should have time for us. I must warn you, though. My uncle can come across as being somewhat..." Daniel paused, looking for the right word. "Cantankerous. His bark, however, is worse than his bite. Even so, be forewarned."

* * *

The man accompanying Daniel back to the table from the bar looked to be in his early seventies, yet was remarkably nimble on his feet. His gray hair and beard framed alert eyes that continuously scanned the interior of the pub, taking notice of what was going on in every corner of the vast room. He nodded to a few customers who were making their way to the pub's exit, having finished their meal. He was wearing a dark-blue shirt with sleeves rolled up to just above his elbows, tucked into gray corduroy belted pants. Brown laced shoes completed his wardrobe. As the two of them approached the table, Brian noticed that the uncle's bare forearms were unusually large. For a couple of seconds, an image of Popeye the Sailor appeared in Brian's mind. Brian attributed the obvious arm strength to many years of lifting beer kegs and cases of bottled beer and other beverages. Clare and he stood up to greet Daniel's uncle.

"Uncle, I would like you to meet the Hansens," Daniel said, introducing his uncle to the current occupants of the table. "This is Brian Hansen and his wife, Clare. This is my uncle, Padraig McGuire."

Reaching out across the table, Brian extended his arm and shook hands with the uncle. Brian was aware that the person in front of him was giving him a rather intense once-over, evaluating this stranger in his pub. Firm handshake completed, the man's penetrating eyes softened as he looked at Clare and nodded.

"Why don't we all sit down," Daniel said, pointing to the chairs around the table.

Daniel opened the conversation by saying, "Padraig, the Hansens are looking to purchasing some property nearby. They are particularly interested in a property that might become available—"

"The Ryans," Padraig interrupted.

"How did you know? I only just found out yesterday that they were interested in selling," a perplexed Daniel asked.

"Daniel, Daniel, me lad." Padraig gently chastised his nephew, patting his arm. "By now you should know that the owner of a village pub knows all and sees all. Sometimes we know what the other feller's going to do before he does. So, you two are interested in the Ryans' property?" Padraig asked, turning in his seat to look at the two people sitting across from him.

"Hansen. Is that Swedish?" Padraig asked before they could respond to the previous question, changing the direction of the conversation and looking directly at Brian.

"Norwegian," Brian responded. Brian noted that Padraig also spoke with a pronounced lilt like his nephew.

"So, we're to be invaded again by the raiders from the north!" Padraig proclaimed, still staring at Brian.

Brian wondered if it was just him or if the others sensed that the room had just become a little bit darker. He could feel Clare's hand gently squeezing his left thigh under the table. Over the years, and many supper club dinners, this was Clare's nonverbal signal to him to be quiet and not be baited. The subject of politics could be very provoking.

"Padraig. They are both Americans. Clare, in fact, her ancestors are from Ireland. Higgins and McCarthy," Daniel quickly chimed in, trying to calm the waters.

With his eyes still on Brian, Padraig slowly turned his head toward Clare. Finally, with his head almost completely turned toward Clare, he shifted his eyes away from Brian to her, a smile appearing on his face. The room now seemed brighter to Brian.

"You don't say. Why, lass, you're right at home," Padraig said.

"County Cork," Clare volunteered, anticipating Padraig's next question.

Raising his left hand and pointing at Brian with his thumb, Padraig said to Clare, "What is a fine lass like you doing with a heathen like him?"

More thigh squeezing, this time with greater intensity.

"We all have our crosses to bear," Clare responded with a broad smile, looking Padraig straight in the eye.

Brian turned to look at Clare and felt another, even harder squeeze of his thigh. *If this goes on much longer, I'm going to need stitches and new pants,* he thought.

Padraig let out a loud laugh and clapped his hand on the table loudly, drawing stares from the young couple sitting three tables over from them. He smiled at Clare and Brian and then said, "Welcome to our humble village. I wish you both luck with the property."

"Um, Padraig, there is something we'd like to discuss with you concerning the property," Daniel cautiously said. "The Hansens have their eyes set on the Ryan property, but they have a . . . concern." Daniel paused. "You see, they wouldn't be living here on a full-time basis. They will continue live in America and plan to visit here several times during the year. Their concern is that when they are not here, the property will be unoccupied."

"True. True. A good point," Padraig agreed, nodding his head, drumming the fingers of his right hand on the tabletop.

"They are looking for someone to live in the house on a full-time basis, both while they are here and while they are in America. The person would live in the house rent-free." Daniel raised his eyebrows and looked at the potential buyers to see their reaction, since they hadn't discussed this beforehand. Seeing that they both nodded in agreement with his statement, he continued, "Well, I thought this might be a good opportunity for Moira and Maureen. They might stay in the house. I wanted to see what you thought."

Padraig looked at his nephew like he was a complete stranger. He stopped drumming his fingers and started to move his right hand around in a tight circle on the table. He continued to stare at his nephew without saying a word.

"Mr. McGuire," Clare said, trying to get Padraig's attention. Padraig looked away from his nephew to the woman sitting across from him. "Mr. McGuire, if we are able to purchase the house, we'd be very pleased if Moira and her daughter would like to live in the house. I can assure you the only thing we'd ask of them is to keep an eye on the place when we're not there and let Daniel know if something needs to be taken care of." This time it was Daniel's turn to nod, and Clare noticed his agreement.

"She is not a maid!" Padraig exclaimed with raised eyebrows.

"We don't want a maid. Moira would not be a maid," Clare responded.

"She'll not be a maid," Padraig repeated more forcefully, his hand having stopped moving around in circles.

This is going well, Brian thought. *At this rate, we can forget living in this quaint little village. Time to cut our losses and move on. Enjoy the rest of our vacation.*

"Mr. McGuire. We are not looking for a maid nor a dishwasher nor a laundress nor a cook," Clare calmly explained. "When my husband and I are visiting Ireland, we will treat your niece and her daughter as family. For every meal. Every meal, whether it be breakfast, lunch, or dinner, there will be four place settings at the *same* table. One for your niece. One for your niece's daughter. One for the heathen, here, and one for me." Clare nodded toward her husband.

Oh great, now she's calling me a heathen too, Brian thought, giving his wife a sidelong look.

Clare continued, "We will all eat together, unless your niece prefers not to. I will be the one doing the cooking. You have our word on that. We will arrange to have all the bills taken care of. She will not have to worry about that. I don't know what her current living arrangements are," Clare paused before continuing, "but in the house, they will each have their own separate bedroom and bathroom and the run of the place rent-free. The house is close enough that Moira can walk here to the pub. In addition, we will pay Moira one thousand euros a month to keep an eye on the house, no strings attached."

One thousand euros a month. Hadn't thought of that. Brian leaned back in his chair and momentarily gazed up at the ceiling. He knew that back home, monthly property association fees could easily amount to twice that. Lowering his head to look at Daniel's uncle, Brian nodded his agreement.

"They each would have their own bedroom—and bathroom?" Padraig asked, mulling over what he had just heard. "And one thousand euros a month?" Padraig started moving his hand around in a circle on the table again.

"Yes," Clare answered, keeping eye contact with the pub's owner.

Silence. The four people at the table exchanged glances among themselves without saying a word. The silence went on for quite a while.

Padraig finally voiced his thoughts aloud. "If Moira did agree—mind you, she might not—that would give her and her daughter more space than what they have now."

More silence. Then, Padraig, in a determined voice, said, "I don't know anything about you two."

"Very true," Clare responded. "I'm sure Daniel performs reference checks on potential clients. We have no problem if he did a reference check on us and shared it with you and Moira. Also, how about we do this: If Moira agrees, we'll have a trial period of, let's say, a couple of months—or less, if Moira and her daughter find they don't like the arrangements. Their call. They can either go back to where they are now living, or we'll help them try to find another place. In the meantime, you're more than welcome to visit to make sure everything is on the up and up. Also . . ." Clare paused for a couple of seconds for emphasis. "If we don't think things are working out from our perspective, we'll let everyone know. It's a two-way street."

Padraig's right hand once again stopped moving in a tight circular pattern on the table as he looked back and forth between Clare and Brian, finally settling on Clare. "Higgins and McCarthy, you say?" Padraig asked.

"Yes Mr. McGuire," Clare responded.

His hand started up again. "Okay. Let's see what Moira thinks," Padraig said, looking at his nephew, who took his cue and left his seat in search of his cousin.

Daniel found Moira in the kitchen and walked with her back to the table. He pulled up another chair for himself so that Moira could sit next to her uncle. Moira sat down and anxiously looked around at the four other persons at the table.

Obviously, Daniel had not given her a heads-up, Brian thought, as he looked at the new arrival with a comforting smile.

"Daniel, why don't you explain to Moira what these people would like to propose?" Padraig said, nodding at his nephew.

Although Daniel's presentation was rather brief, he touched on the key points, including the one thousand euros a month. Moira seemed to be deep in thought, staring at the empty space in the middle of the table. The others at the table waited patiently for Moira's reply. Finally, she lifted her head up, tucked an errant strand of hair behind her left ear, turned to look at her uncle, and asked, "What do you think?"

Padraig turned in his chair to directly face his niece, and said, "Ah, Moira, it really is your decision to make. Before you decide one way or the other, I think it would be a good idea for you to take a look at the place. See what you think of it." Taking hold of Moira's hands in both of his, Padraig continued, "Moira. You, Maureen, and I will always have a home together, no matter where you two live. We are family."

Brian's eyes widened as he looked at Padraig. *He does have a heart. Who would have thought?* He stole a glance at his wife and could see that Clare was also visibly taken by Padraig's reference to *home.* As he kindly looked upon the woman sitting across from him, Brian hoped they might be another step closer to their dream of owning a house in Ireland.

They just might be.

4

FOLLOWING PADRAIG'S SUGGESTION, the prospective buyers (Brian and Clare), the prospective caretaker (Moira) and the prospective commission earner (Daniel) had all piled into Daniel's car and took the short trip to the Ryans' house. Once inside, Daniel provided another tour of the downstairs area, including the two garages. Clare noticed how Moira paid particular attention to the kitchen and laundry areas. In the kitchen, Moira explored the insides of cabinets, tested the burners on the range, inspected the insides of the refrigerator and checked out the hot and cold water pressure of the faucet. In the laundry room, she opened and closed doors on the washing machine and the dryer and checked out the insides of more cabinets until she was satisfied. Brian and Daniel had withdrawn to the dining room, taking seats at the table while the women conducted their inspections.

Having covered the downstairs, the upstairs was next. Clare beckoned Moira over to the staircase leading to the B and B side. Clare told Brian and Daniel they should remain downstairs, to give them some breathing room. Once on the landing, Clare directed Moira to the bedroom in the front of the house. Clare opened the bedroom door and stepped aside to allow Moira to enter the room. Just inside the entrance to the bedroom, Moira stopped and looked around the room. She then went over to the head of the bed against the wall and paced off distances. Clare looked at what Moira was doing, puzzled. Moira took a couple of steps into the bathroom, quickly surveyed the surroundings, then returned to the bedroom.

"Moira, it looked like you were pacing off distances in the bedroom. Is there something wrong with the room?" Clare asked.

"I was just trying to figure out how I would get another bed in the room," Moira answered.

"Why would you want another bed in the room?"

"For my daughter, Maureen."

"Why would you—" Clare began, before nodding her head in understanding, realizing that Daniel had glossed over the sleeping arrangements, not mentioning two bedrooms.

"Moira. That would be your bedroom and your bedroom alone. Come with me." Moira followed Clare along the landing to the rear of the house. Clare opened the other bedroom's door and pointed into the room. "This would be your daughter's bedroom. Or this could be your bedroom and the other bedroom your daughter's. You both would have your own bedroom and bathroom. We wouldn't expect you to share a bedroom with your daughter. You both need your own space."

Moira's face brightened as she looked around the room. She entered and surveyed the bedroom and then walked into the bathroom, where she spent some time checking out the layout, as well as the shower's water pressure. Outside on the landing again, Clare showed Moira the closet in between the two bedrooms and then took Moira across the landing to show her the other bedrooms to complete the tour of the upstairs.

* * *

While Moira and Clare had been viewing the upstairs quarters, Daniel and Brian had taken this time to discuss the next steps required, should Moira agree to stay at the property.

"You'll need an attorney," Daniel said, as the women made their way across the upstairs landing. "My cousin is an attorney. His office is in Galway, a little over an hour away."

"Is there anyone that you're not related to?" Brian asked.

"Well, yes, actually. I'm not related to the Ryans, by the way. If you'd like, I could give you the names of other attorneys," Daniel answered, somewhat defensively.

"No, no, that's fine. Probably best to keep this all in the family," Brian responded.

"If Moira agrees to stay at the property, you're going to have to move quickly and make an offer and see what the sellers' reaction is. That is, if you both want the house. Then, there will be the paperwork—the contract, the home inspection, etc. How long are you and your wife planning on staying in Ireland?" Daniel asked.

"We're scheduled for two weeks in Ireland—including two nights here in Doolin, although, if need be, we could extend our stay in Ireland by another week. Don't know if we can extend our stay at the local B and B though," Brian answered.

"When we get back to the pub, I'll call my cousin and see if he'll block off some time for us tomorrow afternoon, that is, if Moira says yes and it's okay with you and your wife."

"That's fine," Brian replied, as he and Daniel watched the women make their way down the opposite staircase from the one they took up to the second floor.

The rest of the property tour involved going outside and spending some time on the patio. Moira was particularly interested in the setup for hanging up clothes to dry, pushing against the upright posts to see how sturdy they were. The group reentered the house and went out the front door and across the pebbled driveway to the parked car. Daniel locked the house up after them, and they all climbed back in the car and drove back to the pub. It was obvious that three of the occupants in the car were anxiously waiting to find out what Moira thought of the house, but Moira remained quiet during the short trip back. The group entered the pub with Moira in the lead. She stopped by the bar and turned to face the others.

"Is it alright if I give you my answer tomorrow morning?" Moira asked. "I would like to discuss this with my daughter."

"Yes of course, tomorrow will be fine," Clare responded.

With that settled, Moira turned and headed to the kitchen door in the rear of the pub. Daniel, Clare, and Brian adjourned to an empty table. Brian offered to buy drinks, but no one was thirsty. They agreed to meet again tomorrow in the pub at nine in the morning. Brian knew that he and Clare would spend an anxious night wondering what Moira's answer would be. Daniel asked where they were staying. It turned out that the owner of the B and B was yet another cousin of Daniel's.

5

THE OWNER OF the charming B and B, where they had stayed five years before and were now staying again, greeted them with a warm and welcoming smile as they came through the front door. In Brian's mind, the woman didn't look like she had aged a day since their previous stay. A good deal shorter than Clare, the woman had a bubbly personality. Her blond hair was short and swept from her face. The floral blue dress she wore was bright and very becoming. After five minutes in her presence, he felt like he had known her his entire life, and for her part, the woman said she remembered them from their last visit.

They were shown to a room on the first floor with a spectacular view overlooking expansive green fields, with the ruins of an old stone cottage located off to one side. The land gradually rose up the side of a nearby hill. More gray drystone walls crisscrossed vivid green fields, displaying vertical and horizontal patterns as the fields extended upward toward the crest of the hill. A few white cottages dotted the landscape.

The bedroom itself was comfortable-looking, with a queen-sized bed, light-blue bedspread, and fluffy pillows in dark-blue pillowcases stacked high against the headboard. Side tables with reading lamps were located on either side of the bed. Across from the bed was a small dresser with a mirror. Next to the dresser was a wardrobe cabinet for hanging up clothes. There was one cushioned chair in the far corner by the window. A cozy room. The bathroom, which the owner pointed out had been remodeled since their last visit, was immaculate. She also mentioned that the room would be available, should they want to stay an additional night or two. This was said with a knowing smile. Not normally being a suspicious person—well maybe a little suspicious, although Clare would say very suspicious—Brian wondered just how much information was being telegraphed among the locals.

Once outside their room, the owner showed them a common area where breakfast would be served and reminded them of the hours when breakfast would be available. Declining an offer of a glass of whiskey or an ice-cold beer, they informed the owner that they were going to take a walk down to the quay. Holding the door open for them, the cheerful woman bid them a farewell and told them to mind the traffic.

"Tourists, you know, they're not the best drivers. Except for you folks, of course."

* * *

Retracing their steps down the lane, they came to the road they had taken when they arrived from the airport. To the left was the pub they had been in earlier. They turned to the right and slowly walked along the left side of the road down toward the quay, away from the village shops and the pub. A lone horse was grazing in a nearby field.

"What do you think?" Brian asked.

"We'll know tomorrow morning," Clare responded.

They walked in silence for some distance and then Clare said, "That poor woman. I can't imagine what her life has been like. Raising a child on her own. She and her daughter sharing a bedroom. Did you see her at lunchtime? She was on her feet hustling back and forth nonstop."

After they had walked on a little further, Brian spoke. "That Padraig is some character. I must admit, I didn't know what to make of him at first. Then, when he talked about Moira and her daughter and him being family and having a home together, well, that caught me off guard."

Having arrived at the quay, they could see the concrete pier off to the right, where passengers would board sightseeing boats that would depart for either the towering Cliffs of Mohr or the rugged beauty of the Aran Islands. The water gently lapped against the sides of the concrete boat slips, which were protected by an extended stone jetty. Two small buildings nearby sold tickets for the different trips. Both were closed now. Venturing beyond the buildings, they came to a low, relatively flat unprotected rocky expanse that went out for thirty or so yards, disappearing into the awaiting sea. Rolling waves periodically crashed onto the rocks, causing a spray to fly up into the air. A gentle onshore breeze brought with it a briny fragrance. As evening approached, the day's bright blue sky was starting to fade, being replaced by a reddish glow while the setting sun took up position just to the west over the water. Shadows danced across the sea whenever the sun's last rays would momentarily disappear behind drifting clouds. Far off in the distance, the Cliffs of Mohr soared upward above a blue sea. A lone sightseeing boat could be seen in the distance, nearing the base of the cliffs. Brian and Clare stood on the rocky area in silence, holding hands and absorbing the sights and sounds of their immediate surroundings. While there were other people around and about, to them this place, at this moment, was theirs and theirs alone. They were oblivious to intrusions. They felt a renewed sense of freedom, of exhilaration as they watched the surging waves come closer and closer before ultimately crashing on the nearby rocks. Tomorrow they would find out if the sense of inner peace they were feeling now was fleeting or would endure.

As he watched the waves crashing on the rocks, Brian reflected on the life he shared with Clare. Marriage and the growing pains two people experience as they start out on a new adventure together. Children and the added responsibilities that come with them, as well as the way in which time seems to pass by in the blink of an eye. One day you were bringing a newborn home from the hospital and then seemingly the next day you were watching the newborn, now an adult, saying "I do" at their wedding ceremony. Then the sound of another generation of children laughing and crying. Grandchildren seemingly forever asking questions that begin with the word "why." Attendance at children's recitals and plays.

He smiled as he thought back on the days gone by. They were now two empty nesters who, over time, had escaped the abyss of divorce and whose life together endured because of a deep sense of commitment to each other and because of an enduring love. Two people who thrived on a common belief that tomorrow would bring new adventures, new challenges, and a love that would grow even stronger. For them, there would always be another tomorrow.

* * *

They returned to the B and B just in time to witness a younger couple enter with their suitcases. Retrieving their own suitcases from the trunk of their car, which they had parked earlier at the B and B, they followed the other couple into the house. Their plan was to freshen up and then head down to the pub for an early dinner and an early night. It had been a long day. They would miss the traditional Irish music session in the pub later that night, but sleep beckoned.

When they returned to the pub, they sat at the same table where they had been that morning. Brian placed their food and drinks order at the bar and paid. He didn't see Padraig there. Two young men were moving back and forth behind the bar, serving pints and taking meal orders. Back at the table with silverware and liquid refreshment, Brian nursed a pint of lager while Clare nursed a half pint as they waited for the arrival of their meals. The pub started to fill up as people occupied the various tables throughout. The dinner crowd was definitely larger than the noontime sitting, good food, drink, and the evening's music entertainment no doubt the appeal. The noise level was much greater than before. Brian found himself having to speak louder and lean closer to Clare to hear her comments.

Brian noticed Moira as she hustled back and forth with a tray containing plates of food. There were two other servers helping at this hour. Padraig's familiar face could now be seen drawing fresh pints of beer along with the two other barmen. A young man approached Brian and Clare's table with two plates of baked salmon, mashed potatoes, and steamed carrots. He put the meals down on the table and departed. Brian and Clare ate without saying a word to each other.

They were just finishing the last of their respective meals when a shadow appeared over the front part of the table. Brian looked up to see Moira standing with an attractive teenage girl dressed in a pullover sweater and jeans. He nudged Clare's leg and she also looked up. Brian put his fork down on his plate and started to stand, but Moira waved him back down.

"I'll just be a second, but I wanted you to meet my daughter, Maureen," Moira said, as she turned toward her daughter.

"It's a pleasure to meet you," Brian responded, smiling. She looked like a younger version of Moira, he thought. Slightly taller than her mother. Bright green eyes. *A bit shy,* he thought. *Who wouldn't be, meeting two strangers for the first time?* The one big difference he noted was her youthful face, which had so far been spared the hard times that her mother had experienced.

"It's nice to meet you both," the young lady politely responded, hands fidgeting with the bottom portion of her sweater's sleeves.

"Nice to meet you, too," Clare said.

"Well, we don't want to keep you from your dinner. I wanted my daughter to meet you both," Moira said, and then gently ushered her daughter away from the table.

"A good sign?" Clare asked, when they had finished the last of their meal.

"You mean Moira wanting to introduce her daughter to us? Maybe. How old do you think Moira is?" Brian asked, as he saw mother and daughter disappear through the door to the kitchen area.

"Moira is thirty-six and her daughter is fourteen," Clare answered.

"How—" Brian started to ask.

"I asked Daniel."

Brian smiled. He should have known his wife would ferret out that detail. "Do you want anything else to drink?" Brian asked.

Clare looked at her almost-empty half-pint glass. "No, I don't think so. How about you? My treat."

"No thank you. If I have another pint, I'll fall asleep right here. Do you want to head back?" Brian asked, as he pushed his empty plate toward the center of the table.

"Yes," Clare answered, and got up from her chair. Their table was immediately occupied by a young couple who had quickly moved across the floor from the front of the bar with half-filled pint glasses in hand.

Brian and Clare headed out through the pub's exterior door. The sun had completely disappeared, to be replaced by darkness below and twinkling stars above. They walked up the road and turned to the right onto the narrow lane. Light spilled out from the downstairs windows of the few cottages along this stretch of the lane. Once away from the pub and the ambient light of the village, they continued to stroll up a darkened lane toward their B and B. Occasionally, they stopped to look up at the incredibly bright stars that were scattered across the clear night's sky as far as the eye could see. While they both would have loved looking at the endless stars longer, they were tired from the day's events. Tomorrow, however, they might enjoy the starry view even more, should they receive good news.

6

NOON THE NEXT day saw Clare and Brian standing by Daniel's car in the parking area up the road a short distance from the pub, waiting for Daniel, who was inside with his uncle. The morning had passed by rather quickly. Around 9:00 a.m. they had met up with Daniel and Moira in the pub.

"Yes." Moira had told them that she would like to accept their offer, if they still wanted her. That is, if the sale went through. Was it alright, though, if her daughter could see the house and the two bedrooms? It being Saturday, her daughter didn't have school. With the homeowners still in Dublin and the house vacant, Daniel had offered to take mother and daughter to the house. Moira, however, didn't feel comfortable entering the house without the prospective new owners. So, Daniel had driven Moira and her daughter as well as Clare to the house.

Brian, meanwhile, had begged off a return visit. He wanted to go back to the B and B and get his papers in order for their meeting with the attorney in Galway. Brian was notorious for his to-do lists, and he wanted to add a couple of items to the list he had started earlier that morning for the 2:00 p.m. meeting Daniel had scheduled with his cousin, the attorney. Daniel had called his cousin yesterday afternoon, and the cousin had indicated he would be in his office pretty much all day Saturday, catching up. If everything looked like a go from Daniel's end, Daniel would call in the morning to confirm a time for an afternoon meeting, which he had done.

Daniel opened the car doors for Brian and Clare. With everyone buckled in, they were off to Galway, with Brian in the front passenger seat and Clare in the back. The first half of the trip took place on mostly rural roads. Daniel tried to make small talk. In response, Brian and Clare limited their contributions to mostly one- or two-word responses, concentrating their attention on the narrow road that snaked ahead. As the car sped through bends in the road or negotiated steep uphill climbs or downward descents, Brian clenched his arm rest with his hand and held his breath. Of course, Daniel was an experienced "wrong side of the road" driver, but even so, viewing the road from the opposite side, at what seemed like an impossibly high rate of speed, provided a whole new, very scary perspective for Brian. Once on the relative safety of the long straightaways of the highway, Brian was able to relax a little.

"How did the visit to the house go this morning?" Brian asked.

"I thought it went well," Daniel responded. "Didn't you?" he said, with a brief look in the rearview mirror at Clare in the rear seat.

"Yes, I thought so. Brian, you should have seen the look on Maureen's face when she saw the bedrooms. What a smile. Although Moira seemed somewhat reserved. But I think that's because it's a big change for her."

"Definitely, but a positive change, I think," interjected Daniel.

"Brian, do you have your to-do list?" Clare asked, like he wouldn't be caught dead without it.

"Yes, why?"

"You need to add a desk to the list. Right now, there isn't a desk for Maureen to do her homework on. She'll need her own study space. I thought the area with the seating on the upstairs landing would be a good location for the desk. And a chair. Add a chair also to the list," Clare said, tapping the back of Brian's headrest.

"Added," noted Brian, as he wrote the new additions on a pad resting on his lap.

"Probably wouldn't be a bad idea to get her a computer, a laptop. I assume there's Wi-Fi in the house," Clare added.

"Wi-Fi is already on the to-do list. I don't know if there are different requirements for PCs over here versus the US," Brian answered.

"If I may," Daniel said, as he slowed down for a truck up ahead, lumbering up a rather steep incline, "we have a very good techie-type person back in the office. He does all our in-house computer work and he set up and maintains our website for the agency. I could ask his advice. I have to laugh; one time I went to ask him a question and he asked me to wait a minute because he said he was in the cloud. Well, needless to say, my idea of what a cloud was and his were two different things."

"That would be good, if you could," Brian said. "In fact, if he could pick up two new laptops and the necessary software and have him do whatever needs to be done to set them up and running, that would be most helpful. Let me know how much they cost, and we'll reimburse you, if that's alright." Looking back over his right shoulder, Brian looked at Clare and said, "We'll need a PC over here. That way we wouldn't have to take one back and forth on the plane."

Daniel found a stretch of the road without any oncoming cars and passed the slow-moving truck. They continued to speed along the highway for period of time, and then Daniel started to slow the car down. Their first traffic roundabout was up ahead. Brian paid close attention to how Daniel positioned the car in a specific lane of the highway as he slowly approached the roundabout and then how he eased the car to the left around the roundabout and out the exit on the far side, accelerating down the highway.

"I suppose there's a science to these roundabouts," Brian commented.

"Yes," Daniel answered. "Although, I have to admit that I've been known to go around once or twice, myself. Usually, the traffic runs pretty smoothly around them. The problem occurs when you have someone not paying attention, or . . ." Daniel's voice trailed off.

"A foreigner is driving," Brian said, completing the sentence.

"Well. Yes. Non-natives, so to speak, can make the roundabouts rather challenging." Daniel looked briefly over at Brian, who was looking at the fields off to his right. "No offense."

"No offense taken. This non-native has caused more than one near-miss in his travels over here," Brian replied, nodding his head in agreement.

After another forty minutes of travel and a half dozen more roundabouts, they arrived at their destination in Galway. Along the way, farmlands gave way to suburban houses, which then gave way to shopping centers on the outskirts of the city. The city was congested with cars, causing them to crawl along in the heavy traffic until they finally arrived at a parking garage. Daniel took the machine-produced ticket and proceeded up a ramp until he found a vacant parking space. Once outside the parking garage, Daniel pointed across the street at the three-story brick building where his cousin worked.

They entered the office building and, after looking at the directory on the first-floor wall, made their way to the cousin's office on the second floor, where introductions were made. Conor McGuire looked remarkably like his cousin Daniel. *Definitely a family resemblance,* Brian thought, as he shook the attorney's hand. He looked to be perhaps ten years older than Daniel. His brown hair was longer than Daniel's, with the sides starting to show some gray. Black-rimmed glasses gave him a rather dignified look. The man before them displayed an air of confidence. Dressed casually, he was wearing a light-blue golf shirt, khaki slacks, and loafers.

They moved from Conor's office and adjourned to a nearby conference room. The long oak conference table, upholstered chairs, oriental carpet, and surrounding cherry wainscoting presented a very formal, rich setting. Brian thought, *This is where important decisions are made or presentations are given to key clients.* He had been in similar conference rooms many times in his consulting career. The four of them took up seats at one end of the conference table.

"So, you want to buy a house?" Conor asked, once they were all seated, looking from Brian to Clare.

"Yes. Daniel here has been most helpful in our search," Clare said for them both.

"You do realize that while you may purchase property in Ireland as a nonresident, you're not automatically entitled to declare residency in Ireland." It was a statement, rather than a question. Conor continued, "There are certain unique circumstances where residency may be accomplished, with the appropriate approval."

"Yes, we're aware of the residency issue, and no, we don't intend to apply for residency in Ireland," Brian said.

"Well, that's grand. Have you settled on a price for the property?" Conor looked at his cousin, arching his eyebrow.

That question led to a back-and-forth review and discussion of the current owners' asking price. Daniel handed out three folders to the others, different from the ones he had used the other day in the pub. These folders contained information about a limited number of comparable real estate sales in the immediate and neighboring counties where the Ryans' home was located. He spent the next twenty minutes walking through the material in detail. At the conclusion of Daniel's presentation, Brian voiced their intention of matching the requested sales price, having agreed with Clare the previous evening that the homeowners' sales price was reasonable. Daniel's analysis confirmed their thoughts about the offering price of the house. Conor voiced his support with their decision.

With the others looking on, Daniel took out his phone and made a call to the homeowners. The call was very brief. Daniel smiled as he completed the call and laid the phone on the table. "The Ryans have accepted your offer, subject, of course, to the appropriate due diligence review." With that announcement, Clare patted Brian's hand with a big smile on her face. Brian looked visibly relieved and used his pen to check off the first line item at the top of his to-do list.

The offer of the house accepted, further discussions centered on that to-do list. Conor briefly left the conference room to made copies of the list for everyone so they could all follow along. During the next two hours, items such as property survey, title search, home inspection, property appraisal, operating expenses, utilities and other bill payment requirements, etc., etc., were reviewed. As part of the review, the group also discussed who would be responsible for following up on each of the items.

Brian noted his and Clare's concern about establishing a formal process for receiving and processing bills promptly, since they would be part-time residents. The fact that the buyers were going to pay cash eliminated the need for a mortgage, which simplified things. For the most part, Conor's firm would handle the items on the list, including receiving and paying bills promptly, as they already had in place procedures that they currently used for other clients in similar circumstances. The firm would charge a reasonable monthly fee for these services. Conor would set up a bank account that Brian would fund on a periodic basis. Conor's firm would draw from the account for property-related expenses and would also maintain auditable records and provide a detailed monthly statement of all expenditures.

Toward the end of the meeting, Daniel brought up the fact that their cousin Moira and her daughter Maureen would be taking up residence in the house to keep an eye on the place, on a full-time basis.

Conor put his pen down on the table, leaned back in his chair, and removed his eyeglasses and rubbed his eyes before putting his glasses back on. He looked at Daniel and nodded.

In a somber voice he said, "It will be good to get the two of them out of that room over the pub. They'll have separate rooms, finally?"

"Yes, and their own bathrooms," Clare responded. "Oh, that reminds me. We told Moira that she would not have to take care of any bills, which we have addressed today, and we have also agreed to pay Moira one thousand euros a month to keep an eye on things. Can you include that as something your firm will take care of?"

"Yes. Very good. That should be no problem," Conor answered, smiling, while making a note on his pad. "Very good!" Conor repeated without looking up from his pad.

"Oh, cousin. Does our dear uncle know about Moira and Maureen moving?" Conor teased.

"Yes, and remarkably, he seems okay with the arrangements," Daniel replied. "It took some convincing. Though, I believe it was Mrs. Hansen's Irish ancestry which finally won him over."

"So, you two have met Padraig?" Conor smile grew larger as he looked back and forth between Brian and Clare.

Both nodded.

"And survived. Will miracles never cease." Conor chuckled, shaking his head.

At the conclusion of the meeting, contact information was exchanged, both phone and email. Conor assured them that within the coming week, while they were still in Ireland, everything that needed to be nailed down, would be. Brian mentioned that he and Clare would see if it might be possible to extend their stay at their current B and B through the end of the following week, if need be, making themselves available should Daniel or Conor need them. He noted that he didn't think it would be a problem, since Daniel's and Conor's cousin, who owned the B and B, was very accommodating and, curiously, very knowledgeable of their plans. Brian raised one eyebrow and gave the two men sitting across from them a knowing smile.

* * *

The new week saw a flurry of activity. Conor's office set up a bank account to handle payments related to the operation of the house. Brian had funds wired into the account, and an automated process for replenishing the account was established. The real estate contract was signed by both the sellers and buyers with a closing date in two weeks. With the contract signed, Brian finally felt a sense of relief. The uncertainty of not knowing whether they would be able buy a house in Ireland was eliminated. Clare and he now had the second house they had wished for.

Daniel had both good news and not-so-good news for Brian and Clare. The good news was that the sellers did not need all the furniture in the house they were selling. As it turned out, their parents had quite a bit of furniture that the sellers were going to incorporate into the house they had purchased outside of Dublin. So, the B and B furniture, as it became known, was no longer needed by the sellers. Nor did they need the downstairs furniture in the sitting area at the front of the house nor the kitchen and dining area furniture. Either the sellers had enough furniture coming with their parents, or their old furniture was not suitable for the layout of the house they had purchased. To avoid both moving and storage costs, they were willing to let this furniture stay with the house and included it as part of the purchase price. Daniel reported that the sellers had taken into consideration the fact that the Hansens had met their asking price, resulting in a quick, haggle-free transaction. The not-so-good news was that the sellers wanted the other two bedrooms' furniture.

For the Hansens it meant that Moira and her daughter could move in at the end of two weeks if they wanted. Their furnishings were all set. It also meant that Brian and Clare needed to purchase bedroom sets for two rooms, as well as the desk and chair for Maureen. Clare had decided that for now they would hold off on converting the other bedroom into a wardrobe. A trip to the stores in Galway was required. Clare also opted for new mattresses and box springs for the B and B bedrooms. In addition to new furniture, a couple of month's inventory of such basics as laundry and dishwasher detergent, paper towels, and toilet paper was purchased. New towels, sheets, and pillowcases, including duplicates, were also acquired for all the bedrooms. Silverware and kitchen utensils were added to the list of items needed and purchased. The new checking account was put to the test.

Brian and Clare wound up extending their original two-week visit to Ireland by another week to accomplish all the errands. They changed their flight to a new departure date and the car rental was extended. It just so happened that their room at the B and B was still available, even though the rest of the rooms had been booked solid. The B and B owner's smile and wink said it all. At the end of the second week, the sellers' moving truck had arrived, packed up the appropriate furniture and contents, and departed for Dublin. During the beginning of the third week, Moira and Maureen moved into their new quarters, which now included new mattresses and box springs. Brian and Clare followed a couple of days later, once their bedroom furniture had arrived.

Padraig himself made several house inspections under the guise of needing to talk to his niece about something at work. Brian and Clare found it interesting that, over the course of a couple of days, Padraig's discussions with Moira took place in every room in the house, even the bathrooms. Brian did remind Clare that she had told Padraig he was more than welcome to visit the new house as often as he liked.

On the day before Brian and Clare were due to fly out of Shannon Airport to return to the United States, Daniel arrived with two new laptops, one for the Hansens and one for Maureen, along with a printer and printer supplies. Daniel's decision to also include a printer was met with approval from both Brian and Clare. While Moira initially protested the gift of the PC for her daughter, her protest softened when she saw how Maureen's face lit up. Daniel's techie office friend would come by another day to set everything up and give Maureen an introduction to the new PC. He would also be available by phone, should Maureen have any technical questions.

On the morning of their trip to the airport, last-minute instructions were discussed. Another review of phone numbers and email addresses: Conor Maguire's for anything to do with house; Daniel Maguire's as backup to Conor. In retrospect, Brian realized the family connections made life easier for everyone involved, especially for Moira. Clare's and Brian's phone numbers and email addresses and even their son's and daughter's contact information, just in case, were provided. Also, in the far-right kitchen drawer was an envelope with some money for any essentials that needed immediate replenishment or for anything that they had overlooked.

Finally, hugs all around.

7

Eighteen Months Later

OVER THE EIGHTEEN-MONTH period that had transpired since the purchase of the house, the group dynamics had proven interesting. During this time, Brian and Clare had taken six trips to Ireland. Each visit lasted, on average, two weeks, with the shortest being one week and the longest, three weeks. While they had intended for their son and daughter and their grandchildren to join them on some of these visits, thus far, that had not happened. School, summer camps, and Disney World had been some of the deterrents to a visit. *Disney World? Not to worry,* Brian thought. There would be plenty of time for them to visit. He had to admit that he could understand how his elementary-school-aged grandchildren just might find Disney World to be more fun and exciting. And, truth be told, he thought it was probably a good thing to keep the overall number of participants in the new household to a minimum as the American and Irish contingents interacted in this new, untested environment.

True to her word, when Brian and Clare had visited, Clare initially had made sure that there were four place settings on the dining table for every meal. Clare's vision of four people sitting together for all their meals had been derailed by the simple fact that Moira (and sometimes Maureen) often took her meals at the pub. One of the perks afforded to bartenders, servers, cooks, and anyone else who worked at the pub, was a free meal when they were scheduled to work. While initially disappointed, Clare had to admit that a person would have to be crazy to pass up a free meal, especially since the food at the pub was quite good. The fact that Brian and Clare also ate at the pub occasionally, enjoyed a pint or two, and then hung around for the music sessions had added to the lack of a quorum at the dinner table on some nights.

Expectations had to be modified.

The time when all four of them had been available for dinner were most Sunday evenings. On one of their very early visits back to Ireland, Clare discovered that Moira and Maureen's Sunday evening meals had usually included Padraig. Maureen had mentioned this to Clare in passing one morning when she was getting ready to go to school. Padraig had not been to any Sunday dinners whenever Clare and Brian returned to Ireland, which, in Clare's mind, was something that needed to be corrected—immediately. The correction took place after Clare made a visit to the pub the next morning. So, Padraig was included in the Sunday evening meals. Padraig's one and only attempt to decline Clare's invitation to Sunday dinner was no match for her persistence. Or, as Padraig later noted, "The Irish blood flowing through her veins had not thinned, over time nor distance, her being away from Eire."

The first Sunday dinner attended by Padraig started off on the wrong foot, or more correctly, with the wrong chair. With five people for dinner, the evening's meal would be served in the dining room. The dining room table being so long, place settings were located at one end of the table, with one setting at the head of the table and two settings each directly across from the other on both sides of the table. Brian, having been raised to respect one's elders, felt that the seat at the head of the dinner table should rightfully be reserved for Padraig. Clare and Moira took seats next to each other on the side of the table closest to the kitchen. Maureen took a seat opposite them, leaving another seat for Brian next to her.

"Please take this seat," Brian said, standing and holding out the chair at the head of the table for Padraig, who studied the chair in question.

"No, laddie. That there is your seat," Padraig said, nodding toward the chair Brian had his hand on.

"Please, Mr. McGuire," Brian said, still holding the back of the chair and pointing to the place setting at the head of the table.

"Padraig," Padraig said with emphasis, eyes narrowed.

"Excuse me?" Brian asked with a puzzled look.

"Call me Padraig. If you call me Mr. McGuire, I'll be wanting to look over my shoulders, thinking me dear departed Pa is behind me."

Hesitating for a couple of seconds, Brian looked at the man standing in front of him and then said, "Okay, Padraig, please take this seat." Brian still held on to the back of the chair.

"No. This place is for the head of the household. That being you!" Padraig insisted.

Brian stole a quick glance at Clare, whose arched eyebrows and fierce stare moved slowly from Padraig and now remained on him. The stand-off was resolved with—

"Brian. Please sit down!" Clare commanded, with a nod at the chair Brian was holding. "Padraig will sit next to Maureen," Clare finished, in a softer voice.

Once seating arrangements were settled and the two "adult" males in the room sat down, Clare and Moira pushed their seats back in unison and went into the kitchen to get the evening's meal.

"Men!" Clare exclaimed as she entered the kitchen, with Moira trailing right behind her.

Brian ignored his wife's chastisement. He was still trying to figure out what just happened between him and the bearded gentleman seated to his left.

Most Sunday dinner conversations had been rather tame. Discussions about ancestry had been frequent. Maureen's schoolwork was often a topic of interest. Brian and Clare had been the recipients of endless questions about American politics. What did they think about this politician or that politician? The politicians often had Irish last names, of course. Brian and Clare had been frequently asked to explain American foreign policy and they both tried to explain what sometimes was inexplicable, even to them. Thankfully, for the most part, discussions regarding religion had been kept to a minimum. (The heathen was spared any indignities.) All in all, the evening's menu of topics consisted of relatively safe ones. Commenting after their first Sunday meal all together, Brian and Clare had noticed how Maureen was like a sponge, absorbing information. She certainly wasn't shy with the questions she asked nor the opinions she voiced. They both thought that Maureen showed a maturity and an inquisitive nature well in advance of her age.

Meal preparation had been another area where things could go off the rails quite easily, when multiple cooks were involved. Initially, Moira, Clare, and Brian had showed deference to each other's space and meal-prep skills, with only one person at a time in the kitchen when food was prepared.

Yes! Brian also made dinner upon occasion, much to Moira's and Maureen's surprise. And his culinary skills were actually quite good, they both thought.

Gradually, over time, meal prep had evolved into a collaborative effort, with more than one cook in the kitchen at the same time, helping to prepare that day's meal. New recipes were shared, cooking tips were exchanged, and sample food tasting was encouraged. Having a larger commercial refrigerator and stove may have contributed to the successful interplay of all the interested parties.

On the other side of the house from the kitchen, the laundry room saw a similar communal exchange. Initially, the American and Irish contingents had kept their laundry activities separate. Once again, gradually, over time, each other's clothing items became incorporated into shared laundry loads. All parties liked the fresh-air smell of laundry hung up outside on the clothesline, which helped facilitate the integration process. Again, the commercial-grade appliances were useful. While men's undergarments were very distinctive from women's, it took a discerning eye to separate the undergarments belonging to the three ladies, even though the three had distinct body shapes. As would be expected, there had been occasional mix-ups, with one of the women's washed, dried, and folded undergarment winding up in the wrong person's laundry basket.

There were times when Clare, in the privacy of their bedroom, would hold up a particular undergarment by the elastic waistband or strap, ready to put the item on or away in a drawer and then realize that the item was not her size. On some of these occasions, Brian would also be in the bedroom and couldn't help but tease his wife. Clare would hold up a certain undergarment by its strap and it would be obvious that the cup size was too small. Clare would shake her head and place the item in an empty clothes basket. Brian would mimic his wife, shaking his head. Then there were the times when the cup size was, well, obviously too big. Brian's thumbs-up approval would be met with a disapproving stare from his wife. Hands on her hips, Clare would look at her husband like she was confronting a disobedient child. Sometimes Brian would retreat behind the closed door of the bathroom, where muffled laughter could be heard. Clare would set the undergarment off to the side and shake her head, and eventually a knowing smile would appear.

"Some men never grow up!" Clare's loud voice penetrated through the bathroom's closed door to the ears of the immature juvenile.

* * *

Brian and Clare's trips to Ireland had also involved side tours to locations elsewhere in the country. One of the main reasons for acquiring the property had been to use it as a base camp from which they would venture out and explore various sights in Ireland. The country's relatively small size allowed for numerous day trips. On the road by five in the morning, they would return before ten at night. Some of the destinations, like Dublin and Belfast, required overnight stays of more than one night to view all the sights.

Their new house would also serve as a jumping-off point for future trips to other European countries. Revisits to Norway and Scotland were in the planning stages. First-time visits to Switzerland and Sweden were also on the drawing board. A low-fare airline serviced many of these locations, making the trips both practical and very affordable.

* * *

At the end of the eighteen-month period, Brian and Clare once again returned to their home in the United States. Prior to their leaving Ireland, they informed Moira and Maureen that this time they would probably be gone for around six months. Brian had a major systems project that his consulting business would be undertaking, and Clare's architectural business would keep her busy for the duration.

At dinner the night before they left, the four of them—Brian, Clare, Moira, and Maureen—had an open and frank discussion about the previous eighteen months; in particular, they talked about how their combined living experiment was working out. The consensus was that the arrangement was working out remarkably well. Brian thought that the success of the living arrangements, so far, was mainly because Clare and Moira were like sisters, without the sibling rivalry, who very much enjoyed each other's company and respected each other's space. Moira's work requirements at the pub and Maureen's schooling also kept them away from the house for a good amount of time during the week, and on weekends in Moira's case. This, along with Clare and Brian's trips around the country, limited the amount of time that the four of them actually interacted with each other. Ironically, this probably also added to the success of the experiment.

Of course, there were some minor irritations, but nothing that couldn't be overcome. These mostly centered on keeping each other informed of changes in individual schedules. None of the four were bashful about expressing their feelings. In private, before dinner, Clare had remarked to Brian that problems commonly associated with teenage girls—loud music, boys, staying out late, boys—were nonexistent when it came to Maureen. Maureen was focused on her schoolwork. All four agreed that the experimental living arrangement should continue. Brian was relieved that it had worked out so well.

Later that evening, Clare filled Brian in on a conversation she had with Moira after dinner when the two of them were alone. Moira had told Clare that she thought Brian and Clare should be taking money out for her and Maureen's lodging.

"You're kidding me," Brian said, as he placed a pair of socks in his suitcase and looked up at his wife.

"Nope."

"What did you say?" Brian asked, as he folded a pair of undershirts.

"I told her that we felt she earned every penny, and we were very happy to have her and Maureen living here," Clare responded.

"What did Moira say to that?"

"She seemed pleased," Clare said, while refolding one of Brian's undershirts.

"The only reason I can sleep at night with our having two houses on two continents is because of Moira and her daughter. Otherwise I'd be up half the night."

"I know. Now finish your packing; we have an early start tomorrow for the airport. And I know how you like to get to the airport at least *five hours* early," Clare said, giving her husband a knowing wink. "Just kidding."

The following morning, Brian and Clare were off to Shannon Airport. The rental car was dropped off. Airplane tickets were confirmed, and the luggage checked in. Passengers and carry-on luggage were scanned, the duty-free shop checked out, and US customs successfully navigated, all taking place two hours ahead of the flight. The Aer Lingus flight to the United States took off on time. Brian and Clare were once again airborne, he in seat 33A (never to be reclined during the flight) directly in front of Clare's seat 34A (with plenty of leg room).

As expected, seat 32A, directly in front of Brian's seat, was fully reclined for the duration of the flight.

8

Five Months Later

BRIAN HAD BEEN leaning forward in his seat, staring intently at the clean white floor tile directly in front of him. Elbows on his knees, hands clasped together. He was oblivious to the movement around him. He hadn't noticed the young nurse in a blue uniform pushing a trolley across the floor, containing a sophisticated looking electronic monitor. Nor was he bothered by the one errant swivel caster on the trolley, which vibrated back and forth, making an annoying squeaking noise. He had paid no attention to an older nurse who walked determinedly across the brightly lit open space in front of him, head up, eyes looking straight forward, with a clipboard in her hand. Urgent voices at the nurse's station could occasionally be heard throughout the area but went unnoticed by him. While there were a few other chairs in the small waiting area where he sat, whether they were occupied or not, he didn't know. He was oblivious to everything except for that single white floor tile directly in front of him.

Earlier, Brian had checked his watch and had seen that he had been in the waiting area for approximately an hour. Waiting. Waiting to hear how his Clare was doing. The doctor he had briefly met earlier said they would do everything they could, but . . .

There was that word. *But.*

* * *

When Brian had urgently entered the hospital earlier, two police officers had met him just inside. The older of the two police officers, a man in his fifties, had ushered Brian off to a side area, away from the people going in and out of the hospital. The young female officer had stayed by the entrance.

The older officer explained to Brian what they believed had happened. The officer's succinct words felt like someone was stabbing him over and over in his chest. The officer noted that the ambulance had arrived at the scene of the accident as quickly as possible. An alert pedestrian had called 911 as soon as the two vehicles came to rest. Standing on the sidewalk by the intersection, the pedestrian had seen that his wife's vehicle had the green light and had slowly moved forward, proceeding through the intersection cautiously. The driver of the other vehicle appeared to have been on a cell phone and went right through the red light, never slowing down. The other vehicle, a large SUV, broadsided Clare's smaller car, driving it across the road sideways and up onto the far sidewalk, where his wife's car had been pinned against the side of a building. Miraculously, no one had been walking on the sidewalk at that time.

The absence of tire skid marks was evidence that the driver of the SUV had never hit the brakes. What the police officer left unsaid was that his wife's smaller sedan had stood no chance against the larger SUV. The police officer had told him that he would contact Brian later with more information. After getting Brian's address and a telephone number where the police could reach him, the officer had led him over to the hospital's information desk, saying that he hoped his wife would be okay. What else could he say? Years of police experience had taught him it was best to leave it at that.

Brian had looked at the police officer with incomprehension. He had heard the officer's words but was having difficulties understanding them. His Clare was in an accident?

No!

He remembered her taking the car keys off the hook in the kitchen that morning. She had said she was just going to run a couple of errands and would be back by lunchtime.

He had absentmindedly thanked the departing officer as he stood in front of the information desk. Suddenly, his legs had started to buckle. He had instinctively reached out to grab the front of the desk. The alarmed woman behind the desk quickly rose from her chair and helped him sit in one of the chairs in front of the desk. Brian's entire body began to tremble as tears flowed down his cheeks.

* * *

A shadow appeared across "his" white tile and remained there.

"Mr. Hansen," said the familiar voice. "Mr. Hansen." There again, that voice.

Brian slowly looked up and saw the tall doctor he had met briefly before. This was the same doctor who had said he would do everything he could. The doctor looked down at him. The doctor was fitted out in blue hospital scrubs that were stained—red stains. Some sort of gold chain hung down from his neck, barely visible as it disappeared beneath his white undershirt. The doctor moved forward and took a chair next to Brian. Brian swiveled around in his chair to look at the doctor seated next to him, his face a wordless plea for everything to be alright.

"I'm sorry," the doctor said, slowly shaking his head. "We tried our best, but the damage from the accident was too great. The damage to the internal organs and the loss of blood were . . . just too much. Your wife put up an incredible fight. But it was an uphill battle; too much for anyone. I'm sorry."

Brian stared at the doctor, carefully absorbing each word that was directed to him, and finally nodded his head, tears flowing down his cheeks.

"Is there someone we can call to be with you? A son or a daughter?" the doctor asked, as he stood up.

"Yes . . . No . . . Neither one of them live locally. I'll have to call our daughter and son to let them know what happened." Brian turned his head slightly away, now looking at the empty chair where the doctor had sat. A moment of silence passed by. He turned and looked up at the doctor. "My wife . . . did . . . did she suffer?"

"No, I don't think so. We tried to make her as comfortable as possible with medicine." Brian nodded his head, tears still flowing down his cheeks as he turned away and looked down at the white floor tile.

"A member of the hospital will be with you shortly," the doctor said, in a somber voice. "They'll ask you some questions and provide you with some guidance. They'll ask you about funeral arrangements and offer you some information on counseling."

To Brian, the entire situation was so surreal. This was not supposed to happen. He and Clare were both going to live to a very old age. If anything, he would go first, not her. This had to be a cruel nightmare. Maybe he'll awaken and hear Clare downstairs in their home, making her morning cup of coffee and bowl of cereal.

"I'm sorry. We tried our best." The doctor's words brought Brian back to reality and his very real nightmare. "Are you sure you're alright? I know this is a very difficult time for you, but I have to ask, is your wife registered as an organ donor?"

"Yes, she is. Or was. That was very important to her, so whatever you must do . . ." Brian's words trailed off.

The doctor nodded. "We'll proceed accordingly. Thank you. Well, I'm needed back in the operating room."

Brian looked at the doctor, nodded, and mechanically thanked him again. The doctor stepped back, turned, and walked across the floor, disappearing through swinging doors on the far side of the hallway.

Brian didn't have a to-do list for what he had to do next. He knew he would have to go home and call his daughter and son. They needed to hear what had happened to their mother from him and not from someone else. After that, he would try to figure out what else had to be done. What had he done when his parents passed away? Funeral home arrangements, then lawyer. Then . . . whatever . . . He aimlessly wandered across the brightly lit corridor, looking for the elevators, before a member of the hospital staff caught up with him and ushered him into a nearby office.

* * *

Brian was sitting in his favorite chair in the living room. He reached up and loosened his tie. The last of the guests had left. He looked around him; he couldn't remember where he had left his suit jacket. He would find it later. He could hear his daughter and son and both of their significant others in the kitchen, cleaning up, talking quietly among themselves. He couldn't make out what they were saying. No doubt something about Clare . . . or . . . the old man sitting by himself in the living room. The young grandchildren were in the den watching a show that one of their parents had found on the television. *The day must have been a very long one for them,* he thought, as he picked at the material on the upholstered armrest of the chair. Looking back, once he met with the folks at the funeral home, they had taken charge, and he pretty much stepped back and let them tell him what he had to do. He had told them cremation—several times, according to his daughter, who had accompanied him to the funeral home.

He had arrived at the church early, sitting in the front pew. The sermon had been upbeat. It wasn't until the service was over, when he stood up and turned around to leave, that he saw the large gathering of people. Outside the church, he mechanically shook hands, embraced people, and nodded at the kind words that were repeated over and over again by well-meaning passing individuals; some he recognized, others he didn't. Since both he and Clare had decided on cremation for themselves, there was no gathering at the cemetery.

Instead, after the church service, the attendees were invited to his home for catered refreshments, the remains of which were now being addressed by the current occupants of the kitchen. They had been fortunate, he thought. The weather had held out, so the rented tables and chairs that had been set up in the backyard were put to good use. Clare's roses were in full bloom. She was proud of her roses. *Who will take care of them now?* he wondered.

Since Clare's death a week ago, he found himself in a permanent fog. He was aware of what was going on around him, but it felt like an out-of-body experience. He could function, but he felt like retreating from everyone, even from his own daughter and son. He wanted to be alone. Strangely, the one exception to his desire to withdraw from the world was his consulting work, which he embraced with a renewed vigor. For some inexplicable reason, when he immersed himself in the consulting work, he felt like his old self. Work was a safe harbor for him. A place where he could retreat and avoid his new reality—his loss. However, away from work, the fog engulfed him once again.

With the kitchen work completed, the daughter and son and their families would be on their way to their homes. Both families would have four- to five-hour car rides. Tomorrow was a school day for the grandchildren; not to be missed, much to their disappointment, he thought. Coats were retrieved along with containers of extra catered food that were divided between the two departing families. He was told there was food in the refrigerator for him. He shouldn't let it go to waste.

At the front door, more hugs and kisses. Invitations extended to him to visit them. One of them would stop by in a week or two to see how he was doing. A reminder of a two-week family shore rental in August, which he and Mom had previously arranged. Standing on the steps in front of the house, he could see and hear car doors being opened and closed as grandchildren were loaded into the cars. Brian waved halfheartedly as the two cars drove off from the spaces in front of the house. No longer able to see the cars' retreating red taillights that disappeared into the night's darkness, he turned and opened the front door.

Once inside, Brian turned the lock until he heard the familiar click as the deadbolt was engaged. Absentmindedly, he turned off the outside light as he looked over his shoulder at the interior of the house. Slowly moving through various downstairs rooms, he had hoped he might hear her familiar voice again, which would end his nightmare. Retracing his steps through downstairs rooms—nothing. He stopped at the bottom of the staircase. He flicked on the switch for the upstairs hall light. He grabbed hold of the banister and slowly took a couple of steps up the stairs, where he paused. He looked expectantly up to the landing.

There was only silence.

9

MOIRA WAS IN the laundry room, placing the recently washed sheets into the dryer. The threat of rain negated the use of the outdoor clothesline. She hesitated for a minute before retrieving the last of the damp sheets out of the washing machine. She thought she'd heard a sound coming from the other room but couldn't quite make it out. The sheets were placed in the dryer and she set the dial for forty minutes' drying time and turned the dryer on. She entered the dining area, closing the door to the laundry, and started to go across to the kitchen but paused by the staircase. That sound again. She looked up toward the landing. Then she heard her daughter sobbing. Quickly, she made her way up the stairs. At the far end of the landing, she could see her daughter at her desk, looking at her laptop. The sobbing continued.

"What is it, Maureen? Why are you crying?" Moira said, as she rushed across the landing, coming to a stop by the side of her daughter's desk, slightly out of breath.

"Oh Mam, she's dead."

"Who's dead?" Moira couldn't think who her daughter was talking about. None of her daughter's friends had been sick. No one in the village had been ill. Relatives? She drew a complete blank. Not knowing who had died, she started to panic. "Maureen, who's died?"

"Mrs. Hansen."

"Oh, dear Lord," Moira said, as she collapsed into the chair by the side of the desk. "How? When?"

"An automobile accident, last week. Their daughter just sent me an email. Wanted us to know."

"Oh, that poor woman," Moira said, as her eyes teared up. "Mr. Hansen . . . did she say if Mr. Hansen was injured?" Moira asked, with a sense of urgency.

"No, he's alright, Mrs. Hansen was driving by herself when another car ran into her car."

"Oh, dear Lord. Did the daughter say anything else?"

"No. Just that. Wanted us to hear about her mam from her and not someone else."

Mother and daughter sat in silence. The box of tissues on the desk was shared between the two of them. While the Hansens were not family by blood, the short time the four of them had spent together made it seem like they were all one large family. Moira thought of Clare as the older sister she never had. Brian was the thoughtful brother-in-law who just went with the flow. The ribbing that Brian and Clare gave each other was playful, and it was nice to see a couple get along so well together. Something she had never experienced. Moira and Maureen, often bystanders during these sessions, couldn't help but smile.

Moira remembered how Brian and Clare showed a genuine interest in Maureen's studies, listening attentively and engaging in thoughtful conversations. They encouraged Maureen to ask questions and challenged her through thought-provoking discussions on a variety of topics. Moira, rather than being jealous of their influence, was glad to see their interest in her daughter. She was mindful that her work at the pub limited the time she had for her daughter. She also recognized that some of the school subjects her daughter took were beyond her. Moira viewed Brian and Clare as another uncle and aunt to her daughter. And, it would seem, Maureen felt the same way.

Moira didn't say anything to Maureen, but the question of what would become of the house crossed her mind as she dabbed her eyes with a tissue. He would probably sell it, she thought, now that his wife was no longer . . . alive.

* * *

Two weeks later, the status of their future living accommodations surfaced on two fronts.

"Mam, what's to happen to us, should Mr. Hansen sell this house?" Maureen was the first to voice what was now on both their minds, as they sat at the kitchen table eating breakfast.

"We'll have to wait and see. I haven't heard anything from Mr. Hansen. I'm sure he has other things on his mind. This house, well, I'm sure he'll let us know, as soon as he's decided what he's going to do," Moira said, looking out into the dining room.

Maureen looked at her mother and nodded. Then she got up from the table and put her dishes in the kitchen sink before heading upstairs to get ready for school. Moira reached for her cup of tea, started to raise it to her mouth, but then put it down on the saucer as she pondered her daughter's question.

Later that same day in the pub, Moira was bringing out a tray of bundled napkins, each containing a set of clean silverware for the evening meal. She placed the tray on the bar across from where Padraig was standing and setting out cleaned pint glasses. At this afternoon hour, the pub was relatively quiet.

"Have you heard anything from Mr. Hansen? About the house?" Padraig asked Moira, as he inspected another pint glass before placing it on the counter. No beating around the bush for him.

"No. I'm sure he'll let us know in due time. The poor man probably has a lot on his mind right now. I don't feel like we should be bothering him. Maureen asked me the same question this morning." Moira started to turn around, ready to head back to the kitchen.

"Moira. Wait a minute; I want to talk to you," Padraig said, pointing to a bar stool, indicating she should sit down. "If or when he sells the house, you know that your uncles and aunt will be there for you and Maureen."

Moira picked up one of the clean pint glasses that Padraig had placed on the bar and looked at it as though she was inspecting it. "Thank you, Padraig. I . . . I just feel so awful for that poor man. To lose his wife like that. They were so happy together. It's so sad. Maureen got to see for herself what it's like when two people really care about each other. I feel selfish thinking about what will happen to the house and Maureen and me. He lost his wife."

"Now, Maureen. You're not being selfish. I'm sure we'll find out what Mr. Hansen's plans are after he's had some time to mourn," Padraig said, taking the glass from Moira.

* * *

Two months had passed by since Moira and her daughter had heard about Mrs. Hansen's death. Moira's work and Maureen's school had kept them both busy. But the house was always on their minds. Would he just show up out of the blue and tell them that the house was sold? Hopefully he'd give them a couple of weeks' notice.

One day, Padraig had a meeting with a beverage supplier in another town while Moira was at work in the pub. She had made her way to the pub's upstairs area to inspect their old bedroom and bathroom. Both rooms were now being used as storage rooms, full of cardboard boxes, wooden crates, and some broken chairs. Moira surveyed what was once their space, totally dejected. She thought she might use the money the Hansens had been paying her to find some place local to rent. But that wouldn't last very long. She had been saving every cent of that money for her daughter's college education.

The following morning, Moira was putting dirty breakfast dishes away in the dishwasher when her phone rang. She wiped her damp hands on a dish towel and picked up her phone from the kitchen table. She thought she recognized the telephone number but wasn't sure.

"Hello," she answered.

"Moira, this is Conor."

"Oh, hi Conor. How are you?" Moira slowly walked out of the kitchen and took a seat at the dining room table, where she could look outside at the patio area.

"Fine. Fine. I wanted to give you a heads-up. Yesterday evening I received a phone call from Brian Hansen's son. He wanted to let me know that his father would be coming over to Ireland in the next couple of days. The son had spoken to his father about the house in Ireland. The son had told his father that he really needed to figure out what he's going to do with it. The son told me that his father hasn't taken the loss of his wife very well. I believe he used the term "shell-shocked" to describe him.

"Apparently, Mr. Hansen—the father, that is—is still involved in his consulting business and, well, the way the son described it, his father is like two people. When it comes to the consulting business, he's like his old self. He's very engaged in the business and interacts well with others. You wouldn't know anything is wrong. Mr. Hansen's consulting work is his refuge from . . . the tragedy. However, once he's finished with the consulting part of his day, he becomes withdrawn. He seems "lost." That's the word his son used to describe his father—lost. He goes for long walks and appears distant, even to his own children. Anyway, the son and his sister told their father that he should go to Ireland and spend a month or two and figure out what he wants to do with the property.

"He'll be bringing his consulting work with him, so expect him to spend part of the day working. The rest of the day, well, who knows. The son and daughter were hoping that the time over here might help him snap out of his funk.

His word, not mine. So, be prepared." After a brief pause, "How's everything else going there?" Conor asked.

"Oh fine. To be honest, both Maureen and I were wondering what was going to happen with the house. We hadn't heard anything. Which is understandable. The poor man did lose his wife."

"True, but I'm sure not knowing can be very unsettling for both you and Maureen. How is Maureen doing? Still doing well in school?"

"Yes," Moira replied, rising from her chair and walking over to the back window." Did the son say if there's anything special we should be doing for him? For Brian, that is?"

"No. Not really," Conor replied. "He wanted to give us, including you and Maureen, a heads-up. Look, I'm going to give Padraig a call to let him know that Mr. Hansen is coming over so that he's aware of the situation. Also, if you need anything or think Mr. Hansen needs something, please call me. I expect that at some point during his stay he'll either want to come visit with me or for me to come see him. I'll check with you periodically and I'll also let Daniel know he's coming over.

"Moira, his son did emphasize that his father doesn't appear to be a threat to himself, if you know what I mean. He just seems lost. Is everything else fine with the house? From my end, it looks like all the bills are being paid. Do you need any money for anything?"

Moira, lost in thought, barely heard her cousin's last question. "What? No, no we're fine."

"Well, let's keep in touch. Thank you, Moira."

"Thank you, Conor." Moira put her phone away and continued to stare out the window. She suddenly felt a chill as she hugged herself. She found it difficult to picture the person Brian's son had described—"withdrawn," "distant," "lost." Those words didn't describe the man she knew. Well, shortly she would see for herself. Mr. Hansen would be arriving in the next few days.

Later that afternoon in the pub, Padraig told Moira that he had got a call from Conor. Padraig and Moira compared notes about their respective conversations. Conor had told both of them essentially the same thing. Padraig let Moira know that if she needed anything—anything at all—when Mr. Hansen showed up, he would be around, and she shouldn't hesitate to call him. He told Moira that if she thought she should hang around the house for a couple of days when Brian first showed up, he had no problem with that and he would find someone to fill in for her. Moira didn't think it was a good idea. Brian, Moira thought, needed his space, not someone following him around the house. Padraig reluctantly agreed but suggested that maybe they should try to encourage Brian to spend some time at the pub, maybe dinner or lunch, or something.

The next morning, after telling Maureen about the phone call at breakfast, Moira set about stripping the sheets off Brian's and Clare's bed—the thought made her sigh again—and replacing them with clean ones. Fresh towels were hung in the bathroom. Furniture surfaces were dusted and the floor vacuumed. The room was ready. She knew she was specifically *not* to do such things for them—now, for him—but it was the right thing to do.

And so, the wait for Brian's arrival began.

10

THREE DAYS LATER, Brian arrived in Doolin, and the familiar sound of crunching pebbles under the car's tires announced his return to his second home. He got out of the car and stood, looking up at the house. The same house he had seen and visited and lived in before. But as he stood out front, it seemed different. Then again, everything seemed different. Shannon Airport, the rental car office, the car ride, even the roundabouts seemed different.

Once inside the house, he looked around. The only sound was the occasional humming of the refrigerator. Tired from the airplane trip and the car ride, he carried his luggage up the stairs into his bedroom. Once he put the luggage off to one side of the room, he sat down on the bed. He took his shoes off and didn't bother with any further undressing; he just laid down and promptly fell asleep. With Maureen at school and Moira at work in the pub, no one was there to greet him. That would have to wait until tomorrow, because Brian slept straight through the afternoon, the evening, and the night.

When Brian awoke the next morning, he was surprised to find a blanket covering him. He didn't remember covering himself last night. Showered and dressed, Brian paused and looked at the clock radio by the side of his bed and adjusted his watch to reflect the current Irish time. Eight o'clock here. Let's see; there's a five-hour difference, which means its three o'clock in the morning back home, he concluded. So, he could begin to directly communicate back and forth with his clients in the early afternoon—his current early afternoon—which would be their morning, still the same workday. He would block off 1:00 to 2:00 p.m. for any conference calls. The internet would also allow him to communicate 24/7 with his clients. He opened the bottom drawer of the dresser and retrieved his laptop and an electrical cord and plugged the cord into an outlet to charge the laptop. *Strange,* he thought, *I remembered exactly where I keep the laptop.*

As Brian made his way down the stairs, he stopped for a moment, halfway down. He could hear familiar voices coming from the kitchen. At the entrance to the kitchen, he peered in and saw a young woman looking at an open book on the kitchen table while she was eating. Across from her was an older woman who was raising a teacup up to her mouth.

The young woman looked up from her book and saw Brian standing by the entrance. She smiled and said, "Good morning, how was your trip?"

The woman sitting across from the smiling younger woman put her cup down on the saucer and turned to look up at him. She seemed to give him the once-over; he didn't know if it was his clothes or maybe the way he combed his hair. She smiled and said, "Good morning. Can I get you something for breakfast?"

"Um, um, no thank you, I just came down to get a cup of tea or coffee, if there is any? I need to get back upstairs and get on the computer. My work, you know." He fidgeted, shifting his weight back and forth from one foot to the other. For a moment, their names had escaped him. That's it! He remembered the young girl's name was . . . Maureen, and her mother was . . . Moira.

Moira got up and fetched a mug out of an upper cabinet and proceeded to fill it with what looked like tea.

"Milk or sugar?" she asked.

"No thank you, I'll just have it plain." He reached out and took the mug she offered.

"Are you sure I can't get you something to eat?" Moira asked once again.

"No thank you, I'm fine." He turned to go back to his room and paused. He turned back and looked at Maureen. "The trip was fine. Long flight. I have to apologize to you both. When I got in yesterday afternoon, I went right upstairs and fell asleep and I'm afraid I slept right on through the evening and the entire night. Can't remember the last time I slept so soundly. Well, I need to get on the computer for work. Good to see you both." He turned and left the kitchen, holding the mug of tea carefully in both hands, and headed up the stairs. Back in his room, Brian spent the morning with his consulting work.

* * *

Maureen looked at her mother and said, "He seemed like he barely knew who we were. He's lost a lot of weight; the clothes were hanging off him. Did you see the way the end of his belt hung down the front of his pants? Looked like he made a couple of extra holes in the belt."

"Give him some time. Remember, his wife was the more outgoing of the two. I suspect he's also trying to get used to the time difference. You almost ready for school? I'll put the dishes in the sink.

"After school, come down to the pub for an early dinner. We'll have to sort out a meal schedule. I'm off tomorrow night, so I'll cook dinner."

* * *

The next day, the previous morning's scene was repeated. Moira had placed an empty mug on the counter next to the tea kettle for Brian.

"Tonight, I don't have work at the pub, so I'll be making dinner. Is there anything you'd like?" Moira asked.

Brian looked back and forth between Moira and Maureen, then said, "No, I'm fine with whatever you folks would like." Moira noticed his discomfort with the question.

"Okay, I'm thinking of stew. Dinner at six, is that alright?"

"Yes. Thank you," Brian responded. Then he turned and made his way up the stairs with mug in hand.

"I wonder what he did yesterday?" Maureen asked, finishing up the last of her cereal.

"He went for a long walk in the afternoon down to the quay and then along the shore," Moira said. Seeing the curious look on her daughter's face, she continued, "Padraig told the folks in the village to keep an eye out for Brian and to report back to him what the American was up to and where he went during the day."

* * *

Padraig's "sentries" had heard of the American's wife's passing and were only too eager to keep an eye out for him. The American and his wife, they knew, were the ones who invited Moira and her daughter into their home and allowed old man Flynn to continue to work the fields behind the house without charging him rent. Yesterday, two phone calls to the pub: one from the first mate of a boat tied up at the quay, and the second from an old farmer who was out on his tractor plowing his field down near the shoreline, provided afternoon updates on the American's travels. A regular who had come into the pub for his usual early evening pint provided the final update on the American's late-afternoon location.

* * *

"Dining room or kitchen?" Maureen asked. It was later in the afternoon, and she was home from school and was helping her mother get ready for dinner.

"What about them?" Moira asked her daughter.

Maureen was holding silverware along with some napkins ready for place settings. "Are we going to eat in the dining room or in the kitchen?"

"Oh." Moira hadn't thought about where they would be eating. She and her daughter always ate in the kitchen when they were by themselves. The kitchen was cozier. Even when Padraig came up for a Sunday meal, they all ate in the kitchen. Only when both the Hansens and Padraig were here did they eat in the dining room. She looked at her daughter and said, "Why don't we eat in the kitchen; it's less formal."

To say that their first dinner with the three of them together was awkward would be an understatement. Brian sat at one end of the table, looking uncomfortable. Moira and her daughter had sat across from each other on the two sides of the table. Moira served dinner for each of them, ladling the stew into large bowls, placing an extra ladle of stew in Brian's bowl. They ate in silence. The only sound was the clinking noise of soup spoons touching the sides of bowls. Finally, Maureen broke the silence by asking Brian what kind of consulting work he did. Putting his spoon down, Brian leaned back in his chair and looked at her.

"I provide companies with advice on how to use technology—computers—to help improve their businesses." He paused. "For example, one company I'm working with doesn't have a very good inventory system. They use pieces of paper to keep track of the material they use to make furniture. Sometimes they run out of something they need to finish a job. I'm helping them put their inventory on a computer, which will track the material they use and when they should reorder more of an item before they run out."

The mood at the table had changed—less awkward, while Brian discussed his work. Dinner concluded after they each had finished a slice of raspberry pie. Moira informed him that she would have to work tomorrow night, and Maureen would join her for dinner at the pub. Moira asked if he would like to join them for dinner there. Brian responded by saying he'd have the leftovers from tonight, if that was alright with them. Moira nodded.

For tomorrow's lunch, Moira told Brian he could have the sandwich that she'd already made and was in the refrigerator. Brian offered to help with the dishes but was shooshed away. He retreated to his bedroom, leaving Moira and Maureen to finish washing the dishes and put the remains of the meal away in the refrigerator.

After her daughter went up to her room, Moira sat down on one of the kitchen chairs, trying to imagine what Brian was feeling—his sense of loss. She had lost loved ones, her father and her mother, but that was different. Her father's death was sudden, but she was very young when that happened, and she still had her mother. Her mother had lived to ripe old age. Losing her hurt deeply, but it wasn't unexpected. But to lose someone you married and at such a young age, the two of them obviously deeply in love with each other . . . a feeling she probably would never know, she thought as she sighed. She rose from her chair and shook her head. No, she knew she couldn't begin to feel the pain Brian must be feeling. As she left the kitchen, Moira turned off the light and headed up to her bedroom.

11

TWO NIGHTS LATER, Maureen and Brian were finishing up the dinner that Padraig had sent up from the pub, which he usually did when Moira was working evenings.

"Well, I have to get upstairs and crack open a textbook. We're starting a new subject at school, and for some reason, I'm having a hard time understanding the material," she lamented.

"Oh, what subject?" Brian asked.

"Geometry," Maureen replied, shaking her head.

"Why don't you get your book and bring it downstairs, and I'll see if I can help. While you get your book, I'll clean up and put the dishes in the dishwasher." Brian stood up from the table and grabbed both their plates and moved over to the sink. "Let's use the dining room table," he called after her.

Returning with the book, two pads, and two pencils, Maureen took a seat at the dining room table.

"Let me have the book for a minute so I can refresh my memory. What chapter?" he asked, as he took a seat across the table from her.

"Chapter one and two," Maureen said, and slid the textbook across the table.

After fifteen minutes, he placed the textbook on the table and inched it over to Maureen. Then over the next two hours, Brian and Maureen went through the first two chapters, and then two additional chapters, of the book. At times, Brian would use the pad to draw figures to demonstrate information or reference examples in the book. He would ask her questions and ask her to draw corresponding two-dimensional figures and identify various components of the figures. The end of each chapter had a list of questions, which Maureen would attempt to answer. If she had questions about a particular page or the questions at the end of the chapter, Brian would patiently explain what the text was trying to describe and walk her through the solution to a specific problem. Then he'd ask her to solve a similar problem that he would make up. Sometimes he would use items in the room to help explain information contained in the book—for example, calculating the surface area of the dining room table.

"You know, this makes a whole lot more sense to me, and now I'm ahead two chapters," Maureen exclaimed as they finished up. She closed the textbook and set her notepad and pencil alongside it.

"Well, that's good," he said, as he leaned back in his chair. He stared at the back window and saw their reflections in the window. The outside darkness hid the patio and fields beyond. As if talking to himself, he continued, "Sometimes

I found that I would run into a course where I would draw a complete blank. Then what I would do is ask the teacher or another student to help me out with the material. If they took their time and were patient with me, I found that I'd start to understand the material, and the subject no longer seemed so difficult. I'd work on additional problems not assigned by the teacher. Sometimes I'd even come around and like the subject. Just be thankful you're not dealing with solid geometry," he added, with a frown, shaking himself as though he had a chill.

"What's that like?"

So, for the next ten minutes, he tried to explain solid geometry in lay terms, drawing three-dimensional figures. "Got a C in this course. My fault, I didn't ask for help when I should have," he reflected, and then smiled.

"If I need more help, would you . . ." Maureen started to ask.

"Sure, no problem," Brian replied as he looked at his watch. "Sorry for keeping you so long. I'll see you in the morning." He stood and pushed his chair under the table and headed up the stairs to his room.

* * *

The next morning at breakfast, Moira asked her daughter why she'd left her schoolwork out on the dining room table.

"Mam, Mr. Hansen was helping me with a course I'm taking. He's an excellent teacher. He explains things so they're easy to understand. And you know, the entire time, he was like the old Mr. Hansen. I don't mean old, age-wise. It was like he was himself again. If you know what I mean. He said that whenever I needed help with my schoolwork to just ask him and he'd be glad to go over the material with me." Maureen put her spoon down in her empty cereal bowl. "You know, if he didn't want to be a consultant anymore, he would make a great teacher." She picked up her cereal bowl and went to the sink to rinse it out before putting it in the dishwasher. Then she gathered up her schoolwork from the dining room table and headed up the stairs to her room.

Moira's eyes followed her daughter heading up the stairs, textbook and notepads in hand. She thought about what her daughter had just said about last night's tutoring session. She smiled to herself and wondered just who was helping whom.

12

BRIAN'S LATE-AFTERNOON walks continued, rain or shine. Reports by the village "sentries" continued daily. Each day was something different:

"The American was seen down by the quay."

"He's along the shoreline."

The American is up by the stone tower."

"He's along the upper road. Yes, that far, the upper road up past the stone tower."

"He's about three miles out on the road leading north away from the village."

Moira grew concerned. Brian's afternoon diversions didn't seem normal to her. Left unsaid was the fact that there were numerous steep cliffs and treacherous waters nearby where he walked. When Moira voiced her concern to Padraig, Padraig told her that Brian needed time to absorb the loss of his wife, and he was better off walking around the area than seeking answers in the bottom of a bottle of booze.

"Best to leave him alone, but we'll keep an eye out for him all the same," Padraig had advised.

Something that puzzled Moira was the way Brian dressed for his walks. If it was raining before he set off, he would put on his blue windbreaker with a hood and wear a baseball hat. No umbrella. If it wasn't raining, he wouldn't wear the blue windbreaker, just his baseball hat and a sweater if it was cool out. The weather could be threatening rain, but if it wasn't raining, no windbreaker, only a hat and maybe a sweater. And no umbrella. What Moira couldn't figure out was that on those occasions when it did start raining after he began his walks; you would expect that his clothes would be soaked. But they never were.

* * *

It was midafternoon, and Moira had just brought out another tray filled with bundles of silverware encased in napkins for the night's meal. She placed the tray on the bar where Padraig was again arranging clean pint glasses. Next to her, an old-timer named Colm was just settling onto a stool. His was a familiar face in the pub. He and his wife had a little cottage up past the round tower, just off the upper road, and they were known for their generosity. If someone in the village was ill, Colm and his wife would prepare and deliver a hot meal for the sick person and their family with plenty left over to keep the entire family supplied for a couple of days. The only thing they asked for in return was for the person to get well. Now retired, Colm enjoyed a pint every once in a while, so he would occasionally stop in the pub for a pour.

"The weather is threatening, and he went out without his windbreaker again," Moira said, looking at Padraig.

"A pint, if you please," Colm said, locating a beer coaster and placing it on the bar in front of himself next to the money he had laid out on the bar to pay for his pint.

"Maybe the weather will hold out," Padraig answered, pouring a pint of Colm's favorite Guinness part way up the glass and setting it aside to rest. In a minute or two he would finish the pour all the way to the top.

"He'll be fine; he has on his green windbreaker," Colm said, a look of anticipation on his face as he stared at his half-poured pint of Guinness with bubbles making their way up the inside of the glass.

"Who?" Moira and Padraig asked in unison, both turning to look at Colm.

Still staring at the bubbles of his half-poured Guinness, Colm replied, "The American. That's who you're talking about, isn't it?"

"He doesn't have a green windbreaker," Moira said, staring at Colm.

"Well, he does now," Colm answered.

"Are you sure it was him?" Padraig asked, finishing the pour of Guinness and setting the pint on the coaster in front of Colm.

"Yep. Positive. He was walking up past the tower as I was driving down. The hood of his windbreaker was down by his shoulders, and I could see his face clear as day. He seemed lost in thought, didn't take notice of my wave to him. Unless he has a twin, it was him. The American," Colm said, raising the pint of Guinness up to his lips.

Padraig and Moira exchanged looks, both clearly at a loss. "Green windbreaker," Moira said out loud to no one in particular, shaking her head.

The green windbreaker would remain a mystery for the next few days.

13

NORA WAS THE pub's cook. Before becoming the cook, she was on the waitstaff. Before joining the waitstaff, Nora and her husband owned a farm. Ownership in a farm came to an end when her husband quickly developed an incurable cancer and moved on to pastures of a celestial nature. Farming is a tough life for two people, impossible for one, so the farm was sold. With money left over after the mortgage and seed and feed bills were paid off, Nora bought a small cottage on the outskirts of the village.

Padraig liked both Nora and her husband and knew that a waitstaff salary would help Nora out with day-to-day expenses, now that she was alone. In addition to filling a staffing need, Nora's physical size was a bonus. Nora was a big woman. Not obese, but rather, weightlifting big, with broad shoulders and a farmer's muscular arms. Taller than most men, her presence in the pub served as very effective deterrent against any mischievous activity by the pub's patrons. Nora seldom spoke. Most of the time her communication skills were a nod of the head. No one could ever remember seeing her smile.

Nora's waitstaff duties ended abruptly one day two years ago. On that day, Nora physically removed from the pub a despicable customer named Gavin whom nobody in the entire village liked. Gavin had verbally abused one of the other waitstaff, bringing her to tears. Upon seeing the woman in distress, Nora had silently confronted Gavin and hoisted him out of his chair, carried him through the pub's front door and across the street, and tossed Gavin into the field on the other side of the stone wall, where a horse was grazing. Rumor had it that Gavin landed upon a recently deposited pile of manure.

Padraig had not been in the pub for Gavin's "relocation," or as it became known, the Gavin Toss. When Padraic returned to the pub later that afternoon, he heard about what Nora had done. Even though it was the despicable Gavin that Nora had physically removed from the pub, Padraig was concerned about the possible fallout. His concern was greatly lessened when every single patron swore that Gavin had not been in the pub that day. With extreme reluctance, Padraig rewarded the conspirators with a round of drinks—on the house—something no one could ever remember Padraig doing before. With the pub's cook due to depart in two weeks to join her boyfriend in Dublin, Padraig decided, with urging of the pub's staff, to give Nora a chance to be the pub's new cook, away from the pub's patrons. Turned out, Nora was an excellent cook. Her Saturday specials were much favored by the pub's regular and tourist clientele.

14

IT WAS NOW Saturday, a couple of days after Colm's sighting of Brian in the mysterious green windbreaker up by the tower. It was not turning out to be a good day for Padraig. He'd had an argument with the beer supplier about some cases that had arrived with broken bottles. His car was acting up again after he had just had it in for service. One of his bartenders didn't know if they would be able to make it in for the evening shift. The weather was dodgy. Finally, it was two o'clock, and Padraig still didn't know what the special was going to be for tonight's meal. When he asked Jimmy the bartender if he had heard what the special would be, Jimmy just shook his head. Nora was notorious for waiting until the last minute to reveal the Saturday specials.

"That's it!" Padraig said out loud, to no one in particular. He was going to give Nora a piece of his mind. He was going to tell her, in no uncertain terms, that from now on he wanted to know what the Saturday special was going to be by the day before, on Friday. Padraig marched into the kitchen. The noontime meal was over, and he knew Nora would be prepping for the evening meal. When he walked into the kitchen, he saw Nora by the back screen door.

"Nora, I want to talk to you!" Padraig said, in a commanding voice.

Nora was looking out the back door. When she heard Padraig's voice, she turned to look at him; her eyes then drifted over to the clock on the far wall, and then back to Padraig. She raised one finger as if to say *wait a minute.* She stepped outside and looked up at the sky, which had been threatening rain all day. Still looking up at the sky, she blindly reached back into the kitchen and managed to grab a green windbreaker off a hook nearest to the back door, and then she left the building.

Padraig could not believe his eyes. He was standing in the kitchen all by himself. His face turned a beet red. *Enough*! he thought. *I have had it with her. She works for me, not the other way around. Who does she think she is?!* So dumbfounded was Padraig, it took a couple of moments before he stormed across the kitchen floor to go after Nora.

"I've had it," he said out loud, to the empty kitchen.

Once outside, he looked both ways and then caught sight of Nora rounding the corner of a building about thirty yards away. She had the windbreaker in one hand as she marched steadily on toward the lane. As he was about to take off after her, Padraig noticed movement off in the distance to his right, and he stopped. He turned to take a better look and saw Brian walking down the lane, wearing a sweater. No coat, only his hat. Padraig shook his head. *He's going to get soaked, the fool,* he thought, looking up at the massive dark rain clouds quickly closing in from the west.

Padraic continued to follow Nora, making his way around the side of the building. He saw her standing by the corner of the main road where the lane came out. He was just about to yell to her when he saw Brian approaching her. Instead of yelling, Padraig quickly stepped back and took up a position partially hidden by the corner of the building to watch the interaction between Nora and Brian.

Nora stood at the corner of the road and shook her right hand at Brian, as a parent might to a misbehaving child. She was saying something to Brian that Padraig couldn't hear. She then pointed one hand up toward the sky. Brian looked up. Nora took the green windbreaker and put Brian's left arm through the one sleeve. Brian disappeared momentarily as Nora, who was larger than Brian, moved alongside then behind him, where she pushed the windbreaker up on his shoulders. Coming out front on the other side of Brian, she put his right arm through the other sleeve of the windbreaker. Bending over in front of him, she proceeded to zip up the windbreaker. More hand shaking and grabbing hold of the hood of the windbreaker, as if to remind him that it was there. Brian nodded and then continued walking, turning to his right down the road toward the quay. Nora stood there shaking her head with her hands on her hips, watching Brian slowly walk away.

"Well, I'll be," Padraig said softly.

Padraig saw Nora start to turn his way and he quickly retraced his steps around to the back of the pub, through the back door and into the kitchen. Nora was too busy looking over her shoulder at the retreating green windbreaker to notice Padraig. In the kitchen, Padraig stood by the door to the dining area. Nora walked through the door a couple of moments later and looked at Padraig like she had just noticed him for the first time. She gave him a do-you-want-something look.

"Um, Nora, what's the special for tonight?" he asked in a calm voice, his anger completely abated.

"Stew," she replied, making her way over to the prep area.

"Okay. Good," Padraig said. He turned and immediately went out into the dining area.

Moira was heading toward the kitchen as Padraig was coming through the kitchen door heading toward her. He stopped, looked down, then shook his head and appeared to be saying something.

"Padraig. You're talking to yourself," Moira said, as she stopped next to him.

Padraig looked up and smiled. "Come with me," Padraig said. He took Moira by the elbow and headed toward the pub's front door.

"Where are we going?" Moira asked, shuffling alongside him.

"Just follow me," Padraig replied.

Outside the pub, Padraig pointed down the road that led to the quay.

"What am I supposed to be looking at?" Moira asked. Darkening storm clouds overhead threatened rain any minute.

"See that person in the green windbreaker? Way off there," Padraig continued, pointing.

"Yes. There's someone walking down toward the quay. So what?"

"That's Brian."

"Brian doesn't own a green windbreaker," Moira insisted.

Padraig proceeded to explain to Moira what had happened less than five minutes before. How he was going to read the riot act to Nora about always waiting to the last minute to let people know about the Saturday evening special. The green windbreaker hanging on the hook by the kitchen door. Nora intercepting Brian where the lane came out to the road. Nora giving Brian a lecture and putting the windbreaker on him. Finally, Brian heading off down the road.

* * *

Moira stood still, with her mouth open in surprise. Her eyes followed the sight of the green windbreaker moving away from them. For a brief moment, her attention was diverted by a burst of sunlight. The probing sun had found a hole in the gathering clouds through which rays of light had escaped and lit up a section of the darkened fields below, just to the left of where Brian was walking. But as quickly as the sun's rays had appeared, they disappeared, as angry looking dark clouds swept across the sky. Returning her gaze to the green windbreaker, she just caught sight of it as it started to disappear around a bend in the road that led down to the quay.

"So, Brian has a guardian angel down here on earth," Moira said, to no one in particular, shaking her head with a smile.

Heavy raindrops began to fall, bouncing up off the concrete sidewalk. Padraig and Moira quickly retreated to the dry sanctuary of the pub.

The mystery of the green windbreaker was now solved.

15

DURING THE FIRST month back in Ireland, Brian's daily routine had stayed pretty much the same. Work in the morning. Lunch. More work after lunch, then a long walk in the late afternoon. Dinner. Then reading in bed, except for those occasions when Maureen asked him to help her with homework. He seemed to look forward to the homework sessions. To a casual observer, he didn't appear to be losing any more weight, though he didn't look like he was putting on weight, either. A month ago, he had looked frail. Now he looked like, well, someone who managed their weight and exercised regularly, which he did.

* * *

If Brian's work provided him with a temporary escape from thinking about his loss, his daily walks past lush green pastures with grazing sheep or along narrow footpaths by dangerous seaside cliffs provided him with no such sanctuary. Try as he might during his walks, he could not shake the immense feelings of helplessness. The feeling that he had failed to protect his Clare. During his walks, his mind would keep replaying the scene in the hospital—the white tile on the floor directly in front of him while he waited to hear from the doctor about his wife. Then being told she had passed away. He tried taking different routes during his afternoon walks, hoping that a change in scenery would help him ease the anguish that enveloped him. No such luck. There was no escape from that day in the hospital.

Brian had completed his afternoon walk up past the tall granite tower, then along the main road above it. He was entering the village on the way back to the house, crossing the small bridge over a gentle babbling stream, when his right thigh started to severely cramp up. He looked around for a place to stop and rest when he realized he was near the pub, so he hobbled along to the building, cautiously opened the door, and walked in. Once inside, he paused, letting his eyes get accustomed to the darker interior. Off to the left was an empty table away from everyone, where he took a seat. He rested his hands on the top of the table and stretched out both his legs. The tightness in his leg eased a bit. When Brian felt a coin-sized piece of metal embedded in the top of the table, he looked down and saw a number. That would be the number a person would give at the bar when ordering food, he remembered. He wasn't hungry. He just needed to stretch out his legs. Looking around the pub, he noticed small groupings of people on the far side of the room and a couple of people sitting on stools in front of the bar. It was too early for the evening crowd. He was alone in this section of the pub.

* * *

"Do you think he doesn't know that he has to order at the bar?" Rory, the new bartender, asked.

"Who?" Jimmy replied, looking around the pub.

"Over there," Rory said, pointing to a man sitting at a table off by himself.

Jimmy went over to the far end of the bar where Rory was standing and looked where he was pointing. He recognized the American, having seen him numerous times walking around the village. "Ah. No. I don't think he'll be ordering. You tend the bar. I'm going to see if Padraig is around. I'll be right back." Rory quickly assumed a commanding position by the beer taps while Jimmy made his way to the other side of the bar.

Jimmy crossed through the dining area, occasionally glancing over to where the American was sitting, before entering the kitchen. Nora's domain. Nora looked up and stopped cutting the vegetables.

"Padraig?" Jimmy meekly asked.

Nora raised her arm, a rather large knife in her hand. Without saying a word, she used the knife to point to the cellar door. With the weekend coming up, Padraig would be performing the weekly inventory. Kegs, cases of bottled beer, and soda were all kept in the cellar. The spirits and wine were kept in separate location upstairs. Jimmy quickly crossed the kitchen, opened the cellar door, and descended to the cooler depths. Jimmy knew Padraig never liked to be disturbed when he did the weekly inventory. Padraig would make mental notes, not paper ones, of what needed to be ordered, which required complete concentration on his part. The American's appearance in the pub, however, was unusual and required Padraig's attention.

At the bottom of the stairs, along the wall to Jimmy's immediate left, were a few empty kegs waiting to be brought upstairs and stored out back. Further on along the same wall were the full kegs. On the far wall across from where he stood were more kegs, some refrigerated, that had been tapped, lines running from the kegs up through the floor to the bar area above. Over on the right, Padraig was counting cases of bottled beer.

"Um, Padraig," Jimmy hesitantly said, after taking a few steps away from the stairs toward where Padraig was standing.

Padraig turned and looked at Jimmy. He mumbled some words that Jimmy couldn't make out. Then said, "Aw Jimmy. You know better than to disturb me when I'm down here doing inventory. Now I lost count."

"Um, Padraig, there's something you need to see upstairs."

"What is it?!" Padraig demanded.

"Best if you come upstairs," Jimmy said with some trepidation, as he headed back to the stairs. "Best if you come upstairs," he repeated.

Padraig followed Jimmy up the stairs, across the kitchen, and out the kitchen door to the dining area of the pub. Jimmy had stopped just outside the kitchen door and turned to make sure Padraig was behind him. Padraig stopped next to Jimmy and gave him a look as if to say *Well, what is it?!* Jimmy turned and pointed over to where a man was sitting by himself. Padraig looked over in that direction.

"Ah, yes. Good lad. You did right to get me," Padraig said, and patted Jimmy on his back. "You head back to the bar. I'll take it from here."

Jimmy quickly headed off to the bar. Padraig stayed where he was for a moment.

Padraig made his way over to the bar and asked Rory for a Coke in a glass, with ice. He took the soda and a coaster and walked over to the table where Brian was sitting. Brian appeared to be studying the metal insert with the number for the table. When a shadow crossed the table, he looked up. Padraig placed the coaster down on the table and the glass of soda on top of it and carefully slid them both over in front of Brian. Padraig then sat down across the table from Brian.

"You must be mighty thirsty with all that walking," Padraig said.

Brian nodded and reached into his left pants pocket and came out empty handed. He reached in his right pants pocket and pulled out the house keys. He then felt behind him for the back pants pocket but already knew that he had left his wallet back at the house.

"The soda is on the house," Padraig said, noticing Brian searching his various pants pockets.

Brian nodded his thanks, then, by way of an explanation for his being there, said, "Leg cramp."

It was Padraig's turn to nod, and then, after a couple of seconds, he said in a somber voice, "Brian, I just want you to know that I am very sorry to hear about your loss. Clare was a very lovely lass, way too young to depart this earth."

Brian looked at Padraig, then nodded. For the next couple of minutes, they sat in silence. They mostly stared at the pub's outside door, as though they were expecting someone to walk in at any minute. Occasionally Brian would take a sip of the soda. Finally, after a while, Brian spoke. "Padraig, it would be good if you came up for Sunday dinner. I know Moira and Maureen would like you there. And, well, I know I'm not the best of company right now." Earlier in the day, Brian had overheard Maureen asking her mother why Padraig had not been coming for dinner on Sundays.

Padraig turned away from the door and looked at Brian, then nodded and said, "Okay. I'll be there this Sunday."

"I best be going; my leg cramp seems to be easing up. Thank you for the soda." With that, Brian stood and slowly headed across the room and out the door.

16

PADRAIG HAD REMAINED seated, watching Brian leave, favoring his right leg. After Brian had left, Padraic continued to stare at the pub's closed door, lost in thought. He recalled a time that seemed like yesterday but was many years ago when, as a young man, he courted his bride to be—his Clare. As he thought about the sheer joy the two of them felt when they were together, a small smile began to form on Padraig's face. The plans they had made. No dream was too big for them. They would conquer the world. The whole village had turned out for their wedding. A year later, when she told him she was pregnant, he was ecstatic. Both their parents were happy as could be when they heard the news. The soon-to-be grandparents went overboard with gifts and furnishings for the wee one. The small room in the apartment was filled with a crib, blankets, pillows, clothes, and toys—and more toys.

Then the world came crashing down. The doctors did everything they could, so they said, but they couldn't save his wife nor the baby. Tears started to well up as he recalled that day in the hospital. The helplessness he felt. Somewhere inside of him a light had been extinguished. Both sets of parents never got over the loss and, some speculated, it was the reason all four of them had passed away at too early an age. If not for his sister, Moira's mother, he too would probably be dead, having turned to booze to try to ease his pain. But she was relentless and never gave up on him. She dragged him away from the pubs and the bottles of booze and, after much effort, finally got him on the straight and narrow.

When Padraig's sister passed away, he might have lost his way again and done a freefall down a bottomless hole of despair and self-pity. However, her daughter, Moira, needed someone to look after both her and her child. Padraig owed it to Moira's mother to look after the two of them. They gave Padraig a reason for living. After all these years, the loss of his Clare and the baby still hurt; it was a pain that he knew would never go away. As he reached across the table to pick up the empty glass, he shook his head, knowing that Brian's pain would never go away either. Brian might be able to mask the pain, but it would always be with him. He would need all the help he could get from the people around him.

Padraig also knew that Brian would need a reason for going on.

* * *

A couple of days had passed by, and true to his word, Padraig arrived for the Sunday dinner. With him in attendance, the meal wasn't as somber as those before. Padraig spun one yarn after another. The amusing stories kept the evening atmosphere light. While Brian didn't contribute much to the conversation, those around him noticed that he seemed more attentive to what was being said, and sometimes, he gave a glimpse of a smile. At the conclusion of the meal, Padraig said he would be there for next Sunday's dinner. In terms of trying to get Brian out of his shell, as Moira had described it, Padraig thought the dinner was a small step in the right direction. After the meal, Brian had retreated upstairs to his room. Moira and Maureen set about clearing the dishes from the table. Padraig went over to the dining room window overlooking the patio, where he stared into the night's darkness, his thoughts on the debilitated man who had sat next to him at the dinner table.

As Padraig made his way to the front door to leave, Moira quietly reminded him that it was coming up on two months since Brian had arrived back in Ireland, and she was convinced that Brian would shortly tell them of his decision regarding the house.

Padraig tried to comfort his niece, but what was there to say? Time would reveal all. Walking back to the pub, Padraig realized that if Brian did sell the house, lodging for Moira and Maureen would be an issue that needed to be addressed. Their previous rooms over the pub were no longer an option.

17

THIS MORNING, MOIRA found herself outside, taking damp laundry items out of the clothes basket and hanging them on the clothesline. She didn't know whether to scream or cry. She was trembly with emotions. They say that bad news comes in threes. Well, she already had two out of three items of bad news yesterday. First was the letter her daughter had received in yesterday's mail. The letter was from the university up in Galway. For anyone else, the letter would be considered great news. Some sort of scholarship. However, Moira and her daughter suspected that the scholarship probably wouldn't cover all the costs, and they were hesitant to call and find out. They decided that they would call the university early next week. They could only procrastinate for so long.

Moira had some savings, but surely not enough for all four years of college, even with a scholarship. She was convinced that Brian would be selling the house, so the money she was saving by keeping an eye on the house would no longer be available for Maureen's education. No bank would give her any kind of a loan based upon her earnings. A student loan in Maureen's name was out of the question. She would not put that burden on her daughter. She would never ask relatives to help out. Her mother wouldn't accept handouts, nor would she!

What made it so frustrating was that her daughter was so very smart. Everyone said so. All her teachers said Maureen was a very intelligent young woman and should continue her education. Brian had made similar comments to her, based upon Brian and Maureen's evening sessions reviewing her schoolwork. And soon she would need to find lodging for both her and Maureen, once the sale of the house was finalized. That would deplete her meager savings.

Maureen was destined to follow in her mother's footsteps, Moira thought—working in a small village pub. Making up bundles of silverware in napkins, rushing around delivering plates of food, busing empty pint glasses and dirty plates, wiping down tables. Sore feet and chafed hands. What a life. If she was lucky, maybe she might meet a nice fellow. If she wasn't lucky, well... all Maureen had to do was look at her mother to see what the future held.

The second piece of bad news came last night. After dinner, Brian had told her that he would be leaving the following morning for a meeting with her cousin Conor, up in Galway. What had Brian said last night? *There are a couple of items I have to go over with the attorney.* The number one item, Moira thought, would be the sale of the house. Then she and Maureen would be without a roof over their head. She hadn't seen Brian at his normal time this morning. He had a very early conference call with a new client in London. He would be leaving sometime after the call but before noon, he had said.

She obsessed over the two pieces of bad news as she hung laundry on the clothesline. Moira was so deep in thought that she barely paid attention to what she was hanging on the line. The last couple of items she had put up to dry were a couple of Brian's boxer shorts and pairs of his woolen socks with holes in the toes. Absentmindedly, she stuck a finger through one of the holes in the sock she had just hung in front of her. *All his walking*, she thought to herself. The clothesline already held several of his shirts, socks, and other boxer briefs that were gently swaying in the breeze.

Shortly after Brian had arrived back in Ireland, Moira had taken to grabbing his dirty laundry every so often when he went out on his afternoon walks, replacing dirty items with clean ones in his dresser the following afternoon. The fact that he didn't seem to realize what she was doing confirmed for her that the man still had a way to go before he would find himself.

18

BRIAN HAD FINALLY come down the stairs after his rare early morning conference call. His other consulting work would have to wait; he knew that he'd have to leave for Galway soon to see the attorney. There were things he knew he needed to address, the house being a major item. He entered the kitchen and filled his mug with tea. Maureen would already be off to school, he knew. He thought he saw Moira outside hanging up clothes. It felt strange to him to sit at the kitchen table this early in the day. Normally he would grab his tea and head right back up the stairs. He looked around the kitchen as he sipped from his mug, and noticed a letter that was suspended in an upright position between the salt and pepper shakers on the table to his left. A quick glance revealed an address on the outside of the envelope that was the same as this house. When he did get mail, which was rare over here, Moira or Maureen would leave it on the kitchen table.

He reached over and took the envelope and opened the unsealed flap and pulled out a letter. *That's strange*, he thought. The letterhead was for a university up in Galway.

Probably want money, he thought. Brian started to read the body of the letter when he realized it was addressed not to him, but rather to Maureen. Now he felt guilty for looking in the envelope. He was about to put the letter back when he hesitated. His curiosity got the better of him. A scholarship for Maureen. *That's great. She's a very bright kid. Well deserved*, was his first thought. The letter really didn't go into details about what the scholarship covered or the amount. The last paragraph of the letter contained a phone number that should be called to find out the details regarding the scholarship.

He checked his watch. It was time to head up to Galway. He should get a move on. He put the letter back in the envelope and returned it to its place between the salt and pepper shakers.

As he left the kitchen, he looked at the front door and then stopped. He really should go outside and let Moira know he was leaving. He went out the back door onto the patio and headed over to where Moira was hanging up laundry.

"Moira, I'm going to be off to Galway now."

Moira stopped what she was doing and looked at Brian and nodded. Her blank look didn't go unnoticed by Brian. Then she retrieved two clothespins from a pouch hanging on the clothesline and bent over to pull a damp pillowcase out of the laundry basket.

She doesn't seem very happy this morning, Brian thought. *Maybe she's under the weather*. He was about to turn around and head to the back door when he paused. "Moira, I must apologize. I saw the envelope on the kitchen table. I thought it was addressed to me, so I opened it. That's great news. A scholarship for Maureen. You must be very proud," he said, smiling.

Even if she was under the weather, he had expected that Moira would smile at this good news. The expression *if looks could kill* didn't begin to describe the look Brian saw on Moira's face. He thought he could feel the daggers her eyes were throwing his way. He could immediately tell that something was wrong. She pointed to something on the clothesline. A pair of socks with holes were attached to the line with clothespins. Just then a gust of wind lifted the socks and the rest of the laundry, so that they appeared to wave at him. The socks looked familiar to him, as did the pair of boxers shorts next to the socks. *Why, those are my clothes. How? When? Has she been washing my clothes?* He looked from the socks back to Moira, who was shaking her arm, still pointing at the socks with the holes.

"I don't do darning. Do you hear me? I don't do darning!" Moira shouted.

Brian's smile disappeared. He nodded and took a couple of steps backward on the patio, almost tripping on a slightly uneven flagstone. Confused by Moira's eruption, he turned and beat a hasty retreat through the back door into the house and through to the front door, where he picked up a briefcase he had left earlier. He closed the front door and didn't stop until he was safely in his rental car.

What was that about? he wondered.

* * *

It had been almost two months since the last time he had driven a car. He was still taken back by what had happened out back in the courtyard. As he drove down the lane toward the village, he looked cautiously in the rearview mirror. He should be paying more attention to what was up ahead, and not what was behind him. The lane was so narrow that staying on the left side of the road meant driving down the middle. It wasn't until he reached the road the pub was on that he was reminded of the nuances of driving in Ireland. He made a left turn and was immediately greeted by the startling sound of a car's horn. He slammed on the brakes. The car facing him also came to a stop. The front of the two cars were bumper to front bumper, barely inches apart. The driver of the other car was waving at him to move over. Realizing that he was in the wrong, he mouthed a *sorry* then backed up and moved the car over to the left side of the road. He reminded himself that it had been a while since he had last driven in Ireland. Best stay alert.

Throughout the drive, he kept returning to Moira's rather bizarre behavior back at the house. For the life of him he couldn't understand why she behaved the way she did. Was it something he had said? He had mentioned to her he was going to Galway and he had said it was great Maureen was awarded a scholarship. That's all he said. Wasn't it? *Maybe it's something to do with her washing my clothes,* he thought.

Pay attention now! He was coming into the city, traffic was heavy, and he knew he needed to keep a sharp eye out for the street where Conor's law firm was located.

* * *

Up on the second floor of the office building, Brian was standing in front of the receptionist's desk. He still couldn't get this morning with Moira off his mind. He was puzzled by her reaction. Deep in thought, Brian obediently followed the receptionist to a small conference room.

"Mr. Hansen, Brian, it's good to see you," Conor said, standing in the open doorway to the conference room. "My condolences. I was shocked when I heard about your wife. Such a nice lady," he said with all sincerity, as he moved into the room, closing the door behind him.

Conor was dressed in a navy-blue suit, light-blue shirt, and a sharp-looking tie with diagonal red stripes. A far different look from the casual attire he wore when they had last met. Conor shook Brian's hand, indicating that he should not stand up. He took off his suit jacket and draped it over the back of a nearby chair before taking a seat across the small round conference table from where Brian sat.

"Thank you," was all Brian managed.

Having opened a thick file folder in front of him on the table, Conor pulled out a pad and set it alongside the file folder. He then pulled out a thick document from the file and set it off to the other side.

"Now, let's see. I presume that you want to talk about your house and your plans for it," Conor said, as he picked up the document he had previously set off to the side.

"Um, yes," Brian said. He shifted his gaze from the folder on the table in front of Conor and looked directly at the lawyer sitting across from him. He knew Conor was waiting for him to continue. But it wasn't the house he wanted to talk about. Not yet.

"Before we talk about the house, let me ask you a question, or get your opinion on another subject," Brian said, placing his hands on the table.

Conor looked puzzled but said, "Okay," leaning back in his chair.

"This morning, I discovered, by accident, that Maureen was offered a scholarship at the university up here in Galway. I'd opened a letter that I thought was addressed to me; however, it was for Maureen. I'm sure you know that Maureen is an exceptionally bright young woman." Brian paused, saw Conor nod his head in agreement, then continued. "Well, before I left to come up here, I said something to Moira about how she must be very proud that Maureen got a scholarship. The reaction I got from Moira was the last thing I expected. 'Furious' might be too strong of a word to describe it, but it comes pretty darn close. The whole way up here I kept thinking about Moira's reaction and, quite frankly, I'm at a loss for an explanation," Brian concluded, with a shrug of his shoulders.

"Ah, I wasn't aware that young Maureen was offered a scholarship. That's both good news and bad news."

Brian tilted his head and, with a curious expression on his face, said, "Please explain."

"The scholarship is good news. But it probably doesn't cover all the expenses. Full scholarships at the university are very rare. I found that out when my daughter applied to the university. I suspect that's what Moira is thinking. She is also thinking that she doesn't have the money to make up the difference, especially for all four years of a college education. Like her mother, Moira is too proud to ask for help from the family, and a loan is probably out of the question. So yes, it is good news, but for Moira and Maureen it's a tease, so it's also bad news. Therein lies the problem. The uncertainty about their future living arrangements is also probably weighing heavily on Moira's mind, to be perfectly honest," Conor concluded.

Brian's eyes drifted away from Conor and stopped when they came to a lone framed print of the Benbulbin mountain overlooking the city of Sligo that hung on the conference room wall. He sat staring at the print, deep in thought, not saying a word. Early in his career, in his first job, as he recalled, Brian had a boss who said that there are no such things as problems—only opportunities. Maureen's chance to go to college was the opportunity that needed to be addressed.

"Let's forget about the house for a minute," Brian said, as he turned to face Conor. "Let's talk about Maureen going to college. Bear with me. I'm going to throw some ideas out and want to know what you think."

Conor closed the file folder on the table in front of him and inched forward in his chair.

"Let's say money is not the issue. Maureen has been awarded a scholarship. The exact dollar amount we don't know. I will make up the difference for all four years of schooling. I have absolutely no doubt that Maureen will do well in college, so I'm not worried that it will all be for nought. It would be a shame for her to miss this opportunity. I suspect that if I approached Moira and told her I would make up the difference, she would say no." Conor raised an eyebrow and nodded his agreement.

"It seems to me that there are two major challenges that need to be overcome if the plan of getting Maureen to college is to succeed. The first is getting Moira and Maureen to think that the scholarship covers all the college costs, for all four years. The second is to somehow avoid having the college send out information, bills for example, that Moira might see which would spill the beans, so to speak."

Brian was tapping a finger on the table and was about to continue when Conor raised his hand. "If I might interrupt. The second part shouldn't be a problem. First, I'm assuming that we'd set up another account, like we have for your house, currently for utilities and other day-to-day expenses. This new account would be for college-related expenses, whatever isn't covered by the scholarship. You would fund the account, correct?"

"Yes," Brian replied.

"Currently, we have a few clients who have children at the university, where our firm gets involved. We receive the bills directly from the university for their expenses. For example, tuition, room, etc. We process the payments out of our office."

Conor further clarified, "There are situations where the parents' job requires them to work in another country, either on a short-term or long-term basis. They don't want to pull the son or daughter out of the university when they might have only a year or two left.

"I happen to know the dean of admissions over at the university. We graduated together from there, and I play a round of golf with him every other weekend, weather permitting. We also serve together on the board of a local charity. I'll ask him if the scholarship covers all expenses. If he says yes, then we don't have a problem. If the answer is no, I'll talk to him about having his office flag Maureen's account and make sure all correspondence is sent to our firm. I feel confident that we would be able take care of the billing process. Moira would not have to know. I'll also ask him if he knows whether Maureen has already inquired about the scholarship. However, I do have a concern."

"What is it?" Brian asked.

"Please don't take offense, but let's say it's a partial scholarship, we get the billing set up, and Maureen goes off to the university. Then a year later or two years later, something happens to you, God forbid. I think you get my point."

"Actually, that's a very good point. Hadn't thought of it, and well, quite frankly, I should have," Brian said in a somber voice, staring at the table. There was moment of silence before Brian looked up again at Conor and said in a determined voice, "You're quite right in bringing that issue up. Okay. If you can find out from your friend in admissions what we might be talking about in terms of the cost for all four years of schooling, a ballpark figure, I'll fund the account for the total amount. I'll also add a cushion for the unforeseen."

Nodding his head, Brian continued in a faint voice, "No. You were right bringing this up. No offense taken."

For the next few moments, they both stared at the picture on the wall, deep in thought about the other challenge: how to convince Moira that the scholarship covered all the cost of schooling.

Finally, Conor broke the silence. "I don't feel comfortable getting my friend over at the university involved when it comes to convincing Moira the scholarship is all-inclusive in terms of costs."

"Agreed," Brian responded, then added, "Somehow I think if you or I tried to convince her, she would see right through us."

"Yes. I don't think that would work. But how do we convince her? Who would she believe?" Conor started doodling on his pad. "You know, it a crazy idea, but it just might work," Conor said out loud to himself.

"What might work?" Brian asked, his head tilting to the side.

"Padraig. If Padraig told her. I think Moira would believe it, if the news came from him. He's been like a father to her all these years, so . . ."

Brian was skeptical. "Do you think he would agree?"

"Don't know. All he can say is no if we ask him. While you're driving back, I'll give him a call. Before you get home, stop by the pub and see him. Maybe if both of us work on him, he might agree. Before you leave, I'll call my friend at the university."

"We'll need Padraig to be very convincing," Brian said, placing both his hands on the table. Thinking out loud, he said, "How about if Padraig comes up to the house. Said he heard about the scholarship and would like to see the letter. He pretends he is calling the telephone number on the letter to see how much the scholarship covers. However, instead of calling the university, he calls you. He puts on a good show in front of Moira and ends the call, informing Moira the scholarship covers everything. Think that would work?"

Conor looked at Brian and shrugged his shoulders. "It's a long shot—a very long shot. But I can't think of any other way. Hopefully, Moira or Maureen haven't already called the number in the letter. It all depends on whether Padraig will go along. If Padraig agrees to our diversion, let's shoot for him calling here a little after noontime tomorrow from your house. Will Moira be home then?"

Brian thought about the question, then answered, "Yes." He knew she was off tomorrow.

Seeing Brian about to get up, Conor waved for him to remain seated. "Before you go. What do you want to do about the house?"

"The house? Oh, yes. The house." Brian sighed, shaking his head. Remembering what Conor had said about Moira being concerned about the uncertainty of Maureen's and her living arrangements, he felt terrible. *How could he have been so insensitive!* He should have addressed the issue of the house long before now. If Clare were still alive, she would have given him an earful. Then, again, if Clare was still alive... Looking at Conor, Brian said in a firm voice, "*No*, I will *not* be selling the house."

"Fine. Glad to hear it," Conor said with a smile. He then gathered up the materials in front of him and escorted Brian back to his office and pointed to a seat across from his desk. Brian sat down and took a quick survey of the office. He noticed various plaques on the wall behind Conor: diplomas, and a few certificates of appreciation. Brian could hear Conor speaking to his friend at the university admissions office. Occasionally Conor would nod his head and write something down on a pad during the conversation. Conor finally ended the conversation, affirming next weekend's tee-off time at the country club.

* * *

Conor confirmed that Maureen had not received a full scholarship and, from what his friend could tell, Maureen so far had not called to inquire about it. The scholarship covered annual tuition and lab fees. Providing the student maintained an overall B average during the year, the scholarship would be automatically renewed for the following year. What was not covered was room and board, books, incidentals, and computer-related expenses. Looking up from his pad, Conor told Brian an estimate of one year's additional cost, not covered by the scholarship, along with a figure for all four years. Conor also relayed to Brian what the annual dollar amount of the scholarship was worth. A rather significant amount of money. He tore off the sheet upon which he had written the calculations and handed it to Brian. Conor escorted Brian to the reception area and told Brian to keep his fingers crossed. He said he'd give Padraig a call when he got back in his office, before bidding Brian goodbye.

Once again in the car, Brian ran through the meeting again in his mind. Conor, Padraig, and he would all be walking on thin ice. They might, just might, pull it off. That is, if Padraig agreed to play along. The pub would be his next stop. As he drove back to the village, Brian started to notice the vivid green pastures on either side of the road and the occasional whitewashed cottage. He slowed the vehicle to take in the sights. He had driven this route earlier but couldn't recall taking in the surrounding landscape. Up ahead, the roadway followed the contours of the land, with the blue waters of Galway Bay off to the immediate right. Once again, he couldn't recall noticing the bay nor the boats plying its waters.

The old Brian was slowly returning.

* * *

"I told Conor, and I'll tell you the same thing: *you two are crazy*!" Padraig placed a damp towel on the bar directly in front of Brian, who was perched on a barstool. Unconsciously, Padraig started to wipe the already clean surface.

"Then you won't do it?" Brian asked, somewhat deflated, lifting his arms to avoid the swirling towel.

"I didn't say that. I said you two are crazy. And I suppose I am too, for going along with this, this . . ." Padraig finally found the word he was searching for: "charade." Padraig finished wiping down the bar and put the towel in the sink below. "I'm doing this for Maureen's sake. You do know if Moira ever finds out what you're up to, there's no place on earth where you can hide." Padraig stabbed a finger at Brian.

"Me? How about you!" With eyebrows raised, Brian continued, "You're family. I wonder what she would have in store for you if she ever found out about your part in this." Brian smiled. Padraig's face drained of all its color. Brian could see a shiver go through Padraig's body from his head downward. Brian leaned back slightly on the barstool and reflected on the deception that the three of them were about to undertake. A shiver went through his own body as he recalled Moira's outburst earlier this morning.

"Best if we say our goodbyes now then, for tomorrow may not end well—for both of us! A drink, I think, would be in order. Coke? Fine, two Cokes it'll be." Padraig didn't wait for a response and reached behind him and pulled two bottles of soda out of a glass-faced cooler, opened both, and poured the contents into glasses he had filled with ice. He put them on the bar. They drank in silence.

"Seriously, did Conor explain to you your part in this scheme?" Brian asked after a while, as he put his half-full glass down on the bar. Brian knew that Padraig's role was key if they were going to successfully full off tomorrow's deception.

"Aye. Noontime I go up to the house. I'm to first get Moira to show me the letter. Tell her I heard about it. Hopefully she wouldn't ask from whom." From his facial expression, it was clear to Brian that Padraig was going to sacrifice him if asked.

"Then I'm to pretend like I am calling the university to find out about the scholarship. Hopefully she hasn't already called the university. You two brain trusts considered that she might have already called the university?" Padraig asked, jutting his jaw out at Brian before continuing, "I will be calling Conor. I got Rory to put Conor's phone number into my phone." Padraig pointed over his shoulders at a young man pulling a draft pint for a customer.

"Then I'll say something like . . . 'That's great, the scholarship covers all the costs.' If she falls for it, everything is fine. If she knows she's being set up, I'll be out the door before you. Remember the story about the two gents being chased by a bear. You only need to be faster than the other guy. You're the other guy!"

Brian continued to quiz Padraig. "You'll be up at the house tomorrow around noon?"

"Yes. Didn't I just say that?" Padraig paused, stroking his beard. "Let's see now, the reason for me being up at the house. She'll wonder why." Padraig's eyes searched around the pub as if he would find the answer printed on a wall. "I know. I'm returning your wallet that you left behind when you stopped by for a drink on your way back from Galway." Padraig held out his open hand. Shaking his head,

Brian reached into his back pocket and pulled out his wallet. Reluctantly he placed it in Padraig's outstretched hand.

As he drove up the lane to the house, Brian wondered what the odds were that the garda had set up a vehicle checkpoint up ahead, checking driver licenses. Him without his wallet. Then again, that was the least of his worries. He thought about tomorrow.

What have I gotten myself into?

19

THE NEXT MORNING, looking out his bedroom window, Brian could see that it was going to be a beautiful day. At least weather-wise. Hardly any clouds in the sky, the sun shining brightly. After a shave and a shower, he was ready for the new day—or was he? He sat on the end of his bed and tied his shoelaces. He would keep to his normal routine. Go downstairs and get his mug of tea. Say good morning to the ladies and then back upstairs to his consulting work. He stood up and headed downstairs, where his morning tea awaited.

Back in his room, Brian, mug of tea in hand, walked over to the window and looked out across the fields. The look on their faces were pitiful. He didn't think he had ever seen two people look as sad as Moira and Maureen. Normally he would get a good morning. Not today. *I guess they're concerned about the scholarship and what it covers.*

He continued to gaze out the window. Then . . . *You idiot! You complete idiot!* he thought to himself as he slapped his forehead. Some tea sloshed over the rim of the mug held in his left hand. *They both knew you were going to see the law-*

yer yesterday. And why were you going to see the lawyer? The house! They were waiting to find out about the house. And you waltz downstairs grab your tea and head back upstairs without saying a word about the house. He let out a loud sigh. Should he go back down and tell them? Or might it be better to wait until Padraic arrived? It might help distract Moira from the scholarship ploy. *Let them know while Padraic was there, and kill two birds with one stone. Maybe not the best expression, especially today,* he thought.

But he should have already told them.

What an idiot!

* * *

He looked at his watch, which indicated that it was a couple of minutes before noon. He headed downstairs for lunch.

In the kitchen, the atmosphere could best be described as frosty. Maureen was at school. Moira stood by the refrigerator. Seeing Brian, she opened the refrigerator door, reached in and pulled out a plate containing a sandwich made up of last night's leftovers. She pointed to the kitchen table and set the plate down. She reached back into the refrigerator and pulled out another plate with a sandwich for herself. Brian sat down on one side of the table while she sat across from him. Silence. He noticed the letter was still suspended between the salt and pepper shakers. It was nerve-racking to wait to announce his intentions for the house, but it would be a good distraction from the scholarship deception.

Brian and Moira were sitting eating their sandwiches in silence when the quiet was interrupted by a knock on the front door. They could hear the door opening and then closing again. They both looked up from their plates and stared at each other, questioning looks exchanged.

"Anyone home?" Padraig's loud voice boomed out.

"In the kitchen," Moira responded, with little emotion.

"Ah, Brian. You left your wallet in the pub yesterday. Rory found it and gave it to me." Padraig reached in his front pocket and pulled out a wallet and handed it to Brian.

"Thank you, Padraig. I didn't even realize it was missing." Brian took the wallet and slipped it into his back pants pocket.

"Lunch?" Moira asked, barely looking at her uncle.

"No thanks. I had a little something before I came up here."

Padraig stood looking around the kitchen, then said, "Moira, I heard that Maureen got some kind of scholarship from the university up north." Moira's eyes went from Padraig to Brian. Brian could feel the daggers that Moira's eyes shot his way. "Might I see the letter, Moira?" Padraig continued.

Reluctantly Moira reached over and took the envelope from between the salt and pepper shakers and handed it to Padraig. Still standing, Padraig took the letter out of the envelope and started to read it. "Um. Doesn't say how much the scholarship is for, does it? Do you know?" Padraig directed the question to Moira, who shook her head. Padraig walked across the kitchen floor, letter in hand, and continued out of their sight into the dining area. Moira and Brian went back to their sandwiches.

"Hello, is this the admissions office?" Brian could clearly hear Padraig's voice from where he sat in the kitchen. Brian gripped his sandwich tighter in anticipation. "Yes. I have a letter here addressed to my niece's daughter which indicates that she got some sort of scholarship to your university. A Maureen McGuire. Yes. I'll hold."

Right after Maureen's name left Padraig's mouth, Moira's head shot up and her eyes grew the size of saucers. She bolted out of her chair, dropping her half-eaten sandwich on the table, missing her plate. Seeing Moira dash into the dining area, Brian placed his sandwich on his plate and slowly rose from his chair. He then cautiously followed Moira into the dining area, where he saw that she was standing a foot away from her uncle, whose backside rested against the oak sideboard. Brian took a quick look at the back door. *The back door is definitely closer than the front door, should I need to escape,* he thought. Padraig was holding up a hand, indicating that Moira should wait a minute.

"Hush," Padraig said to Moira, then into the phone he said, "What? Oh no, not you. I'm sorry, I'm telling a wee little one here next to me that I'm talking to a very nice gentleman on the phone." With his free hand he tried to shoo Moira away. Moira wouldn't budge.

"Yes, please continue," Padraig said to the person on the other end. "Really. Really. So, just so I've got this straight, the scholarship includes tuition, room, food, all of the fees and the cost of books. That's grand. What's that? Okay. I can see how she might need just a wee bit of spending money if she wants a soda or something. I got it. Thank you very much for your time. And, oh, thank you very much for the scholarship.

"What's that?" he continued. "Absolutely, I know for a fact that Maureen will be going to your university. Yes, you can mark Maureen McGuire down as accepted." As Padraig was speaking, he looked at Moira, nodding his head up and down in an exaggerated fashion, looking for her agreement. Finally, Moira slowly nodded her head up and down in response.

"Thank you, and you have a nice day too."

Moira stood staring at her uncle with furrowed brow and started to tap her foot. In response, Padraig arched an eyebrow as if to say, *What?!* Brian sensed that suspicious thoughts were beginning to stir in Moira's mind. Now was the time for him to step up and cause a diversion.

"Moira, that's great news about the scholarship!" Brian exclaimed.

Moira whipped her head around to face him. Not a hint of a smile. She had the look of someone who thought somebody might have just pulled a fast one on her, but she wasn't quite sure if that was the case. Brian thought it was almost as though gears were turning inside her head, trying to figure out what had just happened. Behind Moira, Brian saw Padraig's expression was one of pure relief as he placed his phone in his pocket. Any minute now, Brian had expected to see Padraig race toward the front door.

"While I have you both here, I have some news. Hopefully, good news." Brian paused to make sure he had the attention of both of them. "As you know, yesterday I went up to see Conor about this property." Moira stopped tapping her foot. "I told him that I am *not* selling. I thought you should both know. Moira, you don't have to answer me now, but I would very much appreciate it if you, and Maureen, would stay and continue to keep an eye on the place."

Moira looked at him with a somewhat confused expression, which eventually turned into one of understanding.

"Okay," was all she said. She turned and gave her uncle a searching look before she headed back into the kitchen and her unfinished sandwich.

Padraig's relief was palpable. He mouthed a barely audible, "Stop by later." Brian knew he meant the pub and gave him a thumbs-up sign. Brian then returned to the kitchen while Padraig headed for the front door.

"I must be getting back to the pub," he called out to no one in particular. The sound of the front door opening and closing followed.

As they sat at the kitchen table, finishing their sandwiches, Brian noticed an immediate change in Moira's demeanor. No words were spoken, but the feeling of gloom had disappeared. What a change from yesterday, he observed. He couldn't put a finger on it, but he felt bit different too. It was like he could see the world around him more clearly. He didn't feel so numb. He realized he actually felt good about something other than work. The woman sitting across from him seemed different from the person who greeted him in the morning or placed lunch on the table in front of him. Now he noticed how green Moira's eyes were and how her hair fell gently to her shoulders. He even found the way she chewed her food fascinating. He had to make a conscious effort not to stare at her, but he was intrigued by this new person who he was just seeing now for the first time. After he finished his sandwich, he picked up Moira's empty plate and placed it along with his own in the sink. He then went on his afternoon walk.

Needless to say, dinner that night was a very upbeat affair. Two pieces of good news in one day. A university scholarship and a home, at least for the foreseeable future. Before his afternoon walk, Brian had briefly stopped by the pub to see Padraig. Padraig looked like he had been put through the ringer. He had been pleased with his amateur acting skills but was also exhausted.

He also said something that Brian didn't quite understand, something about Padraig's nephew Conor telling Irish jokes while Padraig was on the phone to him, and what Padraig was going to do to Conor the next time he saw him. Something that Brian didn't think was anatomically possible. During his walk, Brian called Conor to let him know that he thought their little plan was successful and, fingers crossed, that Moira believed the scholarship covered all expenses. He also asked Conor if he would contact his friend at the university to make sure all correspondence regarding Maureen went to Conor's office.

He would tell Moira and Maureen tomorrow at breakfast that he would be heading back to the United States the day after tomorrow. Work and other obligations required his attention.

But he would come back—*home.*

* * *

Two days later, Brian came down the stairs, suitcase in hand. He walked over to the front door and left the suitcase off to the side. He then proceeded to the kitchen, where he saw Moira sitting at the kitchen table drinking a cup of tea. No Maureen. It was Saturday; *she's probably still sleeping.*

Moira turned in her seat and noticed Brian.

"Cup of tea?" she asked.

"No thank you. If I have a cup, I'd have to make a couple of extra stops on the way to the airport." He smiled and shrugged his shoulders. He looked around the kitchen then said, "I best be on my way. I'll send Maureen an email to let you folks know when I expect to be back in Ireland."

"Send her an email to let us know you made it safely home," Moira added.

He nodded, turned, and went through the dining area and over toward the front door. Moira followed behind him. He picked up his suitcase and was about to open the front door.

"Wait! Wait!" Maureen frantically yelled from upstairs.

Brian and Moira turned to see Maureen barreling down the stairs in her pajamas. As she approached the bottom of the stairs, she grabbed hold of the top of the banister's newel post to help her pivot and swing the direction of her momentum toward the front of the house. She turned and raced across the floor to the front door. She stopped just in front of Brian and looked up at him. She lunged forward, wrapped her arms around him and gave him a long hug. Then she let go and stepped back.

Taken back by this display of affection, Brian was speechless. At that moment, he felt an emotion that had been absent for a long time. He felt genuinely moved by the young woman who looked up at him. Recovering, he smiled and said, "Now young lady, keep up with your studies. No slacking off just because you've been accepted to the university."

"Say hello to your family for us," Maureen said.

"I will."

"Let us know you got home alright," Moira reminded him.

Brian nodded and turned, opened the door, and walked across the stone driveway to the rental car. He placed the suitcase in the backseat and then opened the driver's door and sat down. He started the car and rolled down the window and waved goodbye to the two women poised in front of the open front door. As he drove off, he thought about what Maureen said about saying hello to his family. Moira and Maureen felt like his family too. As he passed the pub—on the correct side of the road—he honked the car's horn twice, then settled in for the hour-plus drive to the airport.

20

A MONTH HAD PASSED since Brian had left for the United States. This Sunday morning was unusual because Moira was in the kitchen first thing, preparing today's main meal. Usually, she would start preparing Sunday's evening meal for the three of them—Padraig, Maureen, and herself—in the early afternoon. Today was special. Today, Moira and Maureen had guests coming for lunch. Daniel and his friend from work would first spend the morning installing new software on Maureen's computer. Maureen would be heading off to the university in three months. Daniel's friend was the computer expert (or "geek," as Daniel referred to his friend).

Moira hadn't been around the last time the person had stopped by when Maureen had first gotten her computer. What exactly the young man would be doing to Maureen's computer was beyond her. The age of the computer or the laptop (*is it the same thing?* she wasn't sure), brought with it a whole new language. Mouse, internet, LAN, modem, notebook, software, WAN, firewall, hard disk, and so on.

Something about the last one—hard disk—*seems a bit indecent,* she thought.

Moira went over to the oven and turned it on so she could bake the two large lamb casseroles she was preparing. She would heat up the rolls she had made last night just before it was time to serve the meal. She sat down at the kitchen table to rest for a minute. Maureen was very fortunate, she thought. Indeed, they were both very fortunate. When word got out that Maureen was going to the university, Moira's uncles and cousins outdid themselves with gifts—clothes, school supplies, and small gifts of cash ("She might need some spending money when she gets to the university," they had said). Moira's protests about the gifts of cash went unheeded.

While Maureen was over the moon with excitement about going to the university, Moira simply was unable to share the same excitement as her daughter. If she were honest, in a way she dreaded the thought of her baby leaving home. Going somewhere where she was unable to protect her from all the strangers she would, no doubt, encounter.

Padraig had sensed her unease about Maureen going off to the university and had offered words of encouragement. "You can't keep her under your wings forever," he had said. "She has to find her own way sometime. Besides, Conor and his family live up by the university, so it's not like no family will be around." Padraig had reminded her that Conor's daughter also attended the university.

The thought of Conor being nearby and his daughter being at the university had helped—a little bit. So did Conor's phone call to her, saying he would stop by the university every so often to see Maureen. His daughter had volunteered to show Maureen the ropes when she got there. Ah well, Moira thought, sooner or later her daughter would have to find her own way.

"I'll get it!" Maureen yelled, as she stampeded down the stairs.

Her daughter's voice had startled Moira and brought her out of her pensive mood. She didn't think she'd heard the doorbell nor a knock on the front door. Maureen must have been looking out one of the front windows and saw the car coming up the lane, she thought. She got up from her seat and took off her apron. "Might as well see what a geek looks like," she said quietly, as she made her way to the front door.

Standing in the foyer was Daniel and a young man who looked to be ten or so years younger than Daniel. Moira looked at the young man. *So, this person is a geek.* He was about an inch or so shorter than Daniel. His ears looked normal. They weren't like the person on that sci-fi show. *What was the character's name? Speck, Spoke, something similar,* she thought. The young man's forehead looked to be normal in size. He was dressed alright—light-colored slacks, dark-blue golf shirt, two loafers (on two feet). She did note the leather thing attached to his belt and the briefcase.

"Moira, I would like you to meet my friend Michael. Michael and I work together at the estate agency," Daniel said, looking from Moira to Michael.

"Pleasure to meet you, Mrs. McGuire," the young man chimed in.

No one corrected Michael regarding his use of the term *Mrs.* How was he to know?

Maureen nodded, then said, "Why don't we move inside?"

As they headed for the dining room, Moira said, "You boys will be staying for lunch. I prepared a nice casserole. I'll not take *no* for an answer." Moira didn't wait for a response and headed back to the kitchen.

Maureen, Michael, and Daniel sat down at the dining room table and reviewed a list that Michael had handed out regarding the new software to be installed and security issues regarding the general use of the computer. Computer security took up most of the discussion, Michael emphasizing the importance of security in the new, less-secured environment that the university represented.

* * *

While Michael's list was being reviewed, Moira pretended to be busy in the kitchen. She was listening to every single word that Michael was saying. She had half a mind to ask for a copy of the list for herself, but she thought better of it. Instead, she would move a pot around, turn the faucet on for a couple of seconds, open cabinet drawers, take plates out, gather silverware to appear busy, the whole time absorbing everything that Michael said or the answers he had to questions raised by both Daniel and Maureen. This went on for a good hour. Finally, she heard papers being put away.

"Now, I'll download the new software on your computer and also check to make sure the security and antivirus programs are functioning properly. I'm going to ask you to key your password into the laptop. I don't want to know what it is nor see you enter it. Okay?" Michael looked at Maureen for confirmation.

"Can I ask you a favor?" Maureen asked in a quiet voice.

"Sure."

"Could you also update Mr. Hansen's laptop? He asked me to ask you. I told him you were coming. He gave me his password before he left. I don't have it written down. I memorized it when he told me it," Maureen said, sheepishly. This after all the discussion about passwords.

"He also said that, if Daniel didn't mind, Daniel could let Conor know what the costs are so that Conor could reimburse whomever for any new software or updates, or whatever else needs to be done for the two laptops."

Michael let out an exaggerated sigh. "This Mr. Hansen must really trust you." Smiling, Michael continued, "Sure, I can update his laptop at the same time I update yours. Same thing, though. I want you to key in his password; I don't want to know it."

Moira could hear the movement of chairs in the dining room. She peeked out into the dining area and saw the three of them making their way up the stairs to the landing where Maureen's desk and laptop were located. Moira looked out the rear window into the patio area and the fields beyond and pondered what Michael had just said: "This Mr. Hansen must really trust you."

* * *

After another hour, both laptops had been updated with new software and the antivirus software had been double-checked. The aroma of the casseroles had permeated throughout the interior of the house. If the three of them were not hungry before, they were now, and they hurried down the stairs to the dining area. The timing was perfect. Moira had place settings for four at the dining room table. This was a special occasion; the kitchen wouldn't do.

Michael moved toward the back of the dining room area and surveyed the two-story wall of glass. Through the upper sections, wispy clouds could be seen slowly floating by. He turned away from the glass wall and moved over to the dining room table, obeying Maureen's mother as she ushered the three of them to their seats. Moira began filling plates with portions of the casserole. Daniel was passing the basket of rolls around to the others after he took two for himself. Michael was commenting about the view outside when Daniel nudged his elbow and handed him a plate full of casserole.

They all dug into their meals. The silence as they ate was proof that the casserole was very good and much appreciated, especially by the two young men, who had willingly accepted an offer of seconds. As they were finishing up their plates, Michael excused himself for a minute and retrieved his leather briefcase from the living room couch. Back at the dining room table, he reached in the briefcase and pulled out a small box that he handed to Daniel.

"You had asked me to remind you and to give this to you this before we left," Michael said, sitting back down in his chair. Daniel nodded and took the box from Michael.

"Maureen, this is for you. Padraig and his brothers and sister, Michael here, and I, thought this would come in handy when you're away." Daniel concluded by handing the box to Maureen.

Maureen took the box and looked from Daniel to Michael, puzzled. She slowly removed the lid and let out a small gasp. "Oh my, oh my. But you shouldn't have. This must have cost—"

"Maureen, it's a gift. There'll be no talk of cost," Daniel interrupted.

"What is it?" Moira asked, leaning closer to her daughter to get a better view of the contents of the box.

"It's a smart phone. She'll need one when she's at the university," Daniel responded.

Moira knew what a smartphone was, and she also knew that it cost a lot of money. Too much money. She was about to protest—

"Maureen, if I may. Let me show you some personal safety features," Michael said, as he inched his chair nearer to Maureen. He took the smartphone in his hand and held it so they could both see it. "This is an SOS feature, which will allow others to locate exactly where you are if there's an emergency. Just press . . ."

Moira was now listening intently to the various personal safety features that Michael proceeded to describe. He meticulously went through each application with Maureen. The entire time, Daniel could be seen nodding his head in agreement with what Michael was saying. When he was done, Michael pulled out the instructions in the back of the box and showed Maureen where she could read about each safety application in more detail. He also pointed out how it could be a useful tool for her schoolwork. He concluded with a warning about not becoming addicted to the smartphone and to use it sparingly. "It's a useful piece of technology, if used properly."

And I thought it was just an expensive toy, Moira thought. She had seen people around the village and, of course, in the pub, constantly pecking away at the screens. Sometimes an entire table of customers wouldn't say two words to each other throughout the meal, their faces buried in their respective phones. She nodded to herself when she thought of what Michael had said about not becoming addicted to it.

"I should mention that Mr. Hansen was insistent that he will pay for the annual service fee. He also said, and I quote, '*No arguments from anyone. Period!*'" Daniel gently slapped the table with his hand for mock emphasis.

"Mam, if it's alright with you, Daniel and Michael said they will take me up to the university when it's time to enroll and move into my dorm. Michael went there and said he would give me a quick tour of the place." Maureen stood up from the table and began to clear away everyone's empty plates.

Moira realized she hadn't thought that far ahead. She didn't have a car, so she couldn't drive her. How she was going to get Maureen up to the university had not crossed her mind. And if Michael knew his way around the place, that would be good, she thought. Daniel would also be going.

"That would be fine and very much appreciated," she said as she looked at Daniel, then over to Michael.

As she entered the kitchen holding the empty casserole dish in her hands, Moira thought that the smile on her daughter's face was proof that she'd had a very productive and exciting day. It was nice of Daniel and Michael to take the time to help Maureen with her laptop, and with Brian's. The smartphone, well, that was icing on the cake. She hadn't realized how many uses it had, particularly the personal safety features.

Especially the personal safety features!

Placing the casserole dish on the counter, she could hear the front door close and then the sound of her daughter racing up the stairs to the landing above. Staring at the empty casserole dish, and pleased she had made a second casserole for that night, she thought, *hope she likes lamb casserole again for dinner.* She smiled as she thought about this evening. Maureen would be telling Padraig all about the day's events and, no doubt, demonstrating her brand-new smart phone. As Moira filled up the empty casserole dish with hot water to let it soak, she thought that Maureen was blessed—no, they were both blessed—with thoughtful relatives and old and new friends.

Moira sat down at the kitchen table and proceeded to fold and refold a kitchen towel. She looked through into the dining room and sighed as she thought how empty the house will be without her daughter. Brian will still be around, but not all the time. He had been traveling quite a bit recently for his consulting business. As she rose from her chair, she thought to herself, *at least there will be fewer dishes to wash.* She placed the kitchen towel on the table and slowly made her way toward the laundry room.

21

Fifteen Months Later

TIME RACED BY. Moira could hardly believe that Maureen had already completed one year at the university and had begun her second year three weeks ago. She missed having her daughter home. That, she couldn't deny. But she also knew that Maureen's education was very important and her ticket to a world beyond the village. When Maureen came home for the summer break after her first year, Moira was surprised at how grown up she looked. Sure, Moira had seen her daughter during Christmas and spring break. Even so, not seeing Maureen on a daily basis, Moira noted that her daughter had shot up at least two more inches in height and seemed to have matured both physically and socially. Maureen displayed a confidence that had not been evident before. Padraig had also noticed a change in Maureen and had mentioned it to Moira. He too had noticed the physical changes in Maureen and was pleased to see her self-assurance while remaining polite and respectful, unlike many of her age group. Moira was grateful that Padraig had made sure Maureen had a job at the pub over the summer so Maureen could earn some extra money for the following year at school.

Unlike other boys and girls her age, in her spare time Maureen continued to bury herself in her books. She was not interested in going with the local lads and lasses to Galway for the nightlife. Just as well, Moira thought. She had heard of a boy in the next village over who had died in a car accident coming home from a night out in Galway two years ago. Alcohol had been involved. Nor had the allure of spending a couple of days in Dublin with her classmates and their friends appealed to Maureen.

One day during summer break, Maureen was sitting outside on the patio, reading. Moira took time away from hanging out the laundry and sat down on the bench beside her daughter. Maureen looked up from the book and smiled at her mother. Nodding her head at the book, Moira had asked her what she was reading. Turned out the book was for an upcoming class Maureen would be taking in the autumn and she wanted to get a head start. Moira was starting to get concerned that Maureen was too focused on school. But what could she say? Certainly, her own behavior in her youth wasn't something to call attention to or be proud of. It just seemed that there should be more to life than books.

During the two times over the summer when Brian returned to Ireland, Maureen did take a break from her normal routine of working at the pub and reading books. Brian got Moira and Maureen to join him on a couple of outings away from the village. As part of these outings, Brian would treat his guests to a nice dinner at a restaurant that he would have scoped out on the internet well in advance. For Moira and Maureen, being served instead of being the servers was a pleasant change. The two of them would compare notes regarding the service, the server's attire, and the table's place settings. Toward the end of the meal, their conversation would turn to what should be next on their list of trips.

While hesitant at first about going on these trips, Moira discovered that she enjoyed these excursions. She was surprised at how little she knew about these places which were, so to speak, in her own backyard. She also liked these trips because it got Maureen away from her books. Moira had also noticed a change in Brian. He seemed to genuinely enjoy being the group's tour guide, introducing them to different places. His smiles and occasional laughter were something new, something she had not seen since his wife had died.

During his visits back to Ireland over the past year, Moira noted Brian still maintained his daily routine of tea, work, lunch, more work, long walks, dinner, then whatever he did up in his room until he fell asleep; read, she supposed. Even with his routine, such as it was, she enjoyed having him around the house, especially during the times when Maureen was away at school. Ever so slowly, she noticed, Brian was getting back to his old self. *If one could ever get completely back to oneself after losing a wife,* she thought. There was a healing taking place and she knew that was good and it would take time.

If she were perfectly honest with herself, she was also changing. She was emerging from what was a self-imposed exile, devoid of hope and happiness, that she had embraced for way too many years. She found that she looked forward to sharing meals with Brian, the two of them alone in the house at lunch or dinnertime. Trying not to stare while they were eating, she would examine his face, his eyes, the way he would occasionally brush his hair back from his forehead. She hadn't really noticed these details before. During one such meal, she came to the realization that she had someone, other than her daughter and uncle, whom she genuinely cared about. She found these feelings to be strange—indeed, somewhat unsettling—and yet, at the same time, comforting.

22

AS WAS USUALLY the case at around four in the afternoon, the pub was relatively quiet. The lunch folks had long gone, and it was still too early for the evening dinner crowd. Moira could relax for a little while; it would be another hour or so before the pub would begin to fill up again with hungry and thirsty patrons. Most of the dinner crowd would bide their time after their meals, waiting for the music session that would start around nine. At this early hour, there were probably around a dozen or so people enjoying a late-afternoon pint and the ensuing conversations. Most of the people were tourists discussing their evening's plans as well as tomorrow's itinerary. These folks had probably already secured tonight's lodgings at the local B and Bs. Some of the tourists congregated at two tables close to one end of the bar, nearest the kitchen. A couple of the tourists were sitting on barstools across from the occupied tables. Away from the tourists, at the very far other end of the bar, were two locals sitting on barstools all by themselves, partially drained glasses on the bar in front of them.

The two locals were a married couple. The man was known simply as "the farmer." His wife was referred to as "the farmer's wife." They had first names, but only the very old folks in the village remembered them. For the most part, people referred to them as the farmer and the farmer's wife, and everyone knew exactly who they were talking about. They also knew the farmer had a reputation for causing trouble. The farmer and the farmer's wife would come into the pub for a late-afternoon refreshment around once a month. From the look of the stains on their work clothes and the mud (or something else) on their work boots and the smell of manure which seem to linger in their immediate area, it was obvious that they had arrived straight from their farm after a hard day's work. The smell might also explain the empty expanse between the folks at the two ends of the bar. Padraig, who was behind the bar, stayed at the end close to the tourists, only venturing to the other end to replenish the farmer's pint.

Farming was a hard life, and it was reflected in their looks. The farmer's wife's weathered face revealed the effects of long days working in the sun. Her heavily tanned face was creased and had a permanent look of being tired. Even her clothes looked tired. A faded green shirt hung from her drooping shoulders. Her jeans were also deeply faded and the areas by the knees looked as though they would give way any day now. Sitting at the bar, her elbows, braced against the bar top, appeared to be the only thing preventing her from falling forward. She stared at the half pint of lager on the coaster in front of her. Since she was the one driving, she would nurse the one beer until her husband was ready to leave. Occasionally she would look over to keep track of the number of pints her husband had. After his fourth, they would usually head out and go home.

Sitting next to her this night, the farmer was already on his second pint. He stared at the half-empty glass in front of him, lost in thought. The stubble on his face was evidence that a razor had been unused for some days. Like his wife, his face could best be described as ruddy. His brown hair was matted down from the day's sweat. His blue work shirt was streaked with farm matter that would be difficult to clean in two or more wash cycles. Unlike his wife, his hands rested on his propped-up knees, except when he would bring a hand up to grab hold of his pint glass. Every now and again he would glance around the pub; with a look of disdain, he would take note of the people at the other end of the bar. His eyes followed Moira as she carried a tray full of clean glasses and set them down on the bar down by the other end.

A well-dressed elderly couple had just come into the pub and taken a seat at a table midway between the group of tourists at one end of the bar and the farmer and his wife at the other end. The older gentleman went up to the bar, and Padraig moved over to the middle of the bar, where the taps were located, to greet him. As the gentleman gave Padraig their early-bird dinner order, Padraig keyed information into the computer in front of him. He already knew the table number, since he saw where the couple was sitting. He then poured out a half pint of lager in one glass, retrieved a wine glass, and filled it with white wine from a bottle from the refrigerator behind the bar. The elderly gentleman paid and took the drinks in his two slightly trembling hands and carefully ambled back to his table, handing his wife the glass of wine before sitting down next to her.

About fifteen minutes later, Moira strode across the pub's dining area to the table where the familiar elderly couple were sitting. In one hand was a small casserole dish of Irish stew, which she placed carefully in front of the lady, retaining the towel she had used to hold the hot dish. She warned the woman that the dish was very hot. In front of the gentleman, she placed a plate containing salmon, mashed potatoes, and string beans. In the middle of the table, Moira placed a basket of warm rolls. She stood chatting with them for a couple of moments and told them if they needed anything else to wave. In a couple of minutes, she would return to their table with extra dinner rolls, on the house.

Having dropped off the extra rolls with the elderly couple, Moira made the rounds of the various tables to see if there were any empty glasses that needed to be picked up or if any of the tabletops needed a swipe with the damp cloth she had in her hand. As she moved past where the farmer and his wife were sitting, the farmer snickered. If she had heard him, Moira didn't seem to pay any mind and kept moving along, looking around the pub at the various tables, returning to the kitchen with a tray containing a couple of used glasses. Hearing her husband's snicker, the farmer's wife turned her head and looked closely at her husband.

"I wonder," the farmer mumbled.

"You wonder what?" his wife asked.

Moira came out of from the kitchen area again and walked over to where Padraig was behind the bar, fiddling with the beer taps. Wondering who was providing the Irish music that evening, Moira looked at Padraig and asked, "Who's playing tonight?"

"Same group as last night. They'll be here again tomorrow night. Then we have a different group lined up for the weekend. Last night's group is new and was pretty good, or at least they were well received last night," Padraig said as he continued to fiddle with a beer tap.

From his place at the end of the bar, the farmer stared at Moira. "I wonder if the American is poking her?" the farmer slurred. "I bet you the American *is* poking her," he repeated, this time his voice much louder, as he continued to stare at Moira. The farmer was now on pint number four.

"Hush," the farmer's wife said, giving her husband a jab to his shoulder with her elbow. "She'll hear you!" The farmer's wife had followed her husband's eyes down the length of the bar to where Moira stood talking to Padraig.

Suddenly Moira's words to Padraig froze in mid-sentence. She had just processed in her head what she had heard from the grubby looking person at the end of the bar. The person she knew as the farmer. She slowly turned away from Padraig and looked at the couple seated all by themselves. Pushing away from the bar, Moira then slowly made her way down to the end of the bar and stopped two feet away from the farmer.

"What did you say." It was more a statement than a question, as she tried to control her anger, hands on her hips.

With some effort, the farmer slid off his stool and stood, barely managing to keep the bulk of his immense six-foot-plus frame upright, one hand grabbing the edge of the bar for balance. He kept his eyes fixed on Moira the entire time; a lopsided grin spread across his face. "I said is he giving you a poke at night, the American?" Behind him, the farmer's wife shook her head and sighed.

Moira slowly beckoned the farmer closer, motioning with a curled finger, a smile now on her face. The farmer unfortunately obliged and staggered closer to Moira, his foul breath invading the space between them. Suddenly, the farmer collapsed, folding over on himself, Moira having driven a well-placed knee into a rather vulnerable location of the male anatomy known by all males and, as it so happens, by at least one female. The man was in agony; the continuous noise he made was a combination of a guttural cough, muffled scream, gasp for breath, and other inhuman noises, which didn't sound like they would end anytime soon.

The sorrowful sound emitted by the farmer did not go unnoticed, as the pub's other patrons became quiet, their eyes drawn to the commotion at the far end of the bar. They were witnessing the agony of a particular male patron who was doubled over, grabbing his proverbial family jewels with both of his hands. The woman, whom they could only see from the back, towered over the whimpering man. Moira looked like a prize fighter, fisted hands on either side of her, waiting for her opponent to get off the canvas so she could hand out more punishment.

Throughout the incident, the elderly couple continued to enjoy their meal, oblivious to what was happening at the bar. The elderly woman reached across the table for another roll, a pad of butter already strategically placed upon a waiting knife. With her finger, she counted the number of remaining rolls in the second basket in the center of the table. The elderly gentleman was surveying his meal, trying to decide the next target for his fork to attack. He also kept a watchful eye on the basket containing the rolls.

Padraig's response to the incident had been delayed. Not because of his age nor any loss of hearing; his hearing was quite good. He had been so focused on the beer tap he had been fiddling around with that he had not taken notice of Moira breaking off conversation in mid-sentence. His working with the tap ceased when he heard a person in agony. Padraig looked up, shook his head, and mumbled something to himself. He arrived on the scene just in time to snatch the farmer's half-full pint glass of lager away from Moira's searching hand.

"Moira," Padraig said, in a calming voice.

Moira looked up from the person who was engaged in a perverse partial genuflection in front of her. She slowly turned her head to Padraig.

"Moira, that's enough. You're needed in the kitchen," Padraig said, in a firm voice.

Heeding Padraig's words, Moira first looked down at her victim, then turned and marched off toward the kitchen with a determined look on her face. She was not going to put up with that kind of talk from anyone.

The group of tourists averted their eyes from her as she passed by.

Looking down at her husband, the farmer's wife said, "I've been wanting to do that for twenty-five years, you moron. Come, let's get you home before she comes back with a *very big, sharp* kitchen knife and neuters you. Would serve you right."

The farmer let out an even louder moan.

Looking down at the heap of a body, Padraig said to the farmer, "Thomas, you're barred from the pub." Looking to the farmer's wife, Padraig shook his head, smiled, and said, "Kathleen, you're welcome any time—without that oaf of a husband!"

Word spread like wildfire about what had happened in the pub to the farmer. There was no need to embellish the story; it was already too good to be true. So, *the Incident,* as it became known, joined *the Gavin Toss* in local pub lore. Given who the victims were and their unpopularity, respect for (and, indeed, fear of) Nora and Moira grew among the pub's regular clientele.

23

MAUREEN HAD COMPLETED her second year at the university and was beginning her third year away at school. Each time Maureen went off to school, Moira would become more melancholy, missing having her daughter around the house. The hectic work at the pub proved to be an effective antidote to her dejection. If she had paid closer attention, she would have noticed that Padraig seem to load up her work hours during the weeks immediately after Maureen's return to school following the summer, fall, spring, and holiday breaks. A more pleasant distraction which took her mind off her daughter's absence were those times when Brian returned to Ireland.

It didn't take long for Moira to realize that Brian visited Ireland more frequently during the summer months and periods when Maureen was home from school. Christmastime was the exception when, of course, he would spend time with his family in the States. At first, she thought the nature of his consulting work probably dictated his scheduled visits. But now, for two years running, Brian's visits exhibited a definite pattern. When he did visit Ireland when Maureen was at school, he would schedule side trips elsewhere in Ireland and the United Kingdom. Some of the trips were for his consulting work, but others, by himself, were for pleasure. She noticed he would keep his time spent at the house to a minimum. When Maureen was home from the university for an extended period, Brian would plan longer stays at the house. He would also plan day trips that included both Moira and her daughter.

Minds tend to wander during idle times, and Moira's was no different. A horrible thought had briefly crossed her mind when she was sorting through some laundry one day. She quickly banished it or at least tried to put it in the back of her mind—not very successfully.

Brian's visits to Ireland became the subject of a conversation between Padraig and Moira one quiet afternoon in the pub.

"Padraig, what do you make of Brian's visits? When Maureen is home from school, his visits are frequent and longer. When she's at school, his visits are less frequent and shorter." Moira started the conversation clearly uncomfortable, not making eye contact with her uncle.

Padraig looked at his niece. He took a damp washcloth and slowly ran it back and forth, cleaning the section of the bar immediately in front of him. He responded with his own question. "What do you think?"

"I don't know. I had a horrible thought," Moira quickly responded.

"Have you ever seen him exhibit any, well, let's say... unusual... affections toward Maureen?" Padraig asked, anticipating where Moira was going with the conversation.

"No!" was Moira's immediate response.

"Do you want my two cents?" Padraig said, putting the dish towel in the sink behind the bar.

"Yes," she replied, now looking directly at her uncle with searching eyes.

"First off, I think Brian is a gentleman, so I think you can dismiss the one thought that has been bothering you. I just don't see it. I think he looks at Maureen with the affection that a father has for a daughter. A very bright daughter."

Moira nodded and appeared slightly relieved.

Padraig continued, "The reason I think Brian is a gentleman is because of you."

Moira erupted. "Me! What do I have to do with anything!"

Padraig quickly raised his hand to stop his niece from interrupting. "Let me finish what I was going to say," Padraig admonished his niece. "I think Mr. Brian Hansen is very much concerned about *your* reputation.

"I think he realizes that tongues are bound to wag about how one man and one woman, who are not married, are sharing the same house together. That, my niece, I believe is why he limits his time here when Maureen is away. That's also why he goes on those trips by himself when Maureen is at school. I think he sees Maureen as a chaperone and feels comfortable spending more time here when she's home. Tongues are less likely to wag if there's a third party in the house. Quite frankly, after your little episode with the farmer, I'm surprised the thought hadn't occurred to you."

Moira stood staring at her uncle, speechless; her mouth was open, but no words came out. Slowly, she began to shake her head back and forth. Her uncle wordlessly nodded his head up and down in response. Moira diverted her eyes away from her uncle and looked to her left and then to her right then finally said to Padraig, "It never occurred to me. I, well, I don't know what to think."

"Just be thankful that our Brian *is* a gentleman and that he cares for both *you* and Maureen," Padraig answered. Once again taking the damp dish towel from the sink, Padraig began wiping down another section of the bar. "He's coming next week, isn't he? I'd be careful what you say to him. He' still not out of the woods emotionally yet."

Moira nodded, turned, and headed back to the kitchen, trying to process what Padraig had just said. As she opened the door to the kitchen, she shook her head again. *Who would even think of Brian and me becoming—well, involved? Nobody, of course!* Then her mind drifted back to the infamous day with the farmer. *Only he would have such thoughts; surely no one else.*

* * *

Padraig, Moira, and Maureen were just about to sit down at the kitchen table for Sunday dinner. Moira had been both surprised and glad to see her daughter appear yesterday morning. After questioning Maureen to make sure everything was alright and determining that her daughter's visit home was nothing more than a spur-of-the-moment decision and a desire on her daughter's part to get a good home-cooked meal, Moira had set about to make a nice Sunday dinner for all of them. On the table was a baked ham, recently retrieved from the oven; a bowl full of fluffy mashed potatoes with a dab (more like a double—actually a triple dab) of butter melting on top; and a side dish of brussels sprouts (Maureen's favorite vegetable, not so

Moira's). Dinner rolls and an accompanied dish of butter also appeared on the table. Maureen had set out place settings, silverware, and plates for three.

The sound of chairs scraping on the tiled kitchen floor stopped once the three of them were seated at the table. With the precision of a drill team, bowls containing the three main ingredients of the meal were passed back and forth until everyone's plates were brimming with food. After brief prayers offered by Padraig, talk was limited as they dug into their respective meals. About the only sound made was that of silverware used to cut the ham and to scoop up portions from their plates.

Moira wondered about the quality of the food offered at the university, seeing her daughter quickly emptying her plate ahead of Padraig and herself.

"Please pass the spuds." With hungry eyes, Maureen looked at the half-empty serving bowl of mashed potatoes on the table by her mother. She had already used her fork to spear another piece of ham for her plate.

As Moira passed the bowl over to her daughter, she was amazed at the amount of food her daughter could eat without putting an ounce of weight around her slender waist. It seemed that the food only fueled her daughter's surge in upward growth. Maureen had to have grown at least three inches since she had started at the university. Moira's eyes drifted down to the bowl of mashed potatoes. She knew that if she took a second heaping spoonful of mashed potatoes as big as her daughter had just plopped on her plate, it would land squarely around her midriff. She was done growing upward. At her age, growth meant outward expansion. She would resist. Or so she thought, as her right arm became outstretched and beckoned for the bowl of mashed potatoes seemingly on its own. *Just one small spoonful,* she thought as she looked at the near-empty bowl. *Waste not want not.* After all, today was special! Her daughter was home.

"I wonder why Brian's children have never come over with him to see this place?" Padraig asked. The question seemed to come out of the blue. Moira looked up from her plate, turned her eyes to Padraig and, after some thought, nodded her head. She also wondered why they had not come visit.

"They don't want to interfere, not now. Maybe sometime later," Maureen answered, as she reached for another roll and corralled the butter dish.

"How do you know that?" Moira asked, somewhat surprised, as she and Padraig both looked at Maureen.

"Uncle Brian's daughter told me," Maureen replied.

"You've spoken to her?" Padraig asked.

"Not spoken to her, no. We've corresponded with each other over the internet. His daughter's name is Mady. Apparently, she and her brother have talked about making a trip over here with their dad but have thought it would be best not to, at least not for the foreseeable future."

"I wonder why?" Moira asked, to no one in particular. She had been momentarily taken back by her daughter calling Brian *Uncle* Brian.

"Mady says they're afraid if they come over here to Ireland, they might spoil things," Maureen replied.

"What on earth could they spoil?" Padraig wondered, as he raised his fork toward his mouth.

Maureen had finished her ham, mashed potatoes, and roll and set her fork down on her plate. She looked from one to the other. "Mady and her brother have noticed that their father continues to improve each time he comes back from a trip over to Ireland. They're beginning to see more and more of the father they once knew." Maureen smiled as her eyes focused on the wall above and behind her mother.

"Each time he returns to them from a trip over here, he tells them a little bit more of what he sees when he goes for his walks here. They know all about the round tower and have even googled it." Seeing she lost the two of them with the word *google*, she clarified. "They use the internet to see a picture of what he's talking about. They enter our town's name and the word "tower," and a picture of the round tower appears. Mady says it looks like just how he described it to her and her brother. He's told them about the quay, the cliffs, and even the pub!"

Maureen's eyes drifted down from the wall to her mother. "They're afraid that if they come over here, they might interrupt his getting better. They refer to his visits over here as his therapy."

Moira and Padraig looked at each other as they considered what Maureen had just told them.

"He even describes to his daughter and son some of the people in the village. They know all about Nora. What she looks like, and that she's a cook and not someone to mess around with." Maureen chuckled as she thought about what she'd just said. "Apparently when he describes a particular person, he sums up that person with one word. You know what word he uses for Nora? You'll never guess in a million years."

Without saying a word, Moira and Padraig both looked at Maureen, shaking their heads. Maureen could see that neither one had a clue.

"Kind," Maureen answered, as a smile grew on her face. "That's perfect when you think about it."

Padraig and Moira looked at each other, both mouthing the word *kind*.

"Gavin wouldn't think Nora is a kind person after she tossed him into the field," Padraig said with a brief chuckle before falling silent.

"The green windbreaker," Moira said in a quiet voice, staring at the empty bowl which once held mashed potatoes.

Padraig looked at Moira and slowly nodded. The story of Nora, Brian, and the green windbreaker had quickly circulated throughout the village, earning Nora immense admiration among the locals.

"Kind," Padraig said, as if testing the associated word. "Yes, kind."

Maureen wiggled a little in her seat and bit on her lip to try to stifle a giggle. "You should hear the word he uses to describe you!" Maureen blurted out, looking at Padraig.

Padraig cleared his throat with a loud *harrumph*. He fidgeted in his seat, uncomfortable with how the conversation had turned.

"When you hear the word, you wouldn't say that it's fitting," Maureen said to Padraig, then continued. "But Mam and I know it fits you perfectly." Maureen looked at Padraig with a smile as Moira gave her daughter an inquisitive look.

"Generous."

Moira turned to look at her uncle and nodded with a smile. The man sitting before her has been incredibly generous to both her and her daughter.

That brought a double *harrumph* from Padraig, as his face turned bright red.

The table grew quiet as they contemplated what they had just heard. Moira was about to ask her daughter what word Brian used to describe her, but she refrained. What if she didn't like the word, or worse yet, what if he hadn't offered a word to describe her? Moira's eyes drifted over to the kitchen window, where she could see the evening's soft remnant of light fading. Soon it would be dark, and the stars, infinite in number, would once again shine brightly. She wondered if Brian talked about her to his daughter and son. And if he did, what did he say about her?

Now, you're just being silly, she gently chastised herself. The three sat in silence until it was broken by—

"What's for dessert?" asked the young lady with an insatiable appetite.

* * *

After Padraig had left to go back to the pub, Moira finished putting the dirty dishes in the dishwasher. Maureen was wiping off the kitchen table.

Moira turned to her daughter and asked, "Why did you call Mr. Hansen 'Uncle Brian?'"

Maureen put the damp cloth down on the table and looked at her mother. She nudged a chair under the table with her knee before responding, "I once called him Mr. Hansen and he asked me not to. He said every time someone calls him Mr. Hansen, he thinks someone is talking about his dad. I knew it wouldn't be polite to call him by his first name. So I said to him, 'How about if I call you Uncle Brian?' He thought about it and said if it was alright with you, it was alright with him. I didn't think you'd mind."

Maureen picked up the damp cloth and walked over to the sink and draped it over the faucet. She smiled at her mother and reminded her that her ride back to the university tomorrow would be bright and early—7 a.m.. Then off she went up to her room.

Moira stared at the damp cloth draped on the faucet and thought about her daughter calling him Uncle Brian. Trying to think of a better way to address Brian, she eventually gave up and turned her thoughts to preparing a care package of goodies for her daughter to take back to school in the morning.

24

ALMOST TWO WEEKS had passed since Moira and Padraig's conversation in the pub about Brian and the timing of his visits to Ireland. Brian's plane had landed at Shannon Airport three days ago and Brian had resumed his normal routine. Tea, work, lunch, more work, long walk, dinner and then bedtime. On this day, Brian's routine took a detour into the pub during his afternoon walk. He was at one end of the bar with a glass of Diet Coke in front of him. Jimmy the bartender had just finished telling him about Moira's run-in with the farmer. As Jimmy was relaying the details of what took place that day, Brian subconsciously crossed his legs. If Jimmy had expected the person across the bar from him to laugh or even smile as he was telling the story, he was to be disappointed. Brian just kept shaking his head. He thought about the deception he and Padraig had carried out regarding the scholarship. Moira's outburst when he had mentioned the scholarship letter when she was hanging out clothes. And now, hearing how she had visited violence upon the farmer, well... he could only imagine what her response would be if she found out how much the scholarship actually covered and who was behind the deception.

Jimmy moved to the other end of the bar to serve a customer who had taken a seat on a stool. Brian stared at his glass of soda. Sensing movement to his right, he looked up to see Padraig approaching.

"Ah, the heathen has returned," Padraig said with a smile, as he pulled out the stool next to Brian so he could sit down. Seeing how pale Brian looked, Padraig grew concerned. "You don't look well. Are you coming down with something?"

"Jimmy was just telling me about Moira and this fellow called the farmer."

"Ah, yes. Moira was in rare form that day. It happened so quickly. Thomas, that's the farmer's name, isn't a little man, either. At least he wasn't until Moira cut him down to size." Padraig chuckled as he thought back to the events of that day.

"Well, *we* have got a problem," Brian said, looking from his glass on the bar to the person sitting next to him. He knew that he went around preaching that there were no such things as problems, only opportunities. But what he was about to tell his fellow conspirator was a problem, a big problem, with no possible opportunity in sight.

"The farmer has a problem," Padraig said, with a laugh. "What kind of problem could we possibly have?"

"During last night's dinner, Moira asked me something. The day after tomorrow, she wants me to take her to the university so she can *thank* someone for Maureen's scholarship," Brian said. "I tried to talk her out of it, but she insists on going."

Padraig's smile disappeared. It was his turn to stare at Brian's glass of soda. "Well, good luck with that," Padraig said, shaking his head. "How are you going to handle it when you get up to the university?"

"You mean how are *we* going to handle it when *we* go up to the university with Moira," Brian said, staring at Padraig.

Padraig's face grew ashen. "Wouldn't it be better if you went by yourself?" he meekly said.

"Oh no, you're going. Remember it was you who called the university and confirmed that Maureen had a *full* scholarship. Surely you want to meet the gentleman you spoke to on the phone that day. We're in this together," Brian said with a sly smirk, which suddenly disappeared as he thought of the various ways the trip could pan out, none of them with a good ending.

"Oh, dear Lord," was all Padraig could say as he slumped forward, placing his elbows on the bar and using both hands to hold his head upright.

"Look, I think I have a plan. I need you to go along with us for it work." So, for the next half an hour, Brian once again conspired with the man next to him on a possible Hail Mary plan for the trip to Galway.

As he rose from his seat, Brian said, "Seven thirty a.m. sharp, the day after tomorrow, be out in front of the pub. I'll mention to Moira tonight that you *really, really* want to go with us to see the university," Brian said with a hint of sarcasm. He paused before he uttered, "Heaven help us."

"Amen," Padraig responded.

* * *

Brian paced nervously alongside the rental car; the crunching noise made by his shoes on the stone pebbles in the driveway was the only sound at this early hour. There wasn't even the usual sound of an occasional bird. Apparently, even the birds wanted no part of what was going to happen today. The morning's air was brisk; however, Brian's goosebumps had appeared much earlier, when he had still been inside the house—nerves. He'd passed on the cup of tea this morning when Moira had offered it to him. He would have enough of a problem controlling his bladder. He heard the front door of the house close, and he stopped his pacing and looked over the top of the rental car. He moved over to the other side of the car to open the front passenger door for Moira, who was approaching across the driveway.

"No. I'll sit in the back. Let Padraig sit up front," Moira said, as she reached for the rear car-door handle.

Brian complied with her wish, edging in front of her to open the rear door for her. She settled down on the seat behind the front passenger seat. While he had seen her in the kitchen first thing this morning, it wasn't until now that he took notice of the blue dress she was wearing. As she swept her legs into the car, Brian could see that lower part of the dress was slightly faded. *Was that makeup she had on?* The floral scent of perfume didn't go unnoticed either as she had passed in front of him to get into the car. *A different perfume from what she normally wore, but very nice,* he thought. Brian closed the rear door and moved over to the other side of the car and took his place behind the steering wheel.

"I told Padraig we'd meet him in front of the pub," he said, looking at his passenger in the rearview mirror. Last night when he had mentioned that Padraig had wanted to go along with them this morning, she had made no comment, which had surprised him. She had only nodded her head. Maybe she had fallen for his excuse that Padraig had said he wanted to see Maureen and the university.

Brian put the car in gear and proceeded slowly out the driveway and down the narrow lane. As they eventually made the left turn onto the road in front of the pub, he caught sight of Padraig standing across from the pub by the picnic tables. He did a double take. Brian had never seen Padraig in a suit. A dark-brown suit and a white dress shirt, with a tie, no less. He pulled the car over to the side of the road across from where Padraig was standing. After looking both ways, Padraig crossed the road and reached down and opened the front passenger door, seeing Moira sitting in the back seat.

"Is this the limousine to Galway?" Padraig bellowed and continued, "My dear man, are you the chauffeur for the day?" He ducked down and looked in the car at Brian. Turning his head to look toward the back seat, he continued, "And who is this fine-looking lass who will be our traveling companion?"

"Padraig, get in the car!" Brian and Moira called out in unison.

With a nervous laugh, Padraig slid into the front seat and closed the door.

"So, tell me, when was the last time you wore a suit?" Brian asked, then continued before Padraig could respond. "Must have been a wedding or a . . ."

"Funeral," Padraig said, completing the sentence when Brian hesitated. The occupants in the front of the car shared a brief knowing look. The fine-looking lass in the back was oblivious to their banter, looking out her window at the rising slope of the mountain with its ever-present stone walls crisscrossing the green fields. The round tower dominated the view, pointing upward at the few slow-moving clouds.

* * *

The trip to Galway had passed by uneventfully. Brian's two passengers had engaged in very little conversation. They both seemed mesmerized by the scenery as they traveled along. Brian suspected that neither one of them traveled far afield from their small village. *This is a rare experience for them,* he thought. The first part of their journey saw them pass large tracts of recently plowed fields, then through small villages with a few stores and whitewashed cottages, and then past more farmland and more villages. As they got closer to the city, farmland gave way to dense housing developments. Housing developments then gave way to busy shopping malls and multiple-story office buildings. The one constant, much to his dismay, were the never-ending roundabouts that he cautiously navigated through, until he approached the inner part of the city. He pointed out Conor's law office building as they drove by. Up a little way was the parking garage where he'd parked on a previous trip. He'd never been to the university and couldn't tell from the website that he had briefly visited last night where precisely visitor parking was on the campus. They would have a bit of a walk over to the university from the parking garage, but it would give him time to consider his plan again before they got on to university grounds.

They left the parking garage and continued along a street until they came to a large open grassy area. This was Eyre

Square, otherwise known as John F. Kennedy Memorial Park. They crossed the square diagonally, coming upon the more central part of the city and a wide pedestrian walkway, which provided safe passage from vehicles. Still early in the morning, they could see various stores, restaurants, and pubs beginning to awaken on either side of the walkway in preparation for the day's visitors. Outdoor tables were being set up in front of restaurants. Empty kegs on hand carts were being exchanged for full ones outside of pubs. The previous night's refuse was being swept up by half-awake store owners and city workers eager to make the city presentable to the influx of people.

Although Brian had visited the city a couple of times before with his wife and thought he had a pretty good idea of the lay of the land, he referred to the map on his phone as he ushered his group onto a narrow side street that led to the River Corrib that flowed through Galway into Galway Bay. As they crossed the river on the Salmon Weir Bridge, they could hear the water rushing by underneath the bridge. Off to the right, a couple of early morning fishermen in green waders could be seen trying to coax fish to take the tiny flies on the ends of their outstretched lines. The rays from the morning sun reflected off the flowing water, making it sparkle. Directly in front of them was the magnificent Galway Cathedral. Brian and Clare had visited inside one summer and took in the splendor of its interior. They paused as Padraig and Moira looked at the green-domed cathedral. Brian didn't know how religious the two of them were, but they certainly seemed transfixed by the imposing structure standing before them. After a couple of moments, they continued their journey past the cathedral and made their way over some canals until they could see the university buildings off to their right.

As they continued to walk along, Brian could only think of the many ways his plan could go wrong. What if she found out what he and his fellow conspirators had done? What would be her reaction? *She would probably be furious,* he thought. Would she pull Maureen out of the university? His stomach started to feel queasy. *Think positive thoughts!*

Brian knew that Moira had arranged to meet Maureen at nine thirty before her daughter's ten o'clock morning class. Moira and her daughter had decided on a central point, a quadrangle that would be easy to locate. Brian's planned subterfuge consisted of him staying with Moira and Maureen while Padraig would go off to a nearby building—any building. Padraig would go inside and spend fifteen or so minutes inside the building, then come out and announce that the admission person who Moira wanted to thank for the scholarship was tied up in a meeting and was unable to meet with them. Then they would leave. Brian knew it was a weak plan, but it was the only one he could come up with on such short notice. Padraig had been unable to improve upon the plan two nights ago at the pub. Padraig did, however, offer to remain behind in the village.

That offer was declined.

The three of them entered a courtyard within the university proper. Large stone masonry buildings surrounded the rectangular area. Moira saw her daughter first. Waving her hands, she surged past Brian and Padraig toward Maureen. Brian looked around and saw, coincidentally, a building off to their immediate left with a large sign out front:

ADMISSIONS. Brian nudged Padraig, who was busy looking from one building to another.

Pointing to the building with the ADMISSIONS sign out front, Brian lowered his voice and said, “That’s the building you want to go into. Spend some time in there. Stay by the front door. When it looks like Maureen is heading off to her class, come out and tell us that the admissions guy is tied up in a meeting. Then we’ll quickly leave before Moira has time to think about what’s happening. Okay?”

Padraig nodded and headed off toward the building. Brian let out a sigh and moved along closer to where Moira and Maureen were talking. Brian noticed a young man who patiently waited off to the side a couple of yards away from the mother and daughter who were engaged in conversation. The young man had a black backpack on his shoulder and a light-blue backpack in his hand. He looked from Brian back to the mother and daughter, shuffling his feet. As Brian approached, Maureen turned and saw him. She stepped forward and gave him a hug, then stepped back and resumed her conversation with her mother. The young man, who Brian suspected was with Maureen, apparently was not to be introduced. This time was reserved only for the animated mother and her daughter.

25

LEAVING THE FAMILY reunion behind, Padraig cautiously approached the steps of the Admissions Building. He paused as a young man carrying books under his arm strode up the granite steps, opened the large glass door, and disappeared inside. Padraig followed the young man up the steps. Once inside, Padraig stood off to one side and looked around the cavernous atrium. Up ahead on his right, he noticed a large directory mounted on a wall. The Admissions Office, he noted, was on this floor, down a long corridor just beyond where the directory was located.

Padraig walked over to the corridor and saw an overhead sign that protruded from the wall on the right above an opening halfway down the corridor. The sign, in bold letters, identified the ADMISSIONS OFFICE. He continued down the corridor. The walls were tiled floor to ceiling, except where interrupted by door openings. The florescent lights overhead illuminated the hallway. Under the ADMISSIONS OFFICE sign was a door which had ADMISSIONS OFFICE stenciled in bold letters on the upper translucent glass panel. Padraig paused. He was supposed to wait by the front door, he knew, but he was curious. He reached out and grabbed hold of the doorknob, and entered what was a rather spacious office area. He didn't notice the woman sitting at a desk to his immediate right. His focus was on the far wall, which was covered with numerous large pictures of the various buildings at the university. Turning to his left, he saw a credenza that ran the entire length of the wall, with neat stacks of different-sized brochures. He took a step toward the credenza and leaned over and spotted a stack of brochures titled Student Aid. He was about to pick up the top brochure when a voice behind him startled him.

"May I help you?" The woman's voice was firm, making it perfectly clear that this was her domain.

Padraig slowly turned around until he was face-to-face with the woman sitting behind a very well-organized desk. A phone was on the desk to the woman's left. To her right were two metal wire baskets marked In and Out, with neat piles of papers in each. A series of low file cabinets were directly behind her. To the woman's immediate left was a low, smaller table with a personal computer centered on top. The woman herself looked to be in her forties, he thought. She wore glasses with dark frames. Medium-length brunette hair; not a hair out of place. Her lavender blouse accented her blue eyes. An attractive woman, he thought, but one that looked like she didn't suffer fools gladly.

"May I help you?' she asked again, staring at Padraig.

"I'm here with my niece to see her daughter. She's a student here." As an afterthought Padraig added, "Not my niece; her daughter is a student."

"Are you lost, then? Do you know where you're supposed to meet them?" she asked, in a firm voice. "What is her name?"

Just as Padraig was about to mumble a response, a tall well-dressed man came out of an open doorway behind and to the left of where the woman was sitting. The man was wearing a pair of neatly pressed gray suit pants, white buttoned-down shirt, and perfectly knotted blue-and-red striped tie. He was tall and athletic-looking. He placed some papers in the Out basket and was about to retrieve paper from the In basket when he noticed the visitor for the first time. He looked up and smiled. Then he looked at the woman sitting behind the desk and nodded as he retrieved the papers from the In basket. He started to turn around to head back through the doorway from which he'd come.

"Maureen McGuire," Padraig stammered, his voice betraying some discomfort.

The man stopped and slowly turned back to look at Padraig. "I know a McGuire. Not an uncommon name. Conor McGuire," he said, nodding to himself in confirmation.

"Conor McGuire is my nephew. He's a lawyer," Padraig voiced with some conviction.

"Yes. The Conor McGuire I know is an attorney. Must be the same person. We play golf together. You're his uncle, you say?"

"Yes sir."

"Are you the uncle who owns the pub in the quaint village he is always talking about?"

"Yes, that I am," Padraig answered, with less discomfort.

"You say you have a relation attending the university? By the way, I'm Dean Kelly," the very tall man said, as he looked the visitor over.

"Padraig McGuire," Padraig introduced himself. "Pleased to meet you. Yes, my niece's daughter is at the university."

"Helen, when is my next meeting?" the dean asked, looking at the woman behind the desk.

"You have a luncheon meeting with Dean Fitzpatrick," she responded, sensing that this intruder was about to breach the inner sanctum that she was sworn to guard at all costs.

"I've got some time. Why don't you come in and tell me about your niece's daughter? I'd also like to hear about this pub your nephew is always going on about," he said, as he ushered Padraig into another room.

* * *

Padraig followed Dean Kelly into another, slightly smaller room. The dean's office. As he entered, Padraig quickly surveyed the room, silently noting the various items of office furniture. What caught his eye, however, was the large window that revealed the courtyard outside, where he could now see Moira and Maureen, as well as Brian and some other young man who was waiting off to the side. Dean Kelly invited Padraig to take a seat on a couch.

After Padraig sat down, Dean Kelly took one of the chairs across from the couch.

"Would you like some coffee, some tea?" Dean Kelly asked.

"No thank you, I'm fine," Padraig replied, staring at the magazines on the coffee table in front of him.

Dean Kelly was seemly lost in thought. Padraig remained quiet, waiting for the dean to continue the conversation.

Then Dean Kelly said to no one in particular, "Maureen McGuire. Conor McGuire." He stared at Padraig, or rather, seemed to stare through Padraig.

Padraig was feeling very uncomfortable as he shifted on the couch, absentmindedly crossing his legs back and forth over each other. He could feel beads of perspiration slowly rolling down his back. He was having regrets about opening the door to the Admissions Office. He was supposed to have waited by the building's entrance, then walked outside and said the Admissions person was not available. And here he was, talking to the very man who was not supposed to be available.

There was no escape. Not now.

"I've got it!" Dean Kelly exclaimed, breaking out of his trance-like stare. "I knew there was something about your niece's daughter. I couldn't put my finger on it for a moment. We send all the university correspondence for your niece's daughter to Conor at his law office. Rather unusual arrangement, but not unheard of. I remember Conor calling me about it some time ago. How does your niece's daughter like it at the university?"

"Oh, she likes it very much. She's a smart lass," Padraig said, recrossing his legs once again. As he leaned back against the couch, he could feel the dampness spread across the back of his dress shirt.

"And this is your niece's first visit to the university?"

"Yes. She came to see her daughter and"—Padraig's gulp was noticeable—"she came here to *thank* someone for her daughter's scholarship." Padraig hesitated before continuing, "But there's a slight problem with that. Well, not a slight problem. A big problem.

"You see, Moira, my niece, thinks that Maureen got a scholarship that pays for everything. Tuition, room, food, books, whatever. The thing is, Maureen's scholarship doesn't cover everything." Padraig looked down at his shoes. "My niece thinks it does," he said sheepishly.

Dean Kelly's eyes widened as he leaned forward in his chair, obviously intrigued by what he was hearing from the pub owner.

Padraig continued, "My niece couldn't afford to come up with the rest of the money for the university. She's too proud to take money from me, Conor, or any of the relatives, and she would never let Maureen take out a student loan."

Padraig slowly stood and pointed out the window with his right hand. Dean Kelly also stood and looked out the window, following where Padraig was pointing. "See those two women talking to each other? That's my niece, Moira, and Maureen, her daughter. See the older gentleman off to the left of them? Well, that's Brian Hansen, an American and"—Padraig paused to think how to best describe Brian's relationship with the McGuire clan and settled on—"a friend of the family. Brian is providing the money for whatever the scholarship doesn't cover. He and Conor worked out this idea, this plan." Padraig paused to catch his breath before continuing, "To make my niece think that all of her daughter's expenses are covered by the university." Padraig had the look of a defeated man, retreating to and collapsing on the couch.

Dean Kelly sat back down on his chair. "So, that's why Conor wanted all of the university correspondence to go to his office."

"Yes."

"And your niece has no idea that the gentleman out there is putting up the extra money?"

"No," Padraig said despondently, shaking his head.

"Does your niece's daughter know where the extra money is coming from?"

"No. She, like her mother, thinks she received a scholarship that covers everything," Padraig said in a barely audible voice.

"Interesting," Dean Kelly said, as he leaned back in his chair. "And now your niece wants to thank someone from the university for the scholarship. A full scholarship..." His voice trailed off, not expecting a response. While Dean Kelly sat deep in thought, Padraig slouched down in the couch, waiting for the lightning bolt to strike.

"Go get your niece and bring her here to this office," Dean Kelly said, suddenly getting up from his chair.

Padraig did a doubletake, not quite sure what he had just heard. He looked up at the man standing in front of him. "You want me to go get my niece and bring her here?"

"Yes. Bring her here. And the gentleman too."

"What are you going to tell her?" Padraig voice betrayed deep concern.

"We'll figure out something. Go get them," Dean Kelly said with a smile.

Padraig slowly got up from the couch and went through the doorway to the outer office.

26

MOIRA AND MAUREEN hugged and said their goodbyes. Maureen went off toward where the young man was standing. She retrieved her backpack, and the two of them headed off on a brick walkway that led to a building at the far end of the courtyard. Brian noticed Moira tilting her head to one side, appearing to take note of the young man with Maureen. Then Moira turned and made her way over to Brian. Brian was waiting patiently for Padraig to come out of the building to his left. After a couple of moments, out came Padraig through the door, slowly waving for them to come his way.

Brian trailed along after Moira, figuring the moment of truth was upon them. All Padraig had to say was that the person is in a meeting, and they could head on home. *Why is he waving like that*? Brian asked himself. Brian and Moira went up the steps to the entrance of the building, where Padraig was holding open the door.

"Come. I want you to meet someone," Padraig said. He took Moira by her elbow and led her through the doorway and over to a corridor off to the right side of the building's interior.

Meet someone—no—no—that's not the plan, Brian said to himself, pausing by the entrance.

Brian stopped just inside the building. He looked around the at the large open area. Then he turned around and looked at the entrance he had just come through. On the other side was his freedom, at least temporarily. Until she caught up with him. *Where are they going?!* With leaden feet, he followed Padraig and Moira across the atrium marble floor. Once in the corridor, he saw Padraig up ahead, pushing open a door on the right side of the hallway through which he ushered Moira. Above the door was a sign: ADMISSIONS OFFICE. Padraig beckoned to Brian to follow. Brian hesitated, then slowly moved down the hallway to where Padraig was holding open the door.

The door made a solid sound as it closed behind them. The three of them were standing in a rather large room. Brian surveyed the surroundings. Padraig was on Brian's left, closest to the door, and Moira on his right. Brian finally noticed a woman sitting behind a desk to the right of where they were standing. He thought she didn't look very happy to have this intrusion. The woman just stared at them without saying a word. He was about to move over to the credenza and look at the brochures when out from a doorway just beyond the woman's desk came a tall man with a broad, welcoming smile. Brian froze.

"Ah, you must be Padraig's niece, Moira. Padraig has been telling me all about you and your lovely daughter." The tall gentleman with a beaming smile strode across the room toward them, hands outstretched. "I'm Dean Kelly," he said, clasping Moira's right hand with both of his.

Still holding Moira's hand, Dean Kelly turned to face Brian and asked, "And you are?"

Trying to understand what was taking place, Brian took a couple of seconds to respond, "I'm Brian Hansen." Knowing he should provide some clarification for his presence in the room, he continued, "I'm an acquaintance of the family's."

Dean Kelly nodded and then turned to Padraig. "Padraig was telling me about your daughter." Dean Kelly turned back to look at Moira. "Since she has been here at the university, Maureen has been on the Dean's List every semester." If he had been expecting a positive reaction from the woman standing in front of him, he was mistaken.

Moira's smile evaporated. "What has she done wrong?" Moira said in an anguished voice. Staring at the confused looking man standing before her, she didn't wait for a response. Moira, trembling, repeated, "What did she do wrong?"

Dean Kelly's jaw dropped, and he released Moira's hand. He took a half-step back. His puzzled expression indicated that he didn't have a clue what Moira was on about.

Padraig started twitching where he was standing, taking a quick look over his shoulder at the door to the corridor. Fortunately, it was Brian who understood the disconnect and he quickly interceded.

Reaching over and gently touching Moira's elbow, Brian said, "Moira, being on the Dean's List is a *good* thing. It means that Maureen has gotten excellent grades. Being on the Dean's List is not a *bad* thing. It's a *very* good thing. What Dean Kelly is saying is that Maureen is a very bright young woman who has consistently gotten excellent grades ever since she started at the university," Brian concluded, looking to the dean for confirmation. Dean Kelly, still taken back, slowly nodded his agreement.

Moira turned to look at Brian, who started to bob his head up and down. She turned slightly to look past Brian to where Padraig was standing; he too was bobbing his head up and down. Moira then turned to look at Dean Kelly, who was now bobbing his head up and down in agreement. Finally, she looked to her right, where the serious-looking woman sitting behind the desk was also bobbing her head up and down. If a person had opened the door and entered the room at that moment, they would have thought it was a bobblehead convention.

Recovering, Dean Kelly now understood the disconnect. "Yes Moira, you should be very proud of your daughter. She is an excellent student. Only students who do very well are on the Dean's List each term. In addition, I am very pleased to say that your daughter has also volunteered to head up several study groups to help other students in their coursework. That is very commendable. Very commendable, indeed. We here at the university are very fortunate to have your daughter as a student," he concluded, with a broad smile.

Moira nodded as a smile slowly reappeared on her face. Then in a somber voice, Moira said, "Dean Kelly. I want to say to you how much Maureen and I appreciate the university's support. The financial support. I want to thank you. I apologize for not coming up here sooner and thanking you. It means a lot to both of us. Thank you." Moira stepped toward Dean Kelly and now took one of his hands in both of her hands.

Looking at each one of them in turn, Dean Kelly said, "Moira it is *our* pleasure to provide such financial support to a very accomplished young woman."

Was that a wink he gave me? Brian wondered, as he then noticed Moira looking down at the coupled hands.

"Moira, dear," Padraig said, breaking the silence that permeated the room. "Moira, I know Dean Kelly is a very busy man. We should let him get back to work."

Moira nodded and released the dean's hand and said, "Yes, we should be going. Thank you again." She paused and turned toward the woman behind the desk, smiled and nodded her head and said, "Thank you."

It was a close call who got to the door first. A photo-finish would have revealed that Padraig just nosed out Brian because he had been standing closer to the door. As Moira went into the hallway, Dean Kelly took Brian and Padraig aside. Dean Kelly poked his head out through the doorway and looked to see that Moira was down the hallway a bit. He leaned toward Padraig and said in a conspiratorial voice, "Tell Conor a generous donation to the local food bank is in order." By way of an explanation, he continued, "Conor and I both serve on the board of directors overseeing the charity that provides food for the less fortunate in this county."

Padraig smiled and nodded, then asked, "What would be a good amount?"

It was obvious Dean Kelly wasn't expecting Padraig's question. He paused and then looked up in the air as though searching for an answer then replied, "Three hundred euros."

Padraig nodded and, without missing a beat, said with a twinkle in his eyes, "Five hundred euros it is." That was payback for when Padraig was on the fake phone call to Conor about the scholarship, and Conor spent the entire time telling Irish jokes, trying to make his uncle lose it.

Dean Kelly smiled and laughed out loud. "Mr. McGuire, it is indeed a pleasure to meet you."

"Please, call me Padraig."

"Padraig it is." Turning to Brian, Dean Kelly continued, "And it is a pleasure to meet you too, Brian. It is not often that this university has such a gifted student like Maureen." Looking back at Padraig, he continued, "Someday I will have to make my way to your lovely village and your very special pub."

"If you do, the drinks and dinner will be on us," Padraig replied, pointing back and forth between Brian and himself.

* * *

Whether it was from nervous exhaustion or sheer relief, neither Padraig nor Brian said a word until they were outside of the building. Moira was about twenty yards ahead of them, crossing the courtyard. Her step was much livelier than when they had arrived before. Brian thought he heard her humming a tune to herself. He had never heard her hum to herself before. Suddenly, his entire body shook from head to toe and then it stopped as quickly as it started. It was as if his body had just purged itself of the extreme anxiety that he'd felt the entire time he was inside the building. When he had been in the dean's office, he felt like he was on pins and needles. If ever there was a time for a panic attack, that was it. He had survived—so far. But how?

Looking at Padraig, who was matching him step by step alongside him, he said in a hushed voice so Moira couldn't hear him, "At some point you're going to have to explain to me just what happened back there in that office. You were supposed to tell us no one was available to meet us. I almost had a heart attack. Although a heart attack would probably be preferable to Moira's knee in a certain vulnerable location," he ended, with a sigh.

"Brian, me lad. Ye of little faith. You send me to do a job and I do a proper job," Padraig said jovially, as they continued to follow after Moira. In a serious tone of voice, Padraig went on, "To be perfectly honest, I'm not quite sure what happened in there. I was staying close to the door, ready to bolt if all hell broke loose. The back of my shirt is soaked. If Dean Kelly hadn't known Conor, I don't know what would have happened. Look at it this way: today was just not our day to meet our maker. Or Moira's wrath."

With Moira in the lead, the three of them headed over the canals, past the cathedral, across the bridge over the fast-flowing Corrib River, and through a narrow side street where they came upon the pedestrian walkway that transversed the city.

27

AS BRIAN AND Padraig trailed after Moira, the tension Brian was feeling from this morning's meeting in the Admissions Office continued to slowly dissipate. The city's transformation from when they had walked through the streets earlier was noticeable. The side streets and pedestrian walkway were crowded with people strolling along, window shopping and venturing in and out of shops now fully open. Even the air was different, with the aroma of lunchtime meals being prepared by the various restaurants and pubs. Brian had suggested stopping for lunch, but when Padraig told them what Nora was preparing for the noontime meal back at the pub, they all agreed to wait.

Moira continued to lead onward through the streets, occasionally slowing her pace to peer into the windows of various shops. Brian thought this was her trip to the big city, and she was going to take her time and enjoy the sights, which was fine by him. They turned onto the wide pedestrian walkway and moved over to their left, retracing their morning steps.

Moira suddenly came to a complete stop. Padraig and Brian closed the gap between them and Moira and stopped just behind her. Before the three of them was a store's very large plate-glass window with various brightly colored dresses on display. Moira slowly walked from one end of the display window to the other, admiring the outfits on the mannequins. Next to the end of display window where Moira was now standing was a brass door with glass panels, marking the entrance to the store.

"Moira, would you like to go inside and browse around? We have time," Brian said to the back of Moira's head.

"Just to look, if I might." Moira said, then entered the store.

Brian caught the door before it had completely closed behind her and motioned for Padraig to go on through. Padraig paused, allowing a middle-aged woman to exit the store holding the handle of a large, rather fancy tote bag with the name of the store printed on the side. As they entered, it was obvious to Brian that this was a strictly a woman's store, no sign of any articles of men's clothing. To their immediate left, a very attractive salesclerk stood behind a counter. *She could be a fashion model,* Brian thought. Long dark hair. Bright-red lips. Dark sculpted eyebrows over emerald-green eyes. And an enchanting smile. The white blouse and salesclerk's immaculate dark-blue dress suit made it clear that this was an upscale women's store.

Brian smiled at the salesclerk, making sure his eyes didn't linger too long. Turning away from the counter, he surveyed the rest of the store. Moira was sorting through a rack of dresses with floral designs. Another rack featured women's business suits, and still others, evening gowns, coats, and so on and so on, until he was unable to determine what the racks at the far end of the store contained. At that distance, the clothing dissolved into a kaleidoscope of colors. Brian knew from previous experience that somewhere near the entrance to the store would be a very small sitting area with some magazines specifically designated for unfortunate bored males who were dragged into the store by their female partners. Many years of shopping with Clare had taught him that there would be such a refuge. Finding it in this store, he took a seat and looked around. He saw Moira heading up a short flight of stairs onto a landing where there was a sign for the dressing rooms. She was holding up an attractive floral dress by its hanger.

Brian surveyed the small glass table in front of him to see if he was interested in any of the magazines neatly arranged on the table. He picked up a magazine and started to flip through the pages, not paying any particular attention to the articles. One magazine down, he picked up another and started to flip through the pages.

He paused and smiled to himself, recalling a time that seemed like only yesterday. Clare had dragged him into a very fashionable upscale store back in the States, *like this one*, he thought as he looked around. The small sitting area, he realized, was very similar in design to the one Clare had parked him in that previous time. Couple of chairs, small glass table, and, he recalled, probably a dozen or so magazines laid out on the table. On the previous occasion, he had flipped through all the magazines not once but twice and was about to flip through them a third time when Clare had finally taken pity and rescued him from his fashion purgatory. He smiled at the memory, recalling Clare's numerous trips to the dressing room. Her modeling various outfits for him before finally making her selections. Shaking his head, he also remembered the sticker shock when he had handed over his credit card to the cashier. But she did look stunning in the clothes, he had to admit. For a couple of minutes, he lingered in the memory.

"Where's Padraig?" Moira asked Brian, now with a different light-blue dress in her hand.

Brought back to the present, Brian looked up at Moira. He had completely forgotten about Padraig. He stood up to look around the store. There, way off in the distance, he could make out the top of Padraig with his full head of gray hair, the rest of his body enveloped by the material on the clothing racks. Padraic wasn't moving, seemingly fixed in one location. Brian directed Moira's attention to where Padraig was standing. With a satisfied look, Moira headed back to the dressing rooms.

Brian sat down, picked up a magazine, and followed Moira's progress up the stairs and across the landing, when suddenly, she stopped. He could see her staring out across the floor below to where Padraig was standing. Brian noticed Moira shaking her head before abruptly turning around and quickly making her way back to where he was sitting with a magazine in his hand.

"Brian, you have to go get him," Moira commanded.

"Who?" Brian responded looking up at Moira.

"Padraig! He shouldn't be there; it's not good for him."

Brian placed the magazine back on the table and got up from his chair. He stood up on his toes to look out across the floor where he had previously seen Padraig. *Still there,* he thought, *still not moving.*

"Why do you want me to get him?" Brian asked, shrugging his shoulders.

"Just get him. Please," Moira pleaded, as she headed off to the dressing room again.

Brian slowly approached the maze of clothes racks, trying to determine which would be the most direct route to intercept Padraig. He started down one aisle that ultimately led to the front display window. There he came upon a young mother looking into the store from the outside. She had her eyes on a dress on the mannequin stationed to his immediate left. A young bored-looking child clung to the mother's hand. When Brian smiled at the child, the child stuck his tongue out at him. *Real nice! The little—*. Tempted to stick his tongue out at the child, he refrained and smiled at the child's mother, who was now staring at the strange man standing next to the mannequin inside the store. Brian turned around and retraced his steps back to the sitting area.

Starting over, he thought his best bet would be the aisle in front of him slightly off to his left. Zigzagging down several aisles, he slowly but surely closed in on Padraig's gray head. He started to get worried when he noticed that Padraig was still just standing in the same spot, almost as if he were in a trance. Finally, Brian could see all of Padraig's body, not just his head, standing at the end of the current aisle he was moving down. Brian was so focused on Padraig that he didn't even notice the women's apparel (or lack thereof) when he finally drew up next to him.

"Padraig, are you alright?" Brian asked, looking at the catatonic man standing alongside him.

Padraig slowly raised an arm and started to point at the clothes racks around him, lips moving but no sound coming out. Brian took his eyes off Padraig and started to follow where Padraig was pointing. The two men were standing at ground zero of the women's lingerie section. Full coverage, the items were not, Brian thought, as he surveyed the tiny, somewhat transparent items of—well—items. *These clothing items were not what you would expect your mother to wear, or you'd at least hope she wouldn't wear.* Quickly putting that thought out of his head, he turned back to look at the man standing next to him.

"Ah, I guess it's been some time since you've been with—" Brian began.

Padraig completed Brian's statement for him. "A woman, you were going to say." Padraig slowly turned his head to look at Brian and continued, "I'll have you know that there are two women in the county who I"—Padraig paused, looking for the right words—"keep company with." Then as an afterthought, Padraig finished, "Not both at the same time, mind you."

Brian looked at Padraig with a new-found appreciation, and smiled.

"I trust you are a gentleman and will keep that to yourself," Padraig said, and waited for a response.

Brian nodded and turned his attention back to the items surrounding them.

Padraig resumed pointing at the various lingerie items and said to no one in particular, "But what the two of them wear . . . the knickers they wear, are more like the size and shape of the canvas material that the fifty-pound bags of feed come in, nothing at all like these things."

The mental image Brian's brain conjured up of two women attired only in canvas feed bags caused Brian to visibly shudder. He hoped Padraig was exaggerating, but then again, maybe not.

"Ah, granny pants," Brian said, trying to shake the mental image.

"Granny pants?" Padraig asked, somewhat confused.

"Yes, granny . . . oh, forget it," Brian responded, not wanting to have to explain or describe full-coverage underwear.

Padraig pointed at another clothing rack to his left containing what some might consider to be brassieres. Both the level of support and coverage were questionable for the various sizes and colors of undergarments clinging seductively to the hangers. Padraig then moved his arm over to his right and stopped at more racks; this time the racks were full of multicolored thongs. Brian's eyes followed to where Padraig's arm was pointing and hoped that Padraig wasn't going to ask him what these items were.

Padraig shook his head and said to no one in particular, "When I was a young lad, I had a slingshot that had more material than those." He pointed again to the racks for emphasis.

Brian stifled a laugh. "Padraig, I don't think people buy these things for their support nor their coverage, if you get my drift." He wasn't about to explain that these delicate items were probably not meant to be worn for any appreciable length of time—*one-and-done undies*. Someone else could give Padraig a refresher course on the birds and the bees.

"Tsk, tsk." The sound of a female voice could be heard from behind where Padraig and Brian were standing.

Brian slowly turned around to locate the source of the double *tsk*, only to see the back of a woman being swallowed up by the sea of clothing as she quickly departed from what she must have thought was the scene of two male deviants. Brian turned back to face Padraig and the intimate surroundings.

As Brian continued to gaze at the unmentionables, he could feel eyes staring at him. He turned to look over his shoulder and saw Moira glaring at him from the landing by the dressing rooms. A sheepish grin crossed his face, only to be met by the daggers that Moira's eyes were sending his way. She shook her head and jabbed her arm toward the door through which they had originally entered the store. Brian nodded once and turned back to Padraig.

Touching Padraig's arm, he said, "Padraig, I don't think it's good for you to be here. Let's go outside and get some fresh air." He used his arm to gently persuade Padraig to turn around. As they started toward the door, Brian looked up and saw Moira still staring at him, slowly nodding her head in approval, pointing with her outstretched arm toward the entrance to the store. Brian shrugged his shoulders and nodded at Moira, continuing toward the entrance, making their way through the racks of clothing. He paused halfway across the floor, tugging gently on Padraig's arm to get him to stop his forward motion. He just couldn't help himself. Padraig had called him a heathen on several occasions in the recent past.

Time for some payback, he thought.

Brian turned to look back at the clothing section where Padraig had stood transfixed. Padraig's eyes followed Brian's. "Padraig," Brian began, "when you are with your lady friends in an intimate moment, it's probably best if you don't imagine them wearing... well, it's best if you don't imagine." Brian left the sentence unfinished as he nodded back toward the women's lingerie section.

As Brian followed Padraig toward the exit, he smiled as he recalled the roller coaster of emotions that had quickly swept across Padraig's face when he mentioned Padraig's lady friends dressed in the intimate clothing they had just left behind. Padraig's furrowed eyebrows and the initial look of incomprehension. Padraig's eyes narrowing as recognition set in—his lady friends and—those items. Then, was that a brief look of horror? *Yep, definitely a look of horror,* Brian thought. Finally, Padraig shaking his head trying to erase the images Brian had implanted.

Brian desperately tried not to laugh as he followed Padraig to the store's exit.

* * *

Once outside, Padraig and Brian stood in front of the store's window, watching people walk by. Moira was still inside, *probably trying on more dresses,* Brian thought. Suddenly, Padraig left Brian's side and scampered across the pedestrian walkway to a pub located directly opposite from where they had been standing. Padraig looked briefly at the notices in the windows in the front of the pub, then opened the door and went inside.

Brian watched Padraig disappear, and he felt something like dread. Brian had never seen Padraig drink anything but soda or water. Never the hard stuff or beer. He had heard stories about Padraig's younger years and his heavy drinking but didn't know if they were true. He never thought to ask Moira. It was none of his business. The longer Padraig was inside of the pub, the greater Brian's discomfort. Maybe he shouldn't have said anything about Padraig's women friends and the wardrobe that he and Padraig had been admiring.

Brian was about to go across the way to the pub to see what Padraig was up to when Padraig came out the pub's door, looked around, and took off toward another pub up a little way to Brian's right.

Outside the next pub, Padraig once again paused to look at the notices in the exterior windows of the building and then went inside. Brian was confused because it didn't seem like Padraig spent enough time inside to enjoy a drink. He was again about to go after Padraig when out he came, slowly making his way over to where Brian was standing. Brian felt uncomfortable about asking Padraig what he was doing but felt he had an obligation to find out. He was spared asking by Padraig himself.

"Just checking to see the layout of the two pubs and to see what they have on tap. Always good to know what the competition is up to," Padraig said.

"See anything?" Brian said, with some relief.

"In addition to the usual ales on tap, both offer a new lager from a local microbrewery. I've heard of it. I was asking the bartenders about its popularity among the customers. Apparently, it appeals to the younger clientele. I might bring it in on a trial basis, see how it goes over. Probably will appeal to the tourists. The old-timers will stick with the Guinness."

Brian, blissfully ignorant about the different types of beer, merely nodded in agreement.

As they were completing their discussion of the nuances of beer drinkers' tastes, the door to the store behind them opened and out came Moira.

"I'm all set, let's go," Moira said.

The three of them headed off toward the car garage. Once again Moira was in the lead, with Padraig and Brian trailing behind. Padraig reached over and took hold of Brian's arm to slow him down, allowing Moira to get even further ahead.

Padraig leaned over toward Brian and, in a very low voice, said to Brian, "The dress." When it was obvious to Padraig that Brian didn't have a clue what he was talking about, he said, "The dress Moira was trying on. In the store." Padraig raised his eyebrows. "We'll go fifty-fifty on the cost."

Brian stopped dead in his tracks. Clapped his hand to his head and nodded his understanding. How could he be so stupid, he thought. Then again, when he had gone into women's clothing stores with Clare, he would assume his obligatory seat in the isolated corner of the store not only while Clare searched for and tried on various looks, but while she took care of the purchase from their joint account.

"You keep her busy, I'll be right back," he said to Padraig. "Tell her I forgot to pick up something that I'd ordered from a store up here."

* * *

Once again in front of the woman's clothing store, Brian opened the door and entered. The very attractive salesclerk looked up from what she was doing at the counter and smiled.

"Did you forget something?" she said in a helpful voice.

"Um, yes. The lady I was with before. She tried on a couple of dresses. Was there one dress that she especially liked?"

"I have the dresses here that she tried on. I was just about to put them back out on the floor racks for display." With that, the salesclerk reached behind her to a clothes rack located behind the counter. She retrieved the two dresses and turned back to Brian, holding a dress in each of her raised hands for him to see.

"Did she like one in particular?" Brian asked, stepping closer to cast a critical eye at the two dresses. *Who am I kidding when it comes to dresses? I don't have a clue,* he thought.

"Actually, your wife seemed to like both dresses. She looked stunning in this pretty flower dress as well as this light-blue dress," the salesclerk said, as she stepped forward with each dress for Brian to see more closely. She looked directly at Brian as she was holding up each dress, her eyebrows raised as if to say it would be too difficult to pick one over the other.

Brian stood looking at the two dresses when he realized that the salesperson thought Moira was his wife. For the briefest of moments, Brian was back in time at a Lord & Taylor store, picking up a present for his wife's forty-fifth birthday. He smiled at the memory.

"If you had to choose one, which would you choose?"

"I don't know that I could. I like them both. And your wife seemed to like them equally," she said, with that captivating smile.

Of course she did! He was running out of time before Moira would soon wonder where he had gone off to.

Brian relented. "Okay. I'll take both dresses. Please, can you put them in a plain box and a plain bag? They're to be a surprise." Brian paused then and said softly to himself, "For my wife."

In the blink of an eye, the salesclerk produced a large box, tissue paper and a plain bag with handles and proceeded to assemble the package. The dresses were neatly folded and individually wrapped in tissue paper. The transaction was finally completed when the salesclerk returned Brian's credit card and sales receipt and handed the bag to him. Brian thanked the young salesclerk and hurried out the front door of the store onto to the pedestrian walkway.

Brian turned the corner around the last building before the park they had crossed earlier on their way to the university, and he caught sight of Padraig and Moira slowly walking down a sidewalk, Moira occasionally stopping and examining a display in a store's window.

Padraig was impatiently looking around until he finally saw Brian making his way toward them. Padraig nodded his approval when he saw the package in Brian's hand.

"Ah there you are. Moira and I were beginning to think you got yourself lost. I see you picked up your parcel," Padraig said.

* * *

"Popular first name," Padraig said out loud to no one in particular, as they drove along the road heading back to Doolin.

After he paused briefly to look down at the instrument panel to make sure he wasn't speeding Brian asked, "What name?"

"Dean," Padraig replied. "We met a Dean Kelly, and I heard that woman in the front office mention to him that he had a lunch meeting with a Dean Fitzpatrick while you two were outside."

Brian slowly averted his eyes from the road ahead and looked at the man sitting next to him. Padraig was looking out his side window, seemingly mesmerized by the passing sights. Turning back to look at the road rising ahead of them, Brian shook his head in disbelief.

"You know Dean is not their first name," Brian said.

"Yes, it is. You met Dean Kelly, and I heard the woman in the office say that Dean Kelly had a luncheon meeting with Dean Fitzpatrick. There are actors with the first name Dean, although I can't think of their last names right now," Padraig said with some authority.

Best to leave it alone, Brian thought. He briefly considered explaining to Padraig that dean was their title but figured the back-and-forth questions and answers about exactly what a dean at a university does would take up the remaining part of the trip and probably would go on into tomorrow and the next day. Life was too short!

They traveled for some distance with no one saying a word. Then Brian sensed someone was looking at him. He first glanced up at the rearview mirror. Moira was still looking intently out her side window at the passing sights. He looked quickly to his left and flinched when he saw Padraig staring at him. He noticed Padraig nodding his head toward the back seat where the package lay. Brian acknowledged Padraig by slowly nodding his own head.

"Moira," Brian began, "could you do me a favor and open the package next to you, please?"

Moira turned her head away from the side window and reached over to the bag. She pulled the box out and placed it on her lap, leaving the empty bag next to her. Using both hands, she lifted the lid off the box and noticed the tissue paper laying across the top. She slid her fingers under the top layer of tissue paper and gently pulled the paper to the side. Looking in the rearview mirror, Brian saw Moira's eyebrows arch upward. He then saw her reach further into the box and pull the dress completely out of the box. More tissue paper was pulled out. After a quick glance at the road ahead, Brian returned to the rearview mirror to see Moira clutch the floral-patterned dress close to her chest with her left hand and reached down and pulled out more tissue paper with her right hand to reveal light-blue material. The other dress. Her head shot up as she looked at the back of Brian's head.

"What's this? Who are these dresses for?" she demanded.

Not quite the response Brian was expecting. Brian noticed how Padraig kept his head turned toward his side window, sinking down in his seat.

"Who are these dresses for?" Moira asked in a louder voice.

More silence. Brian glanced at Padraig again and then reached over and nudged Padraig on his right arm. Reluctantly Padraig looked away from the side window and stared out the front windshield.

"Who—" Moira began, but was interrupted by Padraig.

"Moira, Brian and I thought we would get the dresses for you. A gift."

In the back seat Moira was shaking her head back and forth. "No, no, I can't accept them, we need to turn back and return them." Reaching her arm through the open space between the two front seats, Moira pointed off to the left where there was a side road. "There, you can turn around there."

Brian drove past the road, which angled off to a distant farmhouse.

"There, up on your right, you can turn around there," Moira said sharply, now pointing to a narrow lane.

Brian was at a total loss. He couldn't figure out why Moira was reacting this way. *No good deed goes unpunished,* he thought, as he drove pass the lane.

"There—" Moira started.

"Moira. Enough!" Padraig said in a commanding voice before continuing, "Brian and I were simply trying to do something nice for you. If you don't want the dresses, Brian and I know two lovely ladies who would be very pleased to have them. Very pleased, indeed."

Hearing the words "two lovely ladies," Brian's eyes widened. He wondered who Padraig had in mind and then remembered Padraig confiding to him about his women friends—whose attire included granny pants. *Hopefully he's bluffing,* Brian reassured himself.

"Who?" Moira blurted out, holding the dresses tightly against her chest, looking back and forth at the back of Brian's head and then Padraig's head. With no response coming, she repeated, "Who?"

"Never you mind," Padraig replied. "They'll be very grateful to have those very fine-looking dresses."

Slumping back in her seat, Moira clung to the two dresses as tears started to flow down her cheeks. As the tears continued to flow, she loosened her hands on the dresses and slowly placed them carefully back into the box, making sure the tissue paper neatly separated each. She put the lid back on the box and slid the box back into the bag.

In the front seat, Brian could hear sobs and occasional sniffles emanating from the back seat. He was again at a loss to explain Moira's reaction. Had they insulted her—the way she dressed? Or maybe it was the stress of the trip, meeting with Dean Kelly. Now he felt bad for being the cause of her tears. The remainder of the trip was made in relative silence, except for the sniffles, as farmlands and sweeping pastures with grazing sheep rolled by.

"Sorry," Moira said in a meek voice, as the car neared the little village and the pub. Brian pulled up across from the pub and stopped to let Padraig out. Padraig opened the door and hoisted himself out of the car, closing the door behind him. Looking both ways, he crossed the road and headed toward the pub.

28

AS THE CAR had approached the village, Moira had stared at the closed package next to her on the back seat. She had been shocked by her own reaction and tried to understand it. Brian and Padraig were just trying to be nice to her by giving her a gift—of *two* dresses! Padraig had always been generous to her and Maureen. And Brian, well, he had also been very generous, providing a roof over their heads these last couple of years. Giving Maureen a computer. Moira shook her head. *Why did I behave that way?* Moira questioned herself as she tried to brush the tears from her cheeks.

The dresses are personal. Is that it? she wondered. Was that the reason she snapped at the two of them? She had received nice gifts on her birthdays and Christmas. But that was different. Those types of gifts were expected. Receiving these two dresses was a surprise, one that she was not prepared for. Thinking back over the years, she couldn't remember another time when she'd received such a gift. *I've been alone for all these years. Have I created a wall around me so I might not be hurt again like before, when he skipped out on me? Has it gotten to the point where I don't even know how to accept a gift, an act of kindness?* These thoughts consumed Moira as the car came to a stop across from the pub.

* * *

Brian started to pull the car away from the curb after Padraig crossed the road.

"Stop! Please, stop!" Moira shouted.

Brian immediately braked. Moira opened the rear car door and dashed across the road.

"Padraig, wait, please wait," Moira called after Padraig, who turned around upon hearing his niece. Suddenly Padraig staggered backward as Moira wrapped her arms around him and pressed her head against his chest.

"Padraig. I'm so sorry," Moira said in a muffled voice, her face buried in Padraig's chest. Her steady stream of tears began to produce a dark wet spot on his shirt.

Padraig managed to free his right arm from Moira's grasp. Moira could feel a hand lifting her chin upward. Padraig lowered his head so that both their faces were inches apart.

He shook his head and smiled. "Moira," he softly began, "sometimes you just have to say *thank you,* and leave it at that. All Brian and I were trying to do is give you a nice present for all the things you have done for us. That's all." Padraig used his thumb to wipe away a tear falling down her cheek. She offered a sad little smile and nodded her head in understanding.

"You have a difficult choice ahead of you, young lady," Padraig said, in a serious tone. Moira's body stiffened. "You're going to have to figure out which dress you're going to wear to Maureen's graduation when that time comes."

Moira closed her eyes and nodded once, with a forlorn smile.

Padraig extracted himself from Moira's grasp and pointed to the car where Brian was patiently waiting. "Moira, Brian is a good man. He thinks highly of you and Maureen. He wanted to show his appreciation for all that you have done for him since he lost... since he lost his Clare. It was his idea, getting you those two dresses. He means well."

Moira looked over her shoulder at the waiting car, then turned back and nodded to her uncle. She turned around, wiped tears off her face, and slowly crossed the road. She opened the rear car door and got in. Brian slowly moved along the road and made the right turn up the lane. Once in the driveway in front of the house, Brian came to a stop and turned the car off.

"Brian, I'm sorry for the way I acted." Moira waited for a response and saw Brian nod his head as he exited the car. Moira reached over and grabbed hold of the package, then opened the rear car door and stood on the pebbled driveway with package in hand.

They both arrived at the front door at the same time. Moira looked up at Brian and then said, "Brian I'm sorry for the way I reacted. These dresses are lovely. I..." Moira began but was at loss for words.

Sensing Moira's embarrassment, Brian interjected, "Moira, why don't I put the tea kettle on while you put *your* dresses upstairs in your room."

* * *

Mugs of tea in hand, Brian and Moira sat on the bench on the back patio.

"Padraig called while I was upstairs. He said we should come down to the pub for an early dinner, since we missed lunch," Moira informed Brian. With the earlier drama in the car, appetites had been lost and lunch forgotten. "Five o'clock," Moira added. Brian nodded.

"In a week's time, I'll have to head back to the United States," Brian said. "New client. Not quite sure when I'll be back, but I'll let you know." This time Moira nodded. For a couple of minutes, they sat in relaxed silence.

"What you said about the Dean's List, only a few students make the list?" Moira asked, breaking the silence, looking down at her outstretched legs.

"Moira, your daughter is a very bright young woman. And yes, only a select few of the top students get to be on the Dean's List. And for her to be on the Dean's List every single term is very remarkable." After taking a sip of his tea, Brian continued, "You should be very proud of your daughter."

Moira nodded as she leaned back on the bench and gazed out over the field of flowing wheat. *Yes, I am very proud of my daughter,* she thought. Holding the mug of tea in both hands, Moira knew that the university education would allow Maureen to determine her own future. And that future was not too far off.

Conversation over, they spent the remaining hour before their early pub dinner enjoying their tea and silently watching the puffs of lazy white clouds drift across the blue sky.

29

MIXING UP HIS afternoon routine, Brian visited the pub the next day before his walk, shortly after the lunch hour had ended. Earlier he had taken a stroll down the road to the chocolate shop three doors down and picked up some bars of chocolate for his grandchildren. He had deferred to the lady who ran the shop—milk chocolate vs. dark chocolate, 90 percent cocoa vs. 75 percent cocoa. When he told the shop lady the chocolate was for his grandchildren and their ages (which he guessed at), she made the selections. His role in the shop was reduced to handing over some euros. The bag with the chocolate he was now holding also provided a good cover, should Moira ask him why he wasn't on his walk.

Brian pulled out a bar stool from the far end of the bar and sat down, placing the bag of chocolate on top of the bar. Padraig, seeing him take a seat, wandered over with a Diet Coke in hand and placed it in front of Brian.

"Well, have you heard anything?" Brian asked, raising the glass to his mouth.

"Well, Conor isn't too happy," Padraig replied.

Brian's hand with the glass of soda froze in midair. "Why, what happened?" he asked, immediately concerned.

"Five hundred euros, that's what happened," Padraig said with a chuckle.

Brian smiled and took a sip of his soda. He asked, "Did Conor say anything else . . . about the visit?"

"Not really. He said Dean Kelly had called him and busted his chops about the donation. Dean Kelly also mentioned to him that he thought the meeting went quite well with Moira. He remarked to Conor about how very smart Maureen is and how intelligence in the McGuire family must elude certain *uncles* like Conor." Padraig shook his head and continued, "Conor and I have declared a truce—he won't tell me Irish jokes and I won't make donations to charities on his behalf."

Brian put his empty glass on the bar. He looked around the pub and said to Padraig, "From what I can tell, I think Moira bought the whole story. She seems to be in a very good mood."

Just then, Brian noticed Moira coming out of the kitchen area carrying what looked like a couple of takeaway containers. Looking straight ahead, she made her way across the pub floor to the far side outdoor exit. Brian arched an eyebrow. Padraig, seeing Brian's look, glanced over his shoulder to see what had caught Brian's attention. He also saw Moira with the takeaway containers before she disappeared beyond the far side of the bar.

"Ah, the pub's worst-kept secret," Padraig volunteered, turning back to Brian, who looked intrigued. "Let me freshen up your soda; this may take a little while." Padraig refilled Brian's Diet Coke and placed it on a beer coaster before beginning the story.

* * *

A couple of months back, Padraig had ventured outside the pub after the lunch hour rush to have a look at the facade to see if any painting was required. It had been a while since the woodwork had been painted, and he knew that a worn-down, unattractive-looking pub would draw fewer patrons, so he liked to keep the pub's appearance ship-shape. As he was surveying the front of the pub, he noticed someone coming out from behind the far side of the pub, away from where he was standing. The person was heading up along the road toward the quay. He was surprised to see it was Moira, with two takeaway containers in her hands. She marched up along the road and across the lane and turned right onto the property two houses up. Mr. Byrne's place.

Widower Byrne, who was in his eighties, had lost his dear wife a little over a month ago. The whole village had turned out for the funeral service. Mr. Byrne in the past would come into the pub for a late-afternoon pint, but the years had taken their toll, and he was pretty much housebound.

A week later, at about the same time in the afternoon, Padraig was across the road inspecting the picnic table and the benches. This area was communal, and anyone could use the table and chairs, but he took it upon himself to make sure the outdoor furniture was in good shape. A sudden movement to his left caught his eye. This time he saw Jane, a relatively new pub employee, coming out from behind the pub with takeaway containers, heading up the road and entering Mr. Byrne's property. Coincidence? Padraig didn't think so.

The next day, at approximately the same time after the lunch hour was over, he waited patiently in one of the two outside entranceways to the pub, occasionally leaning out and looking up the road. Sure enough, another person with two takeaway containers appeared from behind the far side of the building. This time it was not difficult to see that it was Nora en route to Mr. Byrne's place. Something was going on, and Padraic was going to find out what it was.

The following day, before the regular lunch crowd and tourists made their way into the pub, Padraig got hold of Jimmy, who was working behind the bar, checking inventory. Jimmy had worked in the pub for too long for anything to get by him. Padraig also knew that it wouldn't take too much on his part to get Jimmy to spill the beans.

"Jimmy, what's going on?" Padraig asked, in an accusatory tone.

Jimmy was caught off guard. "What do you mean?" Jimmy stammered, almost dropping the empty pint glass he was holding.

"Come now, Jimmy. If I was to take you outside after the lunch crowd is gone and we happened to look up the road toward"—Padraig paused for effect—"let's say widower Byrne's place, do you think we might see some people we know carrying takeaway containers?" Jimmy's face turned some interesting shades of red.

"Jimmy!" Padraig said in a loud voice, one eyebrow raised.

"Padraig." Jimmy paused and cleared his throat. "We found out that Mr. Byrne has no relatives close by to take care of him. We also found out that after his wife passed away, he wasn't taking care of himself properly. He wasn't eating right. He had lost a lot of weight. We haven't stolen anything, honest. We each take turns skipping lunch so that Mr. Byrne gets a good meal each day. He doesn't eat much, so what we bring for lunch, well, there's enough for him for dinner, too."

"Jimmy, just who are *we*?" Padraig asked in a lowered voice, tilting his head to one side. Jimmy stood fidgeting, looking over his shoulder toward the entrance to the kitchen.

"Well, Moira, Nora, Jane, myself, and anyone else working days on any given week. We all take turns. Honest, we don't steal, we just . . . give him our meals, the ones we skip," Jimmy concluded, visibly exhausted. "Padraig, I don't want to get the others in trouble. Please, take the lunches out of my wages."

Padraig looked at Jimmy without saying a word but with new admiration for the young man standing in front of him. Truth be told, the only person he was disappointed with was himself, for not thinking of Mr. Byrne.

After a minute, Padraig said, "Jimmy, no one will be getting in trouble, no one will be skipping their meals, and no one will be having money taken out of their wages. You folks did the right thing. Mr. Byrne will continue getting his daily meals. As far as anyone is concerned, you haven't said a word to me about what has been going on. Tomorrow I'll talk to the folks in the kitchen. If anyone asks, I figured this out when I saw people making trips up to Mr. Byrne's place. Okay, Jimmy?"

Jimmy reluctantly nodded, his face full of concern.

* * *

The next day after most of the lunch crowd had departed the pub, Padraig approached the door to the kitchen, the aroma of today's special still lingering. Earlier in the day, his nose had told him the special was pot roast with a thick gravy sauce. Mashed potatoes and cooked string beans were the sides he saw on the plates being delivered to hungry lunch customers. Dessert was bread pudding with raisins, one of his favorites.

Padraig carefully opened the kitchen door and took a step into the kitchen. Over to his left he could see Moira reaching into a very large brown bag containing the dinner rolls that had accompanied today's lunch and would accompany the evening's dinner orders. The local bakery delivered a couple dozen rolls each morning to the pub. Nora stood across from Padraig over by the large industrial kitchen sink, where she was cleaning off a few dirty plates before putting them into the dishwasher. Padraig noticed two empty takeaway containers with their lids open on the preparation table directly across from the large stove. On top of the stove was a very large metal baking pan with its long lid. The metal baking pan was one of four very large pans used to make enough pot roast for both the lunch and dinner meals. Any leftovers after the two meals would be a meal for the evening staff. Next to the baking pan were two oversized pots. Padraig made his way over to the prep table and stood in front of the empty takeaway containers. When he picked up one of the empty takeaway containers, Moira and Nora froze, quickly glancing at each other before looking back at Padraig.

Padraig took the empty takeaway container over to the stove. He took the metal lid off the large baking pan and placed it on the prep table. Condensation from under the lid dripped onto the table. Padraig looked around and found a large serving spoon. He reached into the baking pan and scooped up two large pieces of sliced pot roast and put them in the takeaway container. He looked again at the baking pan and scooped out another smaller slice of pot roast and put it neatly in the takeaway container with the two other slices and nodded his approval. A third scoop contained a liberal amount of the hot gravy. Padraig reached over and retrieved the metal lid and then put it back on the pan containing the pot roast.

"You know, when Mr. Byrne used to come to the pub for a pint, he'd brag about Mrs. Byrne's pot roast. He would describe how tender it was. And the gravy… well, you could almost taste the meal yourself," Padraig recalled, without looking at Moira or Nora. His eyes were on a large pot sitting on top of the stove. He took the lid off and looked in, then he took another serving spoon from the counter and scooped up a generous portion of mashed potatoes. Lid back on, Padraig moved to the next pot and took its lid off. He found another serving spoon and added string beans to the takeaway container. He then put the takeaway container on the prep table and securely closed the lid.

Moira and Nora stood frozen in place, occasionally looking at each other and then back at Padraig. Padraig spied the tray of bread pudding and retrieved the other takeaway container. This time he used a knife to slice a generous portion of the dessert. With a nearby spatula, he lifted the portion out of the baking tray and put it into the second takeaway container and closed it before putting the container on the prep table along with the other container. He looked at

Moira and said, "Don't skimp on the dinner rolls. With the leftovers, he can make nice sandwiches." He turned to Nora and said, "I suppose it wouldn't be too much trouble making a smaller tray of bread pudding when you make a large tray. Bread pudding makes a nice snack and should keep in his icebox." Nora slowly nodded her agreement.

Padraig started across the kitchen floor and stopped at the door to the dining area, where he turned around and looked at Moira and then at Nora. Then he looked at the two closed takeaway containers. After a brief pause, in a determined voice, he said, "No one, absolutely no one, will be skipping any meals!" Padraig briefly looked up at the kitchen ceiling, pondering what he would say next. He lowered his eyes and again looked at the two takeaway containers before saying, "Mr. Byrne is to be considered an employee of the pub . . . part of the kitchen staff. He's the pub's resident food taster." Seeing Nora's eyes narrow, Padraig quickly added, "In name only."

Padraig started toward the kitchen door but stopped again and turned around to add in an understanding voice, "If you're short of staff and need someone to bring the meal up to Mr. Byrne, come get me. I can walk it up." This time when Padraig turned around, he went through the kitchen door. Moira and Nora looked at each other dumbfounded, and then they smiled.

Moira, with three dinner rolls already in her left hand, reached into the large brown paper bakery bag and retrieved another three rolls with her right hand. She opened the lid of the container with the bread pudding, slipped the rolls inside, and closed it up again. Looking over her shoulder, she couldn't see Nora but heard the clattering of metal.

Approaching the sink area, she could see Nora down on her knees searching through the lower cabinet next to the sink where the baking pans were stored. Nora grunted as she straightened up, one hand holding onto a small baking pan, the other hand braced on the front of the sink. She held up the six-by-six baking pan and nodded. With a satisfied look, Nora placed the pan on the counter.

Moira grabbed the two takeaway containers and started off for the rear exterior kitchen door but stopped just short of it. She turned to look at Nora. Nora nodded toward the door to the pub's dining area. Moira smiled and altered course and walked toward the door to dining area. There was no longer a need to slink out the pub's back kitchen door.

The pub's worst-kept secret was secret no more.

30

TWO MONTHS HAD passed since Brian had returned to the United States. Two long months, in Moira's mind. It would be another month before he returned to the village, he had informed her. And summer couldn't come soon enough for her, when Maureen would be home from the university. Moira tried to keep busy by working extra shifts at the pub. Even so, the days seem to pass by at a snail's pace. The house felt empty.

That is, the house *had* felt empty, up until late one night when Moira had a surprise visitor.

* * *

Moira laid in bed, half asleep. Earlier, she had made the rounds throughout the house to make sure all the outside doors were locked and the windows closed. Then she checked the laundry room and the kitchen to make sure the appliances were all off. Once these checks were completed, she turned off the downstairs lights and headed up the stairs to her bedroom, where she changed into her nightgown, pulled the covers down on the bed, climbed in, and drifted off into a dream-filled sleep, which became a restless sleep. During the night, the weather had turned nasty, with gusting winds and a steady downpour of rain that lashed at the windows in Moira's bedroom. Occasional flashes of lightning briefly lit up the sky and invaded her room, creating shadows where there had been none only seconds before. Thunder echoed across the land, adding to her uneasy sleep.

Moira bolted upright in her bed. Was it a dream? She thought she had heard a whimpering sound and a scratching noise. For a split second, she saw her reflection in the mirror on top of the dresser across from the bed when a flash of lightning penetrated the room. The following boom of thunder was deafening. *Must be a dream—the whimpering and scratching,* she thought. But there it was again, after the loud noise from the thunder had rolled on across the fields toward the sea beyond.

Moira slid her legs over the side of the bed, got up, stepped out onto the landing, and immediately looked at the other end of the landing, to her daughter's room. But Maureen was at school, so it couldn't be her making that noise. *Had she locked all the doors? Had someone gotten into the house?* She turned the lights on to illuminate the area downstairs and cautiously made her way down the staircase. At the bottom, she slowly scanned the downstairs, starting with the front seating area. *Nothing.* She started to cross the dining room, heading for the kitchen, when she heard the whimpering and scratching sound to her immediate left, by the outside door to the patio. Slowly she moved over to the door, fearful she would see a strange face looking back at her. The interior light reflecting off the glass door made it difficult to see outside. For the most part, Moira stood looking at her own reflection in the glass. Only when lightning flashed across the sky could she briefly see past her reflection to the outside patio area. She didn't see anyone on the patio. Moira let out a sigh of relief. But then she heard the noise again. The scratching noise was down low on the door.

Moira turned the lock on the door and partially opened the door inward. She let out a scream when she could feel something (or someone) push against the partially open door, forcing her back, before that something made its way inside the house a couple of feet and collapsed on the floor. Moira blinked a few times, trying to make out what exactly had landed near her feet, before she realized she was looking at a drenched animal—a dog. Moira quickly closed the back door and locked it. The dog didn't move. It didn't shake itself as wet dogs are prone to do. Two very sad-looking eyes stared up at her, blinking every so often.

"Well, where's your home?" Moira asked, shaking her head in disbelief. "You're soaked!"

Moira noticed water starting to pool alongside the dog, so she went into the laundry room and found a couple of old bath towels that were eventually going to be cut up and used as dust cloths. She draped one towel over the bottom half of the prone dog and the other on the top half, then got down on her knees and began to rub the dog with the towels to try to dry the poor animal off. The entire time, the dog remained immobile; only the eyes followed what she was doing. Moira stood up, holding two soaked bath towels. She used one less-damp end of a towel to try to soak up the small puddle of water alongside the dog. She then returned to the laundry room and dumped the towels in the sink. On the floor of the laundry room, she formed a makeshift bed for the dog with a couple of bath towels that were supposed to be laundered the next morning.

Moira returned to the damp dog. She tried to get it to follow her into the laundry room, to no avail. She straddled the dog, one leg on either side, and placed her arms behind its front legs to pick it up. With some effort she managed to half carry, half slide the dog into the laundry room and rest it on the towels on the floor. She stood up, exhausted. Then she laid two more towels on the dog's lower body to provide it with some warmth. She stood by the laundry room door, looking down at the dog. The helpless animal looked back at her with sorrowful eyes. She reached over to turn off the laundry room light but thought better of it.

"Good night," Moira said to the dog, as she partially closed the laundry room door. Making her way up the stairs, she wondered who the owner of the dog could be. There was no collar or dog tag. Once she had gotten the dog somewhat dry, she could make out that it was a sheep dog. A nice, very young-looking sheep dog at that. There were plenty of sheep dogs in the county, but she didn't think it was local to the village. *Oh well, tomorrow is another day*. She'd try to find the owner then.

Moira partially closed her bedroom door to darken her room from the downstairs light while still allowing her to hear the dog. As she climbed back into bed, she saw her bedside clock: 2:00 a.m. Moira pulled up the covers and promptly fell asleep. She was exhausted from the night's ordeal.

* * *

The next morning, Moira dressed and went down the stairs and peered into the laundry room. The dog was no longer laying down but was sitting with head tilted to one side, looking expectantly at this morning's visitor.

"Well, I see you're feeling better this morning," Moira said, as the dog tilted its head the other way, as if trying to understand the language of the lady standing before him.

"Come on, you probably have to go outside and do your business." Moira looked around suspiciously at the floor to see if the dog had already done so. Seeing nothing, Moira opened wide the laundry room door and then walked over to the back door, which she unlocked and pulled open. The dog scampered across the floor and went outside onto the patio. Moira watched as the dog sniffed around, first going up to the picnic table, then over to the bench. As she watched the dog, she wondered if it was a female or a male; she hadn't noticed last night. Her question was answered when the dog went over by the entrance to the fields in the back and raised one hind leg and peed on the stone wall separating the patio from the fields. A rather large dark stain cascaded down the wall. The dog—he, apparently—wandered out into the field of wheat and disappeared for a couple of minutes. Then he broke through the tall strands of wheat to reappear, making his way across the patio to the back door and his new-found friend.

At least he's housebroken. She smiled and said to the dog, "You wait outside while I get you something to eat and drink, although I would think you had enough water last night." Moira partially closed the back door and went into the kitchen to find some morsels. The dog waited patiently on the patio, turning his head to follow Moira as she crossed the dining room floor.

Moira returned with two bowls: one filled with water, and one filled with leftovers from last night's meal. She placed the two bowls down on the patio and watched as the dog scarfed up the food, pushing the bowl around with his nose when it was empty to see if anything had been missed or might have fallen out of the bowl. He then slurped up some water. Finished with the water, the dog sat down on the patio and ran his tongue across his nose in what appeared to be a sign of satisfaction. Once again, the dog tilted his head and looked expectantly at Moira, wagging his tail back and forth.

As Moira looked at her new companion, she started to run through her mind what she would have to do to find the dog's rightful owner. She would also have to figure out what she would do with the dog until the owner was found.

* * *

Two weeks had passed by since the dog's appearance at the back door on the stormy night. Moira had called the Irish Society for the Prevention of Cruelty to Animals (ISPCA) several times, but no one had called the organization about a young lost sheep dog. Similar organizations had also been canvassed. She had also alerted the garda, but they too had not received any inquiries about a lost dog. The garda had even alerted units in neighboring counties, but to no avail. With the help of the pub staff, Moira had made up posters seeking the owner of a lost dog, and they were displayed in shop windows in the local and neighboring villages. Even local schools had been canvassed. The absence of a dog collar didn't help. Moira began to suspect that someone, not local, may have dumped the dog, looking to get rid of it.

Moira had a new boarder. She was determined to establish some ground rules right off. The dog could sleep in the laundry room at night; however, it would remain outside during the day except when it was raining, and then its territory was limited to the kitchen and the laundry room. Moira thought about keeping the dog in one of the two garages but decided no; out of sight, out of mind—that could spell trouble. So, the laundry room and the kitchen would be its stomping grounds. The dog was quick to learn that after its meals outside, if it took up a position under the kitchen table, an extra treat might fall from the kitchen table above. Padraig, the few times he had come up for a meal since the dog's arrival, had proven to be a valued ally, discreetly sneaking scraps of food under the table, much to Moira's chagrin and loud protests.

A significant problem was what to do with the dog when Moira went to work. When she worked during the daytime, the dog remained across the street in the area where the picnic tables and benches were located. He would lie down on the stone patio, patiently watching people come and go. Surprisingly, the dog didn't beg when people used the picnic tables for a meal or a pint or two. Then again, the dog didn't refuse a tasty handout when offered. If Moira was working evenings, when it grew dark, the dog would stay behind the pub, by the kitchen back door, where an outdoor light remained lit. The large overhang by the pub's back door provided needed shelter in inclement weather during the day and at night.

The dog's constant presence near the pub didn't go unnoticed by the local garda, who advised Padraig that his four-legged friend needed a dog tag and the appropriate shots to avoid a citation. The friendly advice was quickly heeded, and the services of the local vet were employed. This led to an interesting question—what name to put on the required papers and the dog tag? Everyone, literally everyone—Moira, Padraig, Nora, pub patrons all called the dog, Dog. The dog itself responded to the name Dog. So, the rather unimaginative name of Dog was given to the newcomer and listed on the vet's papers and the dog tag, along with Moira's address and the phone number of the pub.

* * *

Moira enjoyed the company of Dog. She now had a watchdog, a companion, and someone to talk to. If she didn't know better, she thought the dog knew what she was saying, tilting his head to one side or the other as she spoke to him. *If anyone heard me talking to the dog, they would think I'm batty,* she thought. Before, with Maureen at school and Brian sometimes away on business, the house could be a lonely place. Now, she had a constant companion—and one that listened to her!

During the day at home, the dog would obediently spend most of the time outside in pleasant weather and seemed to enjoy helping Moira hanging out the wash on the clothesline, snatching up dropped clothespins with its mouth and placing them in the clothes basket, weaving his way back and forth through drying sheets that hung down almost to the ground. When allowed inside, the dog would obediently stay either in the laundry room or the kitchen, only entering the dining room to cross back and forth between the two areas. In the laundry room, the dog would sometimes get in Moira's way, investigating where the damp clothes were going by sticking his head into the opened dryer door. Moira would patiently wait for the dog to remove his head from inside the dryer while she held another armful of damp clothes ready to load. When Moira was in the kitchen either preparing or cleaning up after a meal, the dog would usually lay under the kitchen table and watch Moira crossing back and forth between the appliances that were the sources of food.

* * *

Throughout the village, people knew that Dog was Moira's. Dog was popular among the pub's local patrons, who would call out a hello to the dog waiting across the road when they either entered or left the pub. Children would cautiously approach the dog, and Dog would allow them to pet him. Sometimes, the children would be rewarded with a wet, sloppy lick across their face if they ventured too close. Tourists found the sheepdog to be part of the allure of the quaint Irish village. One person, however, who lived in the village on a part-time basis, knew nothing of the dog. This was particularly noteworthy since this person had, unbeknownst to him, been providing the dog with housing since his arrival in the village.

Moira's enjoyment of having a new roommate was tempered by the fact that the owner of the house, who was to arrive the day after tomorrow, didn't know about Dog's current living arrangements. She had no idea what Brian's reaction to finding a dog in the house would be. She didn't even know if he liked or disliked animals. He had never mentioned having a pet back in the United States.

No use fretting, she thought, as she continued to fret.

31

BRIAN'S FLIGHT TO Ireland took him to Dublin airport. He had a business meeting in Dublin that he had to attend, followed by an evening meal with the clients. The meal dragged on, so it was rather late before he was able to drive the rental car to the village, and he didn't arrive at the house until after midnight. Not wanting to wake Moira up, he proceeded directly up the stairs to his bedroom.

Tired from the flight, the meeting, and the dinner that seemed to have gone on and on, Brian had slept late the next morning. After a shower, he got dressed and grabbed the rather voluminous file the clients had given him yesterday describing the scope of work their firm had hoped Brian would assist them on. Brian started reading the material as he slowly made his way down the stairs to the kitchen. He briefly looked up and saw the back door was partially open, and he figured Moira must be outside hanging up laundry. In the kitchen, he found a mug and poured himself a cup of tea and made his way over to the kitchen table where he sat down, placing the file in front of him and the mug of tea just off to the right.

He quickly became engrossed in the reading material, while Dog quietly made his way into the house through the back door and into the kitchen, where he laid down under the table. Brian did look up once from the material when he sensed movement, but he didn't see Moira, who he assumed was still outside hanging up clothes. Continuing to read the details of the page in front of him, he searched for the mug of tea with his hand and brought it up to his mouth, took a sip, and returned it to the table. At one point, he scratched an itch on his thigh, then slowly brought his hand back up to turn a page of the document. The itch traveled down to his knee, so he lowered his hand and once again took care of the itch with a quick scratch.

* * *

"I best go inside and tell him about the dog," Moira said to herself with a sigh. Having picked up the empty clothes basket, she made her way to the back door. The back door was partially open. Frantically, Moira looked around the patio area. There was no sign of Dog. She placed the clothes basket down on the patio and quickly went inside. Turning to her right, she glanced inside the laundry room—no Dog. Scanning the dining room area, no sign of Dog. She started toward the kitchen and stopped dead in her tracks. Under the kitchen table, she could see a tail wagging back and forth. She could also hear pages being turned, which sound was also coming from the kitchen. Slowly, Moira approached the door to the kitchen, trying to remain out of Brian's eyesight.

* * *

Brian turned the page and looked up from the file. He thought he heard something but didn't see anyone when he looked around the kitchen from his seat. Maureen, he knew, was at the university. Moira was still probably outside hanging up clothes. *Must be my imagination,* he thought. Brian took a sip of his tea and started reading again. Absentmindedly, he reached down the side of his leg to again scratch the annoying itch that wouldn't go away. Finished scratching, he momentarily held his hand out down by the side of his leg.

Brian's head shot up, his eyes darting around the room. He quickly retrieved his hand from below the table and stared at it. The hand was moist. *What the–* The chair made a scraping sound as Brian hastily pushed the chair back on the tile floor. Cautiously, he lowered his head to peer under the kitchen table, only to be met by a pair of eyes looking back at him. The eyes, he noticed, were attached to a dog. Brian tilted his head to his left and noticed the dog responded by tilting its head to its right, tail wagging back and forth. Brian then tilted his head to his right and the dog tilted its head the other way, still wagging its tail. Brian looked up, confused, and stared across the top of the table. He then looked down at his moist hand. While he couldn't see her, he thought he heard Moira in the living room whispering something.

"Oh, Moira. Would you like to come into the kitchen?" Brian said in a loud voice, looking toward the opening to the dining room.

Brian noticed how Moira reluctantly edged her way into the kitchen, shaking her head, looking down at the dog beneath the kitchen table, giving it a look like it had betrayed her. Moira started to say something, only to be interrupted by Brian.

"Moira, have you been taking on boarders while I was away?" Brian asked, arching his eyebrows.

"I . . ." Moira stammered. "He's house trained," she blurted out.

"I would hope so," Brian responded, a serious expression on his face.

Moira looked back down at the dog with exasperation. Brian tried to hide his smile as it grew. He thought about giving Moira a hard time about the dog but realized he wouldn't be able to keep a straight face.

"Come here, dog," Brian said, holding out his hand. The dog jumped up and approached. "Has she been treating you alright?" Brian asked, scratching the dog behind its ears.

Brian looked up at Moira, who stood uncomfortably on the other side of the kitchen table. "Well, I guess with Maureen at school and me not here a good part of the time, it's probably a smart idea to have a watchdog. What's the dog's name?" Brian asked Moira, still scratching the dog behind its ears.

"Dog," a much-relieved Moira replied.

"Yes, what's the dog's name?" Brian asked again.

"Dog. That his name, Dog, that's what's on his dog tag," Moira explained.

Brian looked at Moira in disbelief, then felt for the collar on the dog's neck. He found the tag. He bent over and started reading what had been etched on it. *Dog.* Brian looked up at Moira incredulously and was about to say something but was at a loss for words. He looked again at the tag and let out a laugh when he saw the address for Dog. "I see from the address on the tag that Dog has already made this his home," Brian said, smiling. He beckoned Moira to sit.

Moira, obviously feeling uncomfortable, took a seat across from Brian. Brian stood up and went over to the teapot, refilling his mug and filling a mug for Moira before returning to his chair.

For the next ten minutes, Moira filled in a bemused Brian on how Dog came to be a part of the household. Dog, disappointed that there were no table scraps, fell asleep under the kitchen table, from where gentle snoring could soon be heard.

In addition to his unofficial day job for the Irish tourism board, entertaining visitors while waiting across from the pub, Dog became Brian's new afternoon walking companion, bringing smiles to passing villagers.

32

THIS HAD BEEN their third trip through the gates into Dublin's St. Stephen's Green over the last three days. Maureen led the way, with Moira following and Brian bringing up the rear. The warm late-August days had been perfect, with no rain and only a few thin clouds slowly gliding across the blue sky. They enjoyed the serenity that the park provided in the early evening with its colorful flowers in full bloom and the park's ponds providing quiet sanctuary for ducks, who occasionally dove beneath the water's surface in search of food. Maureen's leisurely pace provided a needed break from the hustle and bustle of the city's earlier daytime excursions. She found a vacant bench near a pond and took a seat. Moira slid in next to her daughter, and Brian took the end space on the bench. No one spoke; they just watched old and young couples saunter by and the ducks ply the water in the pond.

* * *

With summer coming to an end and Maureen soon to start her fourth year at the university, Brian thought it would be a nice treat to take Moira and Maureen to Dublin for a couple of days. While he wasn't surprised that Maureen had never been to Dublin, he was surprised to find out that Moira had not once, in her entire life, been to Dublin either. Brian had first broached the subject of a visit to the country's capital with Padraig, since he would be taking two of Padraig's workers, Moira and Maureen, away from the pub for a couple of days. Padraig thought it would be a good idea, as long as the trip avoided Friday, Saturday, and Sunday, the pub's busiest days. When asked if Padraig would like to join them, Padraig had begged off; he was too busy at the pub, and apparently Galway was a big enough city for his liking. Convincing Moira and Maureen to go to Dublin was made easier when he told them that the trip would be an early graduation present for Maureen.

So, Brian had arranged two rooms in a centrally located hotel in Dublin for four nights—Monday through Thursday. They would return to the village early Friday afternoon so Moira and Maureen would be able to help at the pub for the Friday evening crowd. Padraig, Conor, and Daniel had all contributed some spending money for Maureen, should she see something to her liking while she was in the big city. Brian had developed a preliminary itinerary for their visits—places to see and places to dine—based upon his previous sightseeing visit to Dublin with Clare. As he thought back to that time, he remembered how Clare had kept him hopping, going from place to place nonstop. He smiled, thinking about how he had been thoroughly exhausted at the end of each day.

For some reason, Brian's attempt at an early Monday start for the trip to Dublin didn't happen. Actually, there were several reasons for the late start. During the morning hours, the women went back and forth, consulting between themselves on what they should pack for the trip. After seeing the two oversized suitcases by the front door, Brian was convinced that if he were to venture into their rooms, he would find empty closets as well as empty dressers. *And where had they found the two ancient, oversized, very heavy suitcases?* Brian decided it was best not to ask.

Then there was the dog. No, Dog was not going with them to Dublin. But the three of them hadn't considered what to do with Dog. After numerous phone calls to find a dog sitter or someone to take Dog, Jimmy from the pub agreed to stay at the house and mind Dog. Brian had commented to both Maureen and Moira that maybe he should have taken Dog with him to Dublin instead of them, since Dog would have had less luggage than the two of them. The look from the two women was enough for Brian to excuse himself to make sure the windshield on the car was clean.

Finally, after lunch, they were off.

When they arrived at the hotel in the late afternoon, their rooms were available, Brian in one room and mother and daughter sharing another room. After checking in, Brian took the rental car in search of a parking garage.

That evening they decided to dine in, and after dinner, they spent the remaining daylight walking around the area of the city close to the hotel. Brian smiled when he saw the excited looks of both mother and daughter as their heads swiveled around, taking in the sights. He soon realized that he had to be ever vigilant, since neither Moira nor Maureen were accustomed to the constant flow and volume of city traffic. A couple of times, Brian had to reach out and grab the women's arms at crosswalks to prevent the potential for serious injury.

Several places that Brian thought Maureen and Moira would like to see were within a relatively short walking distance of the hotel. Nonetheless, on Tuesday morning, Brian purchased three forty-eight-hour tickets for one of the Dublin hop-on–hop-off buses that traveled throughout the city proper and to a few locations on the outskirts. It being a nice day, the three of them took the stairs to the seats in the open-air upper deck of the bus, where they could take in an unrestricted view of the city. They would travel the entire bus route to first locate the various sights and then, depending upon what specifically they wanted to see, would either walk to the location or board another hop-on–hop-off bus for those sights further out from the hotel. Brian enjoyed watching Moira and Maureen point out things to each other on either side of the bus, checking their guidebooks, then eagerly waiting for the next attraction to appear.

Upon completion of the initial bus trip, they had decided to start by walking to Trinity College, then Dublin Castle, with an informal lunch break of fish and chips afterward. The afternoon included Christ Church and a walk along the river Liffey and over the Ha'penny Bridge. Eventually they made their way back to the hotel. After retreating to their respective rooms for a brief break and freshening up, they ventured out again. Up first was some window shopping on Grafton Street and pauses to take in the various musical entertainers along the way before they finally ventured into St. Stephen's Green and made the first of their three evening visits to this scenic park. Brian slowly walked behind the women as Moira and Maureen would periodically pause to bend over and smell the fragrance of the colorful flowers in neatly prepared beds. Afterward, the three of them returned to the hotel for a late dinner and then retired to their rooms for the night for a welcomed rest after all the day's walking.

After breakfast the next day, they took the tour bus and made their way to the historic Kilmainham Gaol Museum then to Phoenix Park and the Dublin Zoo. The zoo was quite a contrast from their visit to the Gaol. For their dinner, Brian had found a nice quiet restaurant that specialized in locally sourced food. With ice cream cones for dessert from Murphy's Ice Cream in hand, Brian, Maureen, and Moira once again made their way up Grafton Street to St. Stephen's Green, where they found an unoccupied bench and enjoyed the remains of their dessert, occasionally licking the melting ice cream off the sides of their cones. When they were finished, they meandered through the park, taking a different path from the one they had used the day before. As the evening sun began to set in the west, turning the sky a warm crimson color, they made their way back to the hotel and another welcomed rest.

After breakfast the next morning, Moira and Maureen decided that shopping would be the focus of the entire day, much to Brian's dismay.

"Shopping? What kind of museum is that?" Brian teased. "Let me check the guidebook, must have missed that important sight."

Maureen and Moira politely smiled and then told him they would enlighten him along the way. As the day wore on, Brian discovered the shopping the women were focused on was clothes shopping. Pacing outside the clothes stores didn't help his sore feet, although he did manage to explore a couple of bookstores along the way.

* * *

Sitting on a different park bench for their last night in Dublin, Maureen, Moira, and Brian continued to observe their surroundings. Three pair of eyes followed the downward flight of a duck flapping its wings as it approached the nearby water, making a controlled landing that resulted in a splash that sent ripples throughout the pond.

Brian broke the silence. "Maureen, what are you planning on doing after this school year when you graduate?"

Moira shuffled uncomfortably in her seat and looked over at her daughter.

"Not quite sure yet. I'll have enough credits to graduate after this fall term. My academic advisor wants me to finish out the school year and take some introductory graduate courses in the spring term in my dual major—computer science and systems engineering. But I don't know. The advisor says the scholarship will pay for the graduate courses. A couple of my professors have encouraged me to take courses in their respective fields."

"When does the university have job fairs?" Brian inquired.

Moira shifted again on the bench and turned to look at Brian.

"They have them at the end of each term. My advisor tells me I should go to them and check out some of the companies," Maureen answered, as she stretched out her legs.

Brian could see Moira was uncomfortable with the subject, not only by her shifting around but also the way she was quiet, looking down at her feet. On more than one occasion, she had mentioned to Brian how much she missed having Maureen around the house. But she had also admitted to Brian that Maureen's education was important and that she knew Maureen would eventually move on. Maureen's future would be elsewhere, away from the village.

"If you want my two cents, take the graduate courses during the second term and check out the companies that show up at the job fairs. The school should give you an advance list of participating companies. I would check out the companies that interest you. Do some research first, find out what the companies do, and when you meet with the company's recruiters at the job fair, ask a lot of questions about the company and the specific position they are hiring for. Also ask about salary and the benefits they offer," Brian said, as he crossed his legs. "Don't commit yourself or sign anything until you have interviewed with all the companies you're interested in. There'll be more job fairs during the second term, so you have time."

Reluctantly, Moira nodded her agreement.

* * *

After an early breakfast the next morning in the hotel's dining room, Brian went to retrieve the rental car, and the women finished packing overstuffed suitcases and waited patiently by the hotel's front entrance. Finally, Brian pulled the car in front of the hotel. He gave the hotel employee a generous tip after the luggage was loaded. The poor man looked like he had strained more than one muscle, heaving the luggage into the trunk of the car.

Finally, Brian pulled the car out into traffic, and they were on their way back to the village.

"Thank you," Maureen said, as she sat back in the rear seat and looked out the side window at the densely packed buildings and the people hustling down sidewalks. "That was fun. Dublin is a lot bigger city than Galway. So much history."

"Yes, thank you," Moira said in a quiet voice, eyes looking straight ahead.

"You're both very welcome," Brian responded. He glanced at Moira, knowing full well she was having a difficult time adjusting to the fact that her daughter might soon be leaving home for good. He knew the feeling all too well, first when their daughter graduated from college and then when their son graduated.

The sound of a blaring car horn reminded Brian that he needed to pay attention to the traffic around him.

33

"HOW'S MAUREEN DOING in school?" Padraig asked, already knowing the answer.

"Fine. She loves it up there," Moira said, as she and Padraig sat at a corner dining table, looking out at the nearly empty pub. It had gone on to 3 p.m. and the pub was quiet except for a few customers sitting at the bar. The lunch crowd had gone, and it would be a while before the pub would start filling up again with the evening crowd. A month had passed since Maureen had begun her fourth year at the university.

"Brian's due back later this evening?" Padraig asked, running his fingers across the top of the table and then looking at them to check if the table had been cleaned after lunch.

"Yes, he flew into Dublin from the States a couple of days ago and had client meetings that were supposed to go through lunch today," Moira said, eyeing Padraig's hand. She knew the table was clean because she had wiped it down not more than thirty minutes ago. Padraig dropped his hand down alongside him, apparently satisfied with the table's cleanliness.

The quiet was disturbed by the sound of Moira's phone.

"Are you going to answer that?" Padraig asked, looking at his niece.

Moira fumbled with her phone before finally putting it up next to her ear. "Hello. Yes, this is she," Moira said into the phone, as she looked over to Padraig, baffled. "Tomorrow or the day after," she said into the phone. "The day after tomorrow would be better." Moira paused. "Ten a.m., yes that should be fine. Can I ask you what this is about? Is Maureen alright?" After a moment, Moira said, "Thank you."

Moira placed the phone on the table and shook her head.

"What's that all about?" Padraig asked, looking at his niece closely.

"It's the university. Some academic advisor wants to meet with me about Maureen. The woman who called, the advisor's administrative assistant, didn't know too much about what the meeting was for. I can't go tomorrow; I need to find a ride up to Galway, and tomorrow isn't enough time for me to arrange a ride."

"Maureen is alright? The woman who called didn't tell you what it was about?" Padraig asked cautiously.

"No, as far as she knew it wasn't anything bad. The advisor has a proposal he would like to run by me."

"Seems odd," Padraig said.

"I need to find a ride," Moira said thoughtfully.

"Perhaps Brian could take you up to the university, he'll be back later today. Ask him," Padraig said, a bit eagerly.

"I don't know. I don't want to be a burden to Brian."

"No, I'm sure Brian will take you. He's good with those university types," Padraig said. "Take him with you to the meeting." Padraig was quick out of his seat. "Let me check the inventory, I want to make sure we received the last shipment of kegs."

Moira watched Padraig quickly stride across the floor toward the kitchen. She was puzzled because she thought that Padraig had told Jimmy less than an hour ago that the inventory was all up to date. *Maybe he's losing it,* she thought.

* * *

Once Brian had arrived at the house later that day and settled back in, Moira asked and he agreed to take her up to the university. When he asked Moira what the meeting was about, she merely shook her head and said the academic advisor had a proposal he wanted to talk to her about regarding Maureen. A subsequent call from the university resulted in a slight change. The administrative assistant had called Moira back and asked if, instead of 10 a.m., the meeting could be moved up an hour to 9 a.m. That was fine with Moira, but she needed to ask her ride if an earlier time would be a problem.

"No, no problem," had been Brian's response.

Brian suggested to Moira that he try to get two rooms in a nearby B and B that he and Clare had stayed at on previous trips to Galway. Moira didn't want Brian to go to all that trouble or expense, but Brian had prevailed by pointing out that he really didn't want to fight the morning rush-hour traffic into Galway, plus it would not be good form to be late for a meeting with the advisor concerning Maureen.

* * *

The following day, Moira was all packed, including one of her new dresses from the store in Galway. Her suitcase—a smaller one than the one she had used for the Dublin trip—was already in Brian's rental car before she walked down to the pub for the dinner shift. Brian had also packed and would have his dinner at the pub. That way, they could take off for Galway directly from the pub. Jimmy, the good lad, agreed to dog sit again, staying the night at the house.

With most of the dinner crowd finishing up their meals and settling in with another pint of liquid refreshments, waiting for the evening's music session to begin, Padraig ushered Moira over to the table where Brian had just finished his dinner. Moira had made a quick change of clothing and was ready for the trip. Padraig walked with Brian and Moira out of the pub and up the road to where the car was parked. The sun, a glowing orange sphere, was just beginning to settle over the western horizon, creating long shadows as darkness started to creep across the land.

Trailing just behind Brian, Padraig halfheartedly said, "I wish I could be going with you two to the university." Brian stopped dead in his tracks, Padraig almost bumping into him. Brian slowly turned around and mouth something inaudible. Padraig smiled.

"What are you two talking about?" Moira asked, as she reached the front passenger door of the car.

"Nothing," Brian said, turning back toward Moira as she opened the car door. "I told Padraig we'd take him with us next time, since he's pals with the deans up there."

Brian climbed into the driver's seat. With the car's headlights on, he slowly reversed the car out of the parking spot. As they drove off, Padraig waved at them from the side of the road, a big smile on his face.

* * *

The female GPS voice told Brian to make the next right turn, and his destination would be on the right. With it being a moonless night, the features of the house were difficult to see as they pulled into the paved parking area in front of the house. Above the front door, a dim light provided a limited view of the immediate outdoor area. Darkness prevailed further out. Moira got out of the car and slowly surveyed the surroundings. Three other cars were also parked in front of the B and B. On either side of the entrance were narrow garden beds of small blooming shrubs and flowers which stretched along the front of the house, disappearing into the outer darkness. Brian exited the car, stood and stretched his legs, and opened the rear car door to retrieve the two small suitcases.

The front door opened slowly, and an older woman gingerly stepped out onto a small landing, smiled, and said, "Welcome." Then she cautiously asked, "Are you Mr. Hansen?"

"Yes," Brian replied. "It's very kind of you to accommodate us at this late hour, Mrs. Murphy." Moira nodded her head in agreement and, together with Brian, walked from the car to where the woman was standing.

"No problem," the woman said. "Please, call me Grace."

Following Grace, their hostess, Brian and Moira entered a slate foyer. A narrow, screened-in porch with a couple of wooden lounge chairs was off to their right. Turning to the left, they stepped through another doorway that revealed a moderate-sized living area. The light-gray wall-to-wall carpet extended out from where they were standing. Three high-back upholstered chairs were set at three corners of the room. A comfortable-looking tan sofa with matching pillows rested against the wall to their immediate right, with end tables holding lit lamps positioned on either side of the sofa. Above the fireplace, a white mantelpiece was adorned with various delicate-looking porcelain figurines. The walls were covered with gold patterned wallpaper. While the room looked a bit dated, it had a cozy feel to it.

Grace appeared to be in her late seventies or early eighties, with neat, stylish gray hair. Age had been kind to her, as her wrinkles were few. The back of her hands, however, revealed protruding veins and dark age spots. Grace had sharp, penetrating eyes with which she examined her guests through round thick-lensed glasses. She was dressed in a gray calf-length skirt and a white blouse. Unlike many her age whose backs would be slightly stooped, Grace had excellent upright posture. Her pleasant smile was welcomed by the two tired travelers. After closing the door to the foyer, Grace turned to greet them again. In her hand were two sets of keys with short metal keyrings with numbers etched on them.

"I may not have heard you correctly on the phone. I couldn't remember if you had asked for one or two rooms," Grace said, as she looked from Brian to Moira and then back to Brian.

"Two rooms," Brian quickly replied.

Moira was oblivious to the conversation. She stood in the middle of the room and continued to look around, taking in her surroundings, finally pausing to look at Brian and the woman. This was the first time that she had ever stayed in a stranger's house, and she felt a little uncomfortable. She caught the tail end of what the two of them were saying, something about two rooms.

"Well then, one room is up the stairs to the right. The other room is on this floor through that hallway. Room numbers are on the keys," Grace said, handing Brian both sets of keys.

Brian turned to look at Moira and said, "I'll take the upstairs room, if that's alright with you." Moira nodded her agreement. "I'll bring your suitcase to your room."

"No need. I can manage," Moira said.

Turning back to Grace, Brian asked, "If I may ask, what time is breakfast in the morning?"

"From seven to nine in the room across from the stairs," Grace responded, pointing to two French doors.

Brian looked at the two sets of keys and then handed one to Moira. "Why don't we plan on getting together at seven fifteen or seven thirty tomorrow morning, if that works for you." Moira nodded her agreement. "I'm pretty tired from the drive, so I think I'll head up to my room." To Grace, Brian said, "Once again, we really appreciate your allowing us to come at this late hour." Grace waved away his comment. She would be up at least another two or three hours, if not more—a curse of old age. The two women watched as Brian ascended the stairs to the landing, turned, opened a door, and disappeared.

"What a gentleman," Grace said, to no one in particular. "Come dear, let me show you to your room. This way."

Moira followed, with suitcase rolling along behind her. As she approached the stairs, she looked through the French doors where breakfast would be served tomorrow morning. Some of living room light seeped through the doors' glass panes to reveal several tables already set up for breakfast, with white tablecloths and neatly arranged place settings. She saw in her quick glance that some of the tables were set for two people while other tables were for four.

Moira continued to follow Grace through a narrow well-lit hallway. Off to her left was an open entrance to what was obviously the kitchen. She could make out two industrial-sized refrigerators on the far wall of the room. Moira slowed her pace and caught sight of the end of a very large stove. The kitchen floor, from what she could see, was spotless—a good sign, Moira thought, reflecting on the kitchen floor in the pub. Seeing Grace widening the gap between them, Moira hurried to keep up with her.

Ahead, the hallway made a sharp turn to the left. The two women continued to where Grace stopped, about a quarter of the way down the hallway. To their immediate right was a door with the number 4 appearing in the center of the upper wooden panel. The bronze number partially reflected a distorted image of Moira's face. Grace opened the door, reached to her immediate right, and flipped a light switch. An overhead light in the center of the ceiling illuminated the room. Next to the bed was an end table with a small lamp. Grace moved over to allow Moira to enter the room and said, "I trust this will be to your liking. If you need anything, please let me know; I'll still be up for a little while longer." Handing the key to Moira, Grace left the room, closing the door behind her.

After locking the door, Moira lifted her suitcase onto the queen-sized bed and opened it. She took out her blue dress—one of the gifts from her previous trip to Galway. She held it up in the air, shook it out, and then carefully hung the dress on a hanger on the wooden rod in the closet, which was next to the open door to the bathroom. Tomorrow morning, she thought, when she took a shower, she would hang the dress just inside the bathroom and let the steam from the shower take out any remaining wrinkles. Although, as she surveyed the dress, she thought the dress looked pretty much free of wrinkles already.

As Moira stood by the closet, she took in the room. While it was rather small, it was functional. Across the floor from the foot of the bed was a vanity with a small upholstered bench seat. In the center of the vanity was a tall mirror. From her angle, she could see the reflection in the mirror of a portion of a small dresser located on the far wall on the other side of the bed. She turned around and moved to the bathroom. From left to right there was a toilet, a porcelain sink, and then a shower. A tight but manageable fit—*for one person at a time,* she thought. Above the sink was a glass shelf with a wrapped bar of soap, a small vial of shampoo, and a small glass wrapped in paper. Across from the sink was a towel rack with two fluffy towels: a large bath towel and a smaller hand towel. A folded cloth shower mat was waiting on the tiled floor by the shower. Inside the shower on a small shelf was another wrapped bar of soap and another vial of shampoo.

Moira returned to the bedroom and slipped out of her shoes, sat on the bed, and got undressed. She then retrieved another hanger from the closet and hung today's pants and blouse inside the closet. With only her knickers and bra on, Moira retrieved a toothbrush and toothpaste from her traveling kit and reentered the bathroom, where she brushed her teeth, rinsed, and dried her mouth on the hand towel.

Next she took a seat in front of the vanity. She stared at her image in the mirror, deep in thought. She was searching the shadows in her mind, trying to bring them into focus. Something that had been recently said. Now what was it?

What a gentleman.

That's it, she thought. The woman had said those words when Brian had headed up the stairs to his room. Moira pondered Grace's words: *What a gentleman.* Brian *is* a gentleman, she thought. Has always been a gentleman. Considerate, polite . . . that's Brian. Moira was about to dismiss the woman's comment as a mere conversation piece when she remembered the woman saying those words after Brian had said that he had reserved two rooms—not one room. *One room—for the two of them to share—together!* Moira's eyes grew wide, and the word "oh" escaped her lips as she just now realized what the woman meant when she said, *What a gentleman.*

Moira probably didn't realize that the face in the mirror just turned a rather bright red. She was grappling with the idea that someone might think that she and Brian would share the same bedroom. *Okay, we share the same house, but not the same bedroom in the house. That's different.* As she stared at herself in the mirror, Moira let her mind wander. She felt their relationship was like two people who were friends. She thought about that for a moment. *Is that all—just friends? But we're more than just friends, aren't we? Why do I feel an emptiness inside of me whenever he's away on his trips? Why do I look forward to seeing him when I hear his footsteps on the stairs when he comes down for his morning tea? Why do I now have these feelings, almost forgotten, that have been awakened?* Moira sat staring at her reflection in the mirror.

I wonder how he feels about me?

Moira slowly crossed the room to the bed and retrieved her suitcase. From inside it, she pulled out a pair of pajamas. She stowed the undergarments that she had just taken off in a plastic bag that she had brought along with her for the wash she would be doing later in the week. Moira sat on the edge of the bed, looking down at her bare feet. She sighed. Perhaps more unsettling than not knowing how Brian felt about her, she realized, was the sudden self-revelation of her affection—her deep affection for the man she would be having breakfast with in the morning. Knowing Brian's feelings for her took on a sense of urgency. Prior to climbing into bed, Moira double-checked the lock on the door to make sure it was secured. She folded back a corner of the bedcovers and then turned out the overhead light before slipping underneath the top sheet and the covers.

Her eyelids grew heavy. She was tired. Three hours busing tables, the trip to Galway, and now the uncertainty that had arisen over the last few minutes was exhausting. She nestled her head in the fluffy pillow. Tears moistened its cover. She closed her eyes and tried to purge her mind of all thoughts, but one thought she couldn't shake loose . . . *What a gentleman!*

34

REFRESHED FROM A morning shower and wearing her new dress, Moira retraced her steps from last night past the kitchen to the open doors of the breakfast room. As much as she tried, she couldn't purge last night's thoughts about her relationship with Brian. As she entered the room, she noticed Brian already seated at a table with the makings of a full Irish breakfast in front of him, minus the baked beans and blood pudding. Moira nodded to the two other couples in the room and pulled out the chair across from where Brian was sitting. In response to his query of whether she slept well, she responded in the affirmative as she sat down.

Looking at Brian's breakfast, she noticed the portions were generous indeed. Once in a blue moon, the pub would offer a full Irish breakfast on the evening menu, but if she were to be honest, the pub's portions were a tad smaller than what was on Brian's plate. As much as she yearned for a full Irish, *with* baked beans and blood pudding, the memory of sitting in front of the vanity last night gave her pause. The elastic waistband on the knickers she put on this morning seemed to tighten around her midriff as she admired the sight on Brian's plate.

Just then, the server stopped by the side of their table with pad and pencil, ready to take her breakfast order. "Cereal, fresh fruit, and yogurt are on the side table," the young server said, pointing to a long, well-stocked serving table behind her against the wall. "Now, what can I get for you from the kitchen?"

"I think I'll just have scrambled eggs, please," Moira said in a somber voice. "Some regular toast too," she added as an afterthought.

"Do you want anything with the eggs? Bacon, sausage, we have sliced salmon, it would be no trouble," the server tempted.

"No, I think that'll be all. Thank you," Moira said, as she carefully placed the napkin in front of her on her lap.

The young server nodded and moved across the room to see if the other couples required anything else.

Just then, a low, rather loud, stomach growl could be heard at their table, and it didn't come from Brian's side. Moira glanced quickly at Brian, but he either didn't take notice or was being polite, she thought, as he continued tucking into some sausage links on his plate.

Moira looked at the side table with the cereal and yogurt and fresh fruit—the healthy food. But those items didn't appeal to her. The rasher of bacon on Brian's plate looked very, very tempting. And the sausage links—well they seemed to beckon to Moira.

"Is that all you're going to have?" Brian asked, as he cut into a sausage. "You really should eat something else." As he finished the sentence, a piece of sausage disappeared through his lips.

Moira looked forlornly at Brian's plate. The server had just finished with the other two couples and was approaching Brian and Moira's table on her way back to the kitchen.

"Excuse me." Moira caught the attention of the server. "Maybe you could add a rasher of bacon—just one—and one sausage link to my order. Please."

The server nodded and smiled. "How about some lovely blood pudding and some baked beans?" the server inquired.

"Maybe some baked beans, just a small spoonful, please." Moira nodded her head in approval at the restraint she had just shown, ordering only one each of bacon and sausage and no blood pudding. She leaned back in her chair and thought, *To hell with the bloody elastic waistband! That's why they're made of elastic!* She stole a quick glance at Brian, who seemed to be focused on his breakfast and not the back-and-forth between herself and the server.

"Moira, have some tea." Brian lifted the tea pot up and filled Moira's cup three-quarters of the way. "I thought we could share a pot. I just wanted a little."

Moira nodded and held the teacup up to her mouth and took a sip. No sooner had she returned her teacup to the saucer then the server was back with her breakfast. Knife and fork in hand, Moira's eyes lit up and she couldn't help but smile as she dug in, making no comment about how the server had doubled the sausage and bacon count that appeared on her plate, as well as what must have been a ladle-full of baked beans. She certainly wasn't going to embarrass the young lass's "mistake" by not eating everything that was on her plate. *Ah the aroma.* Finishing the last piece of toast, the empty plate in front of her betrayed her ravenous appetite.

"I thought we'd drive over to the university rather than walk. The sky looks a little iffy this morning, and there's a fifty percent chance of rain," Brian said, as he placed his napkin on the table. Moira looked up from her plate and nodded her agreement. Brian continued, "It's eight o'clock now. Why don't we meet in the living room in twenty minutes? That'll give us time to freshen up before we leave. It's about a fifteen-minute drive over to the university, and the parking lot is near the building where we're to meet this advisor."

With that, Moira got up from the table, walked over to where the young server was placing dirty dishes on a tray at a recently vacated table, and thanked her for breakfast. They shared conspiratorial smiles.

Brian went up the stairs as Moira continued along the first floor past the kitchen to her room. She was already packed and ready to go; she would just need to powder her nose. After brushing her teeth for the second time that morning, Moira sat down on the bed. She was nervous about the upcoming meeting. What did the advisor want? Maureen was a good student, so surely it couldn't be about her grades. Thoughts about her own relationship with Brian kept surfacing, adding to the uneasiness she was now feeling. Once again, she had a splitting headache. *Nerves.*

* * *

The drive over to the university took twenty minutes, with the heavy volume of morning commuters driving into the city. Still, they arrived at the university with some time to spare. The visitor's parking lot still had several empty spaces. After exiting the car, Brian and Moira crossed the parking area and stood at the beginning of a large grass courtyard bordered on four sides by huge granite buildings. The courtyard was crisscrossed with concrete paths which students were now using to make their way to their early morning classes. Brian pointed to a building off to the right. They followed a walkway, then veered off to a set of steps leading to a rather large, imposing building.

35

"MY APOLOGIES FOR being late," a deep voice said from somewhere behind Brian. Brian had been standing by a wall in Dean Edwards's office, looking at the dean's diplomas and other framed citations. He turned around and extended his hand, which was met by the hand of a very distinguished looking man of average height. Brian introduced himself and briefly explained that he was a friend of the family who Moira had asked to join her today. The dean nodded his understanding.

"I'm Dean Edwards," the immaculately dressed man said, as he used an open arm to corral Brian and usher him to the small sitting area. Brian crossed the room and took a seat next to Moira on the couch. He could see that Moira was very nervous, twisting her hands together. Brian discretely took out a clean pressed handkerchief and handed it to Moira, who began twisting the handkerchief in her hands. Her nervousness must have been noticeable to Dean Edwards, but he chose not to comment.

Dean Edwards reached across the glass coffee table to shake Moira's hand. "You must be Mrs. McGuire, Maureen's mother. It is indeed a pleasure to meet you at last. My apologies, again. My meeting with Dean Kelly ran a bit late. He asked me to say hello to you. He mentioned to me that he had met you a couple of years back. Have you been offered coffee or tea?"

"Yes, we have, we're fine," Moira answered in a timid voice, looking down at the coffee table.

"Very well. Let me explain the reason I asked to meet with you today. Obviously, I wanted to talk to you about your daughter, Maureen." Dean Edwards paused, looking at Moira.

Moira stopped twisting the handkerchief, tilted her head up and looked directly at Dean Edwards and nodded.

"You have a truly remarkable daughter," he said. "Maureen's grades have been exceptional."

Remembering the Dean's List discussion from years ago, Brian smiled to himself.

"All of her professors rave about her, not only about her grades but the fact that she has and continues to lead several study groups, which have helped other students with their coursework. She has enough credits to graduate this semester, in three and a half years. That's also truly remarkable. I understand she plans on staying with us another semester to take some graduate-level courses." Dean Edwards paused and looked from Moira to Brian. Both nodded their agreement.

"I would like to discuss a proposal we have regarding your daughter and her future education. I wanted to run the proposal by you before we discuss anything with Maureen, since there are certain financial considerations," Dean Edwards said, looking at Moira, who had resumed twisting the handkerchief in her hands. Brian considered reaching over and holding Moira's hand but thought it would only draw more attention to her nervousness.

"Okay," Moira said, with certain reservation.

Dean Edwards smiled and continued, "We have an advanced program, for only the most promising students, that allows them to continue with their studies to obtain two advanced degrees—not just a master's degree but also a doctorate—simultaneously. Only the brightest students participate in this program. It is quite challenging. Having said that, our experience has been that the students who successfully complete the program can write their own ticket either in academia or in the business world. With Maureen's dual majors in systems engineering and computer science, well, she would have no problem finding employment." Dean Edwards had been looking at Moira and now turned to look at Brian, who nodded his head to show that he understood what the dean was saying.

Dean Edwards continued, "Completion of the program and the awarding of two advanced degrees can take anywhere from three and a half years to five years."

Brian thought he heard Moira sigh upon hearing the length of the program. He knew that Moira missed her daughter immensely, but he also knew that Moira recognized that education was the ticket for Maureen to escape the limited future the village had to offer a bright, ambitious young woman.

Brian took a pause in the conversation to jump in with a question. "Why the difference in timeframes—three and a half years versus five years?"

Moira watched the dean carefully, waiting to hear his answer.

"Ah, very good question. The difference in program duration relates to . . . the financial considerations I'd mentioned. The university doesn't have unlimited resources. For those who are accepted into the program, the university will cover tuition and books and lab fees. What we have found is that students with limited financial means to cover the additional costs—room and board and incidentals—wind up taking a reduced courseload so they can find part-time employment during the school year and then full-time summer employment. We find that in these situations, five years is a realistic timeframe for successfully completing all the coursework. Some take longer, but rarely do they take less than the five years.

"If the student is fortunate, the summer employment may be with a company that's looking for talented individuals whose area of study aligns with the company's products or the services they provide. Quite a few of our students who have graduated from the program wind up in positions with companies where they had summer employment." Dean Edwards leaned back in his chair and crossed his leg, revealing a very shiny black loafer.

He continued, "The shorter duration, three and a half years, is a reasonable timeframe for those who have the financial means to take a full course load and do not have to seek part-time jobs during the school year. Actually, some of our students take courses during the summer and have completed the program in three years. However, that's very challenging. We try to dissuade students from this approach.

We believe students need the summer away from course-work to refresh themselves."

While Moira continued to twist the handkerchief in her hands, Dean Edwards paused to allow what he had just said to be absorbed by his audience. Brian sat back in the couch and looked around the room, his eyes coming to rest on the dean's shining loafer. Brian nodded to himself and crossed his legs.

Focused on Moira, Dean Edwards took a deep breath. "Now you know why I asked to meet with you today. And why I wanted to talk to you and see what you thought before we even broached the subject with Maureen."

Moira stopped twisting the handkerchief and sighed before saying out loud to no one in particular, "Five years," casting her eyes down to the coffee table in front of her. Neither Dean Edwards nor Brian spoke. The silence in the room was broken by the sound of a printer printing out pages in the next room.

It was obvious that Dean Edwards didn't quite know what to say at this point, so he said nothing. He expectantly looked back and forth between the woman sitting across from him with a mangled handkerchief in her hands and the man sitting next to her. The silence started to become somewhat uncomfortable.

Dean Edwards started to say, "Perhaps you should take some time to—" before being interrupted.

"The three and a half year program," Brian said, slapping his hands on his thighs for emphasis. "That's if Moira here and Maureen agree," Brian concluded, looking at Moira.

Moira slowly raised her head and turned to look from Dean Edwards to Brian. She furrowed her forehead and asked in a barely audible voice, "How?"

Dean Edwards looked from Moira to Brian, back to Moira, and then back to Brian.

Brian looked directly at Moira and said, "Maureen is a very gifted person. This is an opportunity of a lifetime. One that shouldn't be wasted. It would be unfair to Maureen—and you—if Maureen had to undertake the program for five years. You wouldn't see her, Padraig wouldn't see her, and I wouldn't see her, if she had to both work and study for five years. I have the funds available to see Maureen through the shorter program. As a businessman and, more importantly, as a friend, I consider it a very worthwhile investment to make on her behalf—a *very* worthwhile investment."

Moira had opened her mouth to say something when Brian continued, "Clare saw how gifted your daughter is, and if she were alive today, she would insist on supporting Maureen in this endeavor. It would be very important to her—as it is to me."

Moira had no response to that. She leaned back on the couch and continued to stare at Brian.

Dean Edwards saw his opportunity to join the conversation. "Well, if you're both in agreement, I would like to have a conversation with Maureen in the not-too-distant future, if I may?"

Across from him, two heads nodded their agreement—one head reluctantly, still focused on the man sitting next to her on the couch, and the other head nodding rather emphatically.

36

AS THEY LEFT the building, Moira was still trying to take in what had just happened in the dean's office. She understood what the dean had said about Maureen and the opportunity that the program afforded her in terms of the future. But Brian saying he would help Maureen financially and then to invoke his poor deceased wife Clare to stave off her protest, well, that had blindsided her.

Moira had mixed feelings about the arrangement. On the one hand, she understood how the additional schooling would be a great benefit for Maureen. She also knew that Maureen would look forward to the challenge. But she felt uneasy about Brian using his money. And she was trying to sort out her relationship with Brian. Her feelings for him and what his feelings might be for her. Last night in the B and B raised an uncertainty she didn't have before and a anxious need to know.

Brian and Moira slowly walked across the courtyard to the far end, where a restaurant was located just on the outskirts of the university grounds. They were to meet Maureen for an early lunch. They walked alongside each other without saying a word. When they entered the restaurant, they were shown a table for four after Brian had told the hostess that another person was expected. Brian sat directly across from Moira. A waitress came over with a pitcher of ice water, which she used to fill the empty glasses on the table. Brian informed her that they were expecting another guest, so the waitress left three menus. Moira sat staring at Brian, oblivious to her surroundings.

"Hello!" Maureen's cheerful voice broke the uncomfortable silence.

Brian looked up and smiled, then stood up and received a hug from Maureen. Behind Maureen, a young man was standing uneasily. Maureen let go of Brian, moved across to the other side of the table, and bent over to give her mother a hug.

Brian cleared his throat to direct Maureen's attention to the young man who must have had something very interesting on his shoes, from the way he was staring at them. Maureen beckoned him over to the table.

"This is Matthew." Maureen then turned to Brian and said, "This is Mr. Hansen, my Uncle Brian." Maureen then turned toward her mother and said, "And this is my mother."

Moira looked at Maureen's friend and nodded without smiling. She had seen Maureen with this Matthew fellow once before and, seeing him again, wondered if their relationship was serious. After a moment, Moira shifted her eyes to her daughter.

Continuing to look at her daughter, she thought back to the meeting she had just attended and what Dean Edwards had said about how smart her daughter was and the opportunity that the university was now offering her. *More years away from home,* she thought dejectedly. Her eyes drifted away from her daughter over to the glass of water on the table in front of her. She nodded to herself. She knew that the additional education was a great opportunity, not to be missed, and eventually Maureen would have to seek her own way in the world—without her mother.

Looking at Matthew, Brian said, “Please join us for lunch. It would be our pleasure.”

“Oh, we can't.” Maureen interrupted. “There's a special guest lecture in fifteen minutes that we don't want to miss. I hope you don't mind.” Maureen looked to Brian and then to her mother with eyes that begged understanding.

Moira slowly nodded her assent. Brian smiled and nodded before saying, “Go on, don't miss the lecture.” Matthew had already headed for the restaurant door before Brian finished his sentence. Maureen bent over and gave her mother another hug and then hugged Brian before turning around and heading for the restaurant exit where she paused, turned around, and smiled and waved once more before slipping through the door held open by her companion.

Brian sat down as silence once again engulfed the table. Moira took her eyes away from the door where her daughter had just exited and looked across the table at the man sitting there.

Brian reached for the glass of water, bringing it up near his mouth, when—

“How?” Moira began and paused momentarily, dreading what Brian's response might be to the question she was about to ask.

Without taking a drink, Brian placed the glass of water back down and looked at Moira before saying, "How can I? Because both you and Maureen deserve this opportunity. Maureen to continue her education and you so that you can see her over the summer months. For me it was the right decision. You . . . you both have helped me since Clare passed away. I was lost, and you both helped me find my way again," Brian said.

Moira gazed past Brian and looked out the window at a purple flowering rhododendron shrub just outside the restaurant. She nodded to herself. But that was not the question she was looking for an answer to. She already knew why Brian had said he would support Maureen financially with school. Brian was an unselfish man. Yes, she was thankful—not just thankful, *incredibly* thankful that Brian said he would help Maureen. Why couldn't she leave well enough alone and be satisfied with his answer and leave her other question—the one after last night at the B and B—unspoken? Be content with the way things were between him and her? But she had to know the answer to the question her mind—and her heart—wanted so desperately to know: what were Brian's feelings for her?

"How . . ." Moira started then stopped again.

"How," she continued, "have you thought about us . . . our relationship? Have you ever thought of us as more than"—Moira's voice trailed off—"just friends?"

Moira's eyes pleaded for an answer before the tears cascaded down her cheeks. When an answer was not immediately forthcoming, she looked away, totally embarrassed, and gathered up her purse and quickly rose from her chair. Mortified, she paused briefly, standing over Brian, who had remained seated, and said to him, "Can we please just go . . . back . . ." She had almost said *home*, but just then the place in the village didn't feel like home. The house was now a prison for her. She quickly made for the door.

As Brian rose from his chair to go after Moira, the waitress appeared, ready to take lunch orders. Brian apologized, mumbling something had come up and they had to leave, before reaching into his pants pocket to retrieve a twenty-euro bill, which he placed in the puzzled server's hand. Apologizing again, he quickly headed toward the restaurant exit.

Brian hurried after Moira, who had already made considerable gains across the university courtyard, heading to the car park. She made it to the car one step ahead of Brian. Brian stood next to Moira and sighed. He opened the front passenger door for her and closed it after she slipped into the front seat, then circled the car to the driver's door and got in. As he started the car, Brian stole a quick glance sideways, only to see the back of Moira's head. She was looking out the side passenger window.

Having left the busy traffic of Galway city, they traveled through dense suburbs and then out into the open space of vast farmlands. The atmosphere inside the car was like an enclosed tomb. Painfully silent. As they neared their village, off in the distance the round tower could be seen pointing up toward the blue sky. Brian slowed the car as they approached the village proper. The car slid by the village stores, passed the pub, and then made a turn up the narrow lane. Brian turned the car into the driveway, where the unbearable silence was finally interrupted by the sound of crunching tires on the pebble driveway.

37

BEFORE THE CAR even stopped, Moira was out of the car, running for the front door. In she went, not even bothering to close the door behind her. She quickly made her way toward the back of the house. But where should she go? She looked at the kitchen. *No.* The laundry room. *No.* She didn't want to be trapped. She crossed the floor to the back of the house and reached for the handle on the back door.

"Moira!" Brian called after her from the foyer.

"Moira," Brian repeated in a softer voice, now only a few feet away.

Moira held onto the door handle but didn't turn it. She stared at the reflection in the glass door and saw tears flowing down the cheeks of the reflection. The reflection shook its head and then looked down toward the floor. She pleaded with herself. *Why couldn't I have left well enough alone? Why did I have to ask the question in the first place? Why did I have to have to have an answer?* At that moment, she wished the rest of the world could disappear and leave her by herself.

* * *

"Moira," Brian began, "when Clare was alive, I thought... I thought we would live to a very old age... together. There would always be another tomorrow for both of us. Something to look forward to—new experiences, new travels, watch our grandchildren as they grew up, new times to even just sit and hold each other's hands and watch the clouds float by. Then she was gone. There would be no more tomorrows for us... for me. A huge part of me died with her. I felt nothing. I know I should never think this, let alone say it aloud, but I was hoping my time on this earth would end sooner rather than later.

"For some reason I returned to this village after Clare's passing. And, ever so slowly, over time I started to realize there were people, some whom I had never met before, who cared for me.

"Some were strangers who, after a while, I discovered were keeping an eye out for me when I went for my afternoon walks. Others were people who went out of their way to say hello or good afternoon to what must have appeared to them to be a half-dead, unresponsive person.

"Your uncle, the grumpy pub owner, kept me on my toes and wouldn't let me feel sorry for myself. And then there were two caring individuals—a mother and daughter who wouldn't let me quit, wouldn't allow me to waste away, to wait for death to release me from the prison I had created for myself. They showed a kindness and a determination. They insisted I have meals with them. They engaged me in conversation, they challenged me, they wouldn't allow me to drift toward the endless sleep I had so hoped for after I lost Clare.

"The daughter went off to the university and the mother, by every measure a beautiful woman, encouraged me and made me realize how fortunate I was. I felt her kindness. I also felt her occasional bark. I started to feel alive again. I felt a renewed purpose. I began to look forward to tomorrow, especially if I knew she would be there when I woke up."

The reflection's tears seem to subside. Moira let go of the handle to the door as her arm slipped down to her side.

"I had feelings that I never thought I would have again. I wanted to reach out and brush the occasional loose hair back behind her ear. I wanted my fingers to linger a bit longer with the hand handing me a cup of tea in the morning. I so much wanted to reach out and take this woman in my arms and hold her and gaze into her eyes and touch her soft lips with my fingers . . . with my lips."

Brian paused, looking out the back where a lone soft cloud made its way across the sky.

"I was so afraid that if I did try to hold you—to touch you—to say how I felt, I might hurt your feelings, might scare you, drive you away, might make you wish you had never met me. Then I would have lost you also . . . forever." Brian paused and took a deep breath.

"Because I was so afraid of losing you, I hurt you by not telling you my feelings. Believe me when I say I am so sorry; it was never my intention." Brian started to turn away. "I'll be gone in the morning."

* * *

Moira slowly turned around and reached out and took Brian's hand. Hearing his words, she could now see the loneliness he also felt. She realized that the two of them had both been searching for an escape from their self-imposed exiles, but their inability to communicate their feelings had created a wall between them.

Moira looked into his questioning eyes. She tightened her grasp on Brian's hand and slowly moved toward the stairs. At the top of the stairs, Moira turned toward her bedroom, continuing to hold Brian's hand. It had been ages since she had been with a man. While she felt a certain degree of apprehension, she knew that she could trust Brian. As she entered her room, the apprehension she was feeling gave way to a state of serenity, knowing that all would be well, going forward.

* * *

Once in her bedroom, Moira turned around and inched backward until her calves met the side of the bed. Releasing Brian's hand, she reached up to the top of his shirt, hesitated, then slowly started to undo the buttons. When the front of the shirt fell open, Moira took either side of the shirt and slid it from his shoulders, letting it fall down his arms and onto the carpet. She then reached down and unbuckled his belt and released the pants button, allowing his pants to fall around his ankles. Brian slipped off his loafers and stepped out of his pants, pushing them to the side with one foot. Moira then turned around, leaned her head slightly forward and reached behind her head to lift her hair out of the way so Brian could undo the clasp at the top of the dress. He lowered the zipper down as far as it would go. She stepped out of her dress when it fell to the floor, bent over, picked it up off the floor, and laid across the nearby chair.

Moira turned around and looked longingly into Brian's eyes. They slowly moved toward each other and embraced, wrapping their arms around each other. Moira rested her head on Brian's chest while Brian lowered his head onto Moira's shoulder. Her soft hair brushed gently against the side of his face. At first, they could feel each other's rhythmic breathing, then a shudder rippled through both of their bodies, making them tighten their hold of each other. And then the shudder was gone, and they relaxed. The tension they had both been feeling for so long had finally dissipated from their bodies.

Moira leaned slightly forward so Brian could reach behind her to unclasp her bra, which fell to the floor. *Not now, please not now,* Moira said to herself, as she felt Brian's fingers gently touch the skin on either side of her waist. She inhaled slightly, hoping the elastic band on her knickers wouldn't choose now to play hide-and-seek with Brian's searching fingers. She held her breath as she felt his fingers slide under the elastic band on either side of her hips and slowly push her underwear down until it slid unabated to the floor. Relieved, Moira reached over and worked Brian's boxer shorts down until they also fell to the floor. They stood there, staring into each other's eyes, for several moments. Moira could feel her heart beat faster in anticipation. Slowly they found the bed and together laid down across it. As they kissed, their hands gently explored each other's bodies. They paused their kissing, heads drifting slightly apart, and through moist eyes, looked longingly at each other. Knowing smiles crept across their faces as they tenderly held each other.

38

BRIAN SLOWLY AWOKE. Through sleepy eyes, the room seemed different to him. The morning's light was coming into the room from behind him, not from the other side of the room where his feet lay. Instead of the door to the bathroom being alongside the bed to his left, it was across from the foot of the bed. He looked down at the covers, which were also different. Then he remembered. Next to him was an empty unmade side of the bed. No Moira. The bedside clock read 10:00 a.m. He had slept way past the time he normally rose. He slid out from under the covers, gathered his clothes, and went around the landing to his bedroom.

After a brief shower, he sat on his bed, slowly putting on fresh underwear and socks. He paused and looked out the window, where he could see the blue sky above. He let out a loud sigh as he thought about last night and the guilt he was now feeling—betraying his Clare.

When Clare was alive, they had had several discussions about what they should do if the other were to pass away. While he had joked about becoming a monk should she pass away, Clare had insisted that he find someone else. First, she had said, the monks wouldn't want him. And second, he would look silly in a monk's outfit. Then she had gotten very serious and told him in no uncertain terms that he needed to go on with his life, and that meant he should find someone else with which to share the future. He would be selfish if he didn't find someone else, and she would be very upset—wherever she wound up. Besides, she had said, if anything happened to him, she would find someone in short order. Brian smiled as he recalled their last discussion on this matter. Clare had been very adamant, shaking her finger at him.

Brian rose from the bed and walked over to the window. He looked down at the field of flowing wheat, then up a bit to the see the sparkling blue sea far beyond the fields, then up further to the blue sky, speckled with slow-moving clouds. He knew he could never let go of Clare completely, nor did he want to. He closed his eyes, nodded his head, and smiled. He would finish getting dressed and find the woman who had made him feel alive again.

Someone he knew his Clare would approve of—with all her heart.

* * *

Moira had quietly slipped out from her side of the bed, trying not to wake Brian, who was sound asleep. As she put on a pair of slacks and slipped into a pullover t-shirt, unencumbered, she smiled, thinking about the many times they had made love during the night and early morning. She felt—how did she feel? As she looked at Brian sleeping, she tried to put into words what she felt flowing through her.

Joy, happiness, peacefulness, warmth, love. All these now were new to her, different from what she was used to for too many years. Above all, the feeling of loneliness was gone. While she watched, Brian rolled over, his head facing the far wall, away from her. It was very early; she would let him sleep. She should be tired, but she was too excited to just lay there in bed. Besides, there was laundry that needed to be done. Looking out the window, she saw it was a beautiful morning, perfect for hanging the clothes on the line outside.

Making her way down the stairs, she heard scratching at the back door.

"Dog!" she said out loud to no one.

They had forgotten about the dog last night. He must have slept outside. Moira opened the door to let him in the house. Dog looked up at Moira dejectedly, slowly crossed the floor to the laundry room, and sat by his food bowl. Moira, feeling guilty, poured the normal amount into the bowl, hesitated, then poured another half portion. Dog looked at the bowl then up at Moira then back at the bowl and dug in. Apparently, all was forgiven. Moira put the dirty clothes in the washing machine, added detergent, and started the machine.

An hour and a half later, Moira went outside with a full wicker clothes basket and began hanging the damp clothes on the line. Dog laid down on the stone patio and supervised. Damp bed sheets were hung up on the two rows of clotheslines closest to the back door, where they wouldn't block the sun from the remaining laundry. She would slowly fill the remaining clotheslines, working away from the back door. Towels were next. Bending over, she retrieved a towel from the clothes basket and then a couple of clothespins.

* * *

Downstairs, Brian didn't see Moira in the kitchen. He looked around and then went over to the laundry room. No Moira, but the fresh scent of detergent told him that she had recently been in the room. He made his way over to the backdoor, saw the fluttering sheets on the clothesline, and stepped down onto the patio, closing the door behind him. The clotheslines and sheets waved at him in the breeze. He walked past the first row of sheets and stole a glance down the line, but no Moira. He walked past the second row of sheets and saw Moira at the far end of the row. She was bent over with her back toward him, picking through the clothes basket, looking for items to hang on the line. With three damp towels draped across her shoulder, she grabbed a handful of clothespins. Just then, Dog got up on all fours and his tail started wagging enthusiastically. Moira slowly turned her head and looked back over her right shoulder.

"How long have you been staring at my backside?" Moira said, putting thoughts into words as she placed both hands on her hips, turning toward Brian. Moira furrowed her brow and then took the hand with all the clothespins off her hip and shook it at him in mock indignation. Dog inched forward.

"I just got here . . ." Brian let the sentence drag out as he maintained a serious look, then finished with a broad smile, "On the tail end."

"What!" Moira responded, shaking her fist harder. Dog inched a few steps closer.

"But I have to admit that I like the other one better," Brian said, trying to keep a serious face.

"What other one!" demanded a confused Moira, now narrowing her eyes at the man across from her, a determined look on her face.

"The one last night . . . in the flesh," Brian answered with a broad smile.

"Why you!" Moira let fly with the clothespins in the general direction of Brian.

Dog was off and running, chasing down clothespins that flew every which way.

Brian couldn't help but laugh as he approached Moira. Moira broke into a smile as the insolent man neared.

They held each other as Dog scurried around at their feet, picking up clothespins in his mouth, then quickly making his way back to the clothes basket where he deposited them before searching for another hurled clothespin.

Moira removed the damp towels from her shoulder and let them drop into the clothes basket. Arm in arm, Brian and Moira slowly walked to the back door, went through, and proceeded up the staircase nearest Brian's bedroom.

39

"HOW WAS THE trip to Galway?" Padraig asked his niece the next day. She seemed to almost waltz across the pub's floor. And she had been smiling ever since she had entered the pub. *Was that makeup on her face?* he said to himself.

"Great," Moira said, as she continued past Padraig.

Padraig was behind the bar, tapping his forefinger on the middle tap—the Guinness tap. Something is up, he thought, following her with his eyes as she disappeared through the kitchen door. The meeting with the advisor must have gone well or she would not be in such a good mood. But his niece seemed positively ecstatic. *Could the news have been that good?*

"Moira." Padraig beckoned to her as she came out the kitchen door with a tray full of salt and pepper shakers for the various tables. Moira set the tray down on the nearest table and walked over to the bar.

"How did it go up at the university yesterday?" Padraig asked. "Everything go alright?"

"Yes. We met with a very nice man who wants Maureen to continue her education there. They offered her another scholarship. This time a partial scholarship." As if anticipating Padraig's next question, Moira continued, "At the meeting, Brian said—Brian *insisted* that he would cover any additional costs so Maureen could attend school and still be able to come home during the summer."

Moira reached across the top of the bar and picked up a clean pint glass and started to slowly rotate it on the bar in front of her. She looked up at Padraig and said in a serious voice, "I had mixed emotions about him helping out financially, but then he said it was what his Clare would have wanted."

Padraig nodded knowingly. "Yes, that dear lady, if she were alive, she would have wanted that for Maureen." Padraig reached across the bar top and retrieved the pint glass from Moira. "Did anything else happen up there? How was the B and B, nice, roomy?" Padraig pried.

"We briefly saw Maureen. She couldn't have lunch with us. There was some sort of lecture that she wanted to attend." Moira picked up a coaster and then slid it back and forth in front of her. Padraig noticed the smile returning to her face and the way she looked as though she was someplace far away.

"And the B and B, how was the *room*?" Padraig prompted, placing a little too much emphasis on the word.

Moira stopped sliding the coaster back and forth and looked up at her uncle, her smile fading away. She tilted her head to one side.

"For your information, *my* room was very nice. I don't know what Brian's *sep-ar-ate* room was like," she said, looking directly at Padraig. "Would you like the phone number of the B and B so you can ask the hostess to send you pictures of the two rooms each of us stayed in *sep-ar-ate-ly*?"

Sensing his niece's impending eruption, Padraig quickly changed the subject. "How was the breakfast at the B and B?" he asked, averting his eyes.

"Fine," Moira answered, returning the coaster to the small pile to her left on the bar. "Any more questions?" Moira asked sarcastically.

"No, no. Just asking." Padraig picked up a damp towel and walked away from Moira to the other end of the bar. He sensed Moira turning back to her tray. It really wasn't any of his business what she did. He just thought it would be nice if Brian and Moira, well, if they got to like each other . . . better. More than just *like* each other. They might be happy with each other. Heaven knows they both deserved some happiness in their lives after what they both had been through.

Padraig could see Moira slowly shaking her head back and forth as she walked over to the table where she had left the tray of salt and pepper shakers. She picked up the tray and went around to each of the pub's tables, forcefully putting down a salt shaker and then a pepper mill. Padraig pretended to be busy behind the bar, avoiding eye contact with his niece.

40

"SO, YOU TWO have finally hit it off," Nora said to Moira a couple of days after her visit to Galway. Nora was dicing carrots on the cutting board, the two of them alone in the kitchen.

"I don't know what you're talking about." Moira feigned ignorance in response to Nora's comment as she placed dirty dishes in the kitchen sink. Moira looked away from where Nora was standing, a slight smile dancing across her face.

Nora placed the knife down on the cutting board and used her apron to clean her hands. "Come on, now. You've got a permanent smile on your face." Nora paused and gave Moira a searching look. "Is that what I think it is? Why yes, it is—makeup. And you no longer linger around the pub after your shift. You look like a teenage girl who's fallen head over heels in love. Mind you, it's about time you two hooked up. I was wondering when you and Brian were going to realize that you and he were the best thing that could have happened to each other. It was no good for him to go on moping around, and you always looking out for other people but not yourself."

Moira turned around and stared at Nora. She couldn't remember the last time Nora had said more than three words in a row—in an entire day, in an entire week—and now she was rambling on. Moira felt she could confide in Nora. "Is it really that obvious? We were trying to keep our . . ." Moira paused, looking for the right word, "friendship a secret for at least a little while."

"Friendship my eye. It's more than friendship, and it's about time," Nora said, using the knife to sweep the diced carrots off the cutting board into the bowl she was holding.

"You know, if you hadn't landed him soon," Nora said, raising her left eyebrow, "I was thinking about using my vast charms to seduce him." Nora then laughed out loud, shaking her head back and forth.

"Seriously, you two deserve each other and have nothing to be ashamed about. Everyone in the village knows you two are an item. Heck! Everyone in the village knew you two were an item before you and Brian even knew. And everyone in the village is happy for both of you. I'm serious. We've all been hoping for you two to find happiness together."

"Padraig?" Moira asked.

"Yes, even Padraig. Especially Padraig," Nora said in a serious tone. She looked down at the food prep table. "It's a shame that he didn't find someone after . . . well . . . after his loss all those years ago." Nora's voice trailed off. Moira nodded her agreement. Nora reached across the prep table and grabbed a couple of stalks of celery, which she placed on the cutting board and began dicing with the knife.

* * *

"You know, the people in the village know about us," Moira said to Brian, as they sat down for their Sunday morning breakfast the next day. In the background, Dog could be heard making short order of his breakfast in the laundry room.

Brian had begun to raise his cup of tea but placed it back on the saucer without taking a sip. He looked thoughtfully across the table at Moira. Nodding his head, he said, "Good." Then he picked up his cup of tea and took a sip. Placing the cup back down on the saucer again he asked, "Does it make a difference to you that the people in the village know?"

Moira smiled and said, "No, not at all." As she smoothed out the tablecloth, she looked at Brian and said, "We don't have to pretend anymore. I need to tell Maureen, though, before she hears about us from someone else."

Brian smiled and said, "I wouldn't be a bit surprised if Maureen doesn't already know or have her suspicions about us."

"Do you think so?" Moira asked. Seeing Brian nod, she wondered what Maureen would think of their relationship. She didn't think her daughter would object; at least, she hoped she wouldn't.

"What about your daughter and son, what do you think will be their reaction to us—being together?" Moira asked, searching Brian's face.

Brian looked past Moira to the world beyond the kitchen window, deep in thought. Nodding to himself, he replied, "I think they'll be fine with it. They miss their mother, no doubt about that. But knowing those two, they'll be happy for us. And thankful for the woman who helped their father feel alive again." Brian reached across the table to gently squeeze Moira's hand.

Moira nodded and then smiled. With her free hand, she placed a piece of toast on the plate in front of her and reached for the jar of strawberry jam.

"Why don't we go for a walk today. Together," Brian said. Seeing Moira's eyes widen, knowing how long his afternoon walks could be, Brian continued, "Not a real long walk, just a walk down to the quay and back. We can take Dog."

"I would like that," Moira replied with a smile, before taking a bite of her toast.

41

"WHERE ARE WE going again?" Moira asked, as she closed the top of her small suitcase.

"Achill Island, it's just a little way up north. Surely you've heard of it?" Brian replied as he double-checked the contents of his suitcase: underwear, socks, golf shirts, sweater in case it got chilly in the evening. Four months after their first walk together in the village, they were finally going away for a short trip. Jimmy once again volunteered to be the dog sitter.

"We're going to spend four days at a B and B right by the bay up there. It's incredibly scenic. And romantic," Brian said with a smile.

Moira looked up from her suitcase and gave Brian a knowing look before she said, "I trust we are going to see more than the four walls of the bedroom at the B and B."

"Maybe," Brian responded and winked. "Yes, there are plenty of sights. This time of the year, rhododendrons are in full bloom and are everywhere. There are fields of purple rhododendrons. In a couple of places, they grow halfway up the mountains. There are long stretches of white sandy beaches where we can walk. We'll make some side trips too. The food at the B and B is excellent."

Brian paused, thinking about his previous trip to Achill Island—with Clare. As he looked out the bedroom window to the fields beyond, he fondly remembered the trips they had made around the island. The way the setting sun danced across the mountain peaks and how Clare had wanted to visit the island again. With a gentle sigh, Brian returned to the present.

"I told Padraig that I would have you back at the pub Friday afternoon for the weekend rush. And when you finally get your passport, I will take you to the States and introduce you to my family and we can see some of the sights on the other side of the ocean."

Moira smiled and said, "I'd like that." Moira had previously suggested that Brian should invite his family over to Ireland, which he had. But work and the schedule of grandchildren had thus far been obstacles.

Brian picked up his and Moira's suitcases and headed out the bedroom door and down the stairs. Moira started after Brian but then paused. She slowly made her way over to the bed and sat down. A headache, like the one she had the other day, came out of nowhere. She squinted her eyes as the sharp pain seemed to move across her head from one side to the other. The sharp pain was replaced by a manageable dull ache. She got up from the bed, went into the bathroom, and ran some water in the sink, then splashed some water on her face and dried it with a towel. Moira looked at her reflection in the mirror. As the headache dissipated, she said quietly to her reflection, "Probably should see a doctor about these headaches, but that can wait. Rhododendrons halfway up the mountain . . ." Moira smiled, thinking about the sight.

* * *

Yes, the plentiful rhododendrons did cover the mountain halfway up. Moira had asked Brian to pull the car over into a car park by the side of the road so she could get out and slowly take in the sight. The flowers were an incredible deep purple. She had never seen anything like it. The rhododendrons started by the side of the road, traveled across the fields, and then climbed halfway up the mountain, tapering off where the sheer rock face no longer allowed the bushes to take hold. And there were towering hedges of purple rhododendrons in bloom on either side of certain roads, which provided a fairy-tale-like effect. Rhododendrons were everywhere. Brian had been telling the truth.

"Did you know that the rhododendrons are considered invasive?" Brian remarked as they enjoyed their dinner in the B and B's enclosed porch, overlooking the smooth expanse of Keem Bay. The tranquil waters of the bay were nestled among the island's rugged mountains, which soared upward. The rays of the surrendering evening crimson sun cast moving shadows, making the mountains appear to come alive.

So entranced was she by the changing scenery playing out on the mountains across the bay, Moira almost didn't take notice of Brian's comment. "No, I didn't," she eventually responded.

As the server cleared the plates of the remains of poached fish, Brian and Moira contemplated the various choices on the dessert menu. Crème brûlée for her and ice cream with raspberries for him.

After dessert, they took advantage of the remaining light to take a stroll along the sandy beach directly behind the B and B, watching the water from the bay gently lapping over the grains of white sand just a few feet from where they were walking. The occasional empty seashell was picked up, admired, and returned to a new sandy home along the water's edge. Moira paused and surveyed a small grouping of pebbles at the water's edge. She bent over and picked up a smooth, flat pebble that fit neatly in the palm of her right hand. She turned the pebble over, examining it closely, then nodded her head in approval and brushed off the few grains of sand. Holding the pebble in her fingers, Moira bent her knees slightly, slowly pulled her arm back behind her, then whipped her arm forward, letting the pebble fly over the surface of the calm, flat water.

............1..........2........3......4....5..6 skips across the surface of the water before the pebble disappeared into the awaiting depths.

Brian let out a low whistle of approval.

He surveyed the surrounding sand in search of his own pebble, locating one slightly behind where he had been standing. With the pebble firmly held in his fingers, Brian practiced swinging his arm back and forth, back and forth, back and forth.

With a smirk, Moira watched the spectacle in front of her.

Finally, Brian lowered his body, swung his right arm back and, with a mighty effort, followed through with a forward motion before releasing the pebble out over the water.

..........*KERPLUNK!*..........

As soon as the pebble hit the water, it sunk like, well, like a pebble. Not a single skip! The pebble did make a loud noise and a sizable splash, and the outward ripples of water were rather symmetrical.

Of course, Moira couldn't help herself. She moved from where she was standing to a position right by the water's edge. She leaned forward toward the water, raised her right hand up to her forehead just above her eyes, and mockingly pretended to search the waters beyond, moving her head back and forth in an effort to locate the path of Brian's pebble, trying to stifle her laughter.

"Nice, real nice," Brian said, as he absentmindedly kicked the sand with his right foot.

"Oh Brian," Moira managed to say, before she started to giggle again. She moved over to where he was standing, put one arm around his waist, and leaned her head against his shoulder. Finally, after a few seconds, Brian put his arm around Moira's waist before repeating, "Nice, real nice."

After walking about a mile along the beach, they made their way inland as the faint red glow of the setting sun finally disappeared behind a mountain on the far western part of the island. The soft light from the just-risen full moon was now their silent companion.

On their walk back to the B and B, they made a stop along the way at a neighboring pub, where they enjoyed a pint and polite conversation with some local folks before they once again headed for the B and B and the sanctuary of their bedroom overlooking the tranquil bay and the imposing mountains. Brian and Moira stood by the bedroom window, taking in the incredible sights that the full moon illuminated outside. The moon's reflection formed a narrow lighted path across the surface of the bay. Finally, with curtains drawn, their quiet world now consisted of only the two of them in their cozy bedroom. Eventually, the early dawn's light would begin to peek through either side of the curtains and bring with it a new day. They would once again awaken to the sights and sounds of the world around them.

And the delicious aroma coming from the B and B's kitchen, when breakfast was being prepared.

* * *

The four days passed by quickly. Too quickly, as far as Moira was concerned. They would have breakfast and then take their time returning home to the village and her work at the pub. Along the way, they planned on briefly visiting with Maureen. Brian had just left the room and was bringing the suitcases out to the car.

Moira sat at the end of the unmade bed, looking out the window at the bay's waters gently caressing the rock faces of the mountains, which rose steeply. The sun's morning rays reflected off the water, making the bay appear to sparkle, to come alive. Moira also felt alive—incredibly alive. Ever since the first night she had spent with Brian in her bedroom, she had felt joy. Happiness. And as she thought back over the past couple of months together with Brian, she realized she no longer felt the excruciating loneliness that had seemed to pervade every moment of her waking life before. As she stood up, she marveled at how her life had changed so much. Where once she was despondent, she now felt an enduring sense of hope and contentment.

While she prepared to leave to meet Brian in the breakfast room, she suddenly felt sick to her stomach. She moved quickly into the bathroom, raised the seat on the toilet and vomited. She stayed leaning over the toilet for a couple of minutes until she felt there was nothing else left to come up. Rinsing her mouth at the sink to rid herself of an awful lingering taste, she couldn't figure out what had overcome her.

She sat down on the bed for a couple of minutes more until she felt better. She then cautiously made her way to the door and the awaiting breakfast table, and a very light meal.

* * *

After a couple of stops along the way to take in the sights and scenery, they finally made it to the university campus in the early afternoon. By the time they had arrived, Moira was feeling much better. Brian patiently stood off to the side by the car park as mother and daughter conferred, standing on the grassy area of the large courtyard separating the buildings. Occasionally Moira and Maureen would pause their conversation and look at Brian, smiles on their faces. Conversation between mother and daughter would then pick up again, laughter briefly erupting. Then more words back and forth between the two of them. Finally, Moira beckoned Brian over to join them.

"About time!" Maureen scolded him as she quickly embraced him, burying her head in his chest. Just as quickly, she released him and gave him a big smile.

"So, when is the big day?"

"Maureen!" Moira reprimanded her daughter, clearly taken back by her daughter's forwardness, unable to hide a smile.

"I, um, I . . ." Brian had been caught off guard and could only stammer.

"Never mind, marriage is old-fashioned anyway," Maureen said. By the smile on her face, it was obvious Maureen was enjoying his discomfort.

Quickly changing the subject, Brian inquired about how school was going, knowing full well that Maureen would be excelling in all her courses. With a class in ten minutes, conversations quickly drew to a close. As he had with his children when they were in college, Brian slipped Maureen some much-appreciated spending money, this time in euros.

While Maureen headed off to class, Brian and Moira returned to their car and their trip back to the village and home.

42

FOUR MONTHS AFTER their first walk together in the village turned into six months, then eight, and now one year. More trips had been planned and taken. Dublin had been revisited. The other major city, Belfast, with its Titanic Experience and evidence of past turmoil, had both captured their imagination and produced somber reflections of a life and time not so long ago that was so very different from the present. There were also trips to Kinsale, Waterford, Strangford, and Sligo. A tentative trip to the United States had to be pushed back because they still awaited the arrival of Moira's passport, a victim of bureaucracy, the original application having been misplaced within the bowels of a government agency.

During this time, Brian had continued with his consulting engagements, traveling to locations in Europe and the United States. Whenever his work took him to the States, he made sure to visit his children and his grandchildren—and the house that he and Clare had shared for all those years, which he refused to sell. The house had many cherished memories of his Clare, and he could not let go of either the memories or the house.

Like Moira, Brian realized that he could not stop working. He enjoyed meeting with clients, taking on new challenges, and coming up with innovative solutions. His services were still in demand, so much so that he had to turn down work. He could be selective both in terms of the number of engagements as well as their duration. And Brian noticed that his travels away from Ireland served to heighten his desire to return to his other home and Moira. Currently in the States with a client, Brian was literally counting down the hours until he could board his Aer Lingus flight to Shannon.

* * *

For Moira, the year seemed to have flown by. She still enjoyed the work at the pub. Weekends were always busy. There was some staff turnover, but not much. Training the new people fell to her, which she liked; teaching them some of the tricks of the trade and forever telling them that Padraig's bark was worse than his bite. Padraig was Padraig. He didn't seem to age, and time had not tempered his feisty disposition. Padraig had let the farmer back in the pub, so long as he was under the strict supervision of the farmer's wife. Moira had yet to see him.

Whenever Brian went away on business, Padraig would pester Moira, wanting to know when the "heathen" was returning to the village. It seemed that Padraig missed having Brian around almost as much as Moira did. Well, not nearly as much as Moira did.

During this time, there had been some changes in Moira's health, particularly in the morning. Headaches were more frequent. Over-the-counter medication didn't seem to have any affect. And there was the more frequent vomiting. An occasional tingling in her fingers was a new symptom. Moira hid these episodes from Brian and others, although she wasn't always successful. Brian had become increasingly concerned.

* * *

"You alright?" Nora had asked, when Moira came in with a trayful of dirty dishes. Moira walked slowly over to the sink, where she placed the tray down with some difficulty.

"Sit for a moment. The others can clear the tables and finish up," Nora commanded, nodding to Jane, who took the hint and headed out into the pub's dining area. Nora walked around the prep table over to where an exhausted-looking Moira sat on a chair near the kitchen door to the dining area.

"I don't know what came over me. Suddenly, I felt very tired. I just need to sit a minute, it'll pass." She let out a sigh, lowering her head.

Nora wiped her hands on her apron and, with the back of her hand, felt Moira's forehead. "You don't seem to have a temperature. You know you're not a spring chicken anymore. You should let the others take the weekend shifts."

Moira lifted her head to look at Nora. "Did anyone ever tell you that you talk too much?"

"Nope," Nora replied, eyeing her friend closely.

A smile crossed Moira face before she once again lowered her head and closed her eyes.

As much as she tried, Moira could not hide the feeling of exhaustion that frequently overcame her. She knew she had more difficulty carrying trays loaded with plates of dinner meals, making two trips to a table with fewer meals rather than one trip with all the meals, like she used to be able to do. She banished the thought that occasionally played inside her head that old age was catching up with her and that she needed to take it easy. As she sat in the chair resting, she thought, all I need is a couple of nights' good sleep. But she knew that was a lie—something wasn't right. *Maybe when Brian gets back home, I'll ask him to take me up to Galway to see a doctor.* Her thoughts were interrupted.

"Seriously, you need to take it easy," Nora said, in a kind voice.

"Good night, Nora," Moira said, as she slowly rose from the chair, then gently rested a hand on her friend's shoulder. "I'll see you Tuesday," she said, before making her way over to the back door and home.

Nora stood by the kitchen's open screen door, watching Moira being greeted by an awaiting Dog. Nora held the screen door open with her right foot as she looked after her tired friend who, slightly bent over, slowly made her way up the nearby lane. Dog, Moira's ever-faithful companion, stayed close by her side, occasionally looking up at the woman who took him in on that stormy night and showed him kindness.

43

BRIAN WAS SITTING at the far end of the conference table. Earlier, he had completed his presentation, which he thought went well. He half-listened to the conversation being carried on by two of the corporate-types at the other end of the table. He slipped the finger of his right hand under the collar of his shirt, trying to loosen it a bit. He couldn't wait to take his tie off and unbutton the top button of his dress shirt. One of the disadvantages of his consulting work was that he had to dress up and wear a suit and tie for executive presentations like this one. Had to look professional; slacks and a golf shirt wouldn't cut it. He took a quick look at his watch and saw that he had plenty of time to catch the evening flight from Newark Airport to Shannon.

"Well, Mr. Hansen, Brian. Your presentation was very impressive. You came up with ideas that our people hadn't thought of. Ideas that will save us both time and money. Very impressive indeed," the older of the two corporate-types said, nodding his head as the rest of the corporate-types, a half a dozen or so, also nodded their heads in agreement.

"We'd very much like to engage you to help us out on our project and, after the project is complete, for you to continue to assist us in an advisory compacity. If that's agreeable to you?"

It was agreeable to Brian, and he said so. The formal part of the meeting over, he stood up and joined the others in various small group discussions. His carry-on luggage was in the corner of the conference room, and he still had plenty of time to catch his flight. The older corporate-type, the decision maker, had corralled Brian in one corner of the room and was discussing what his firm thought might be some of the additional types of advisory work his firm would like Brian to perform. Brian felt his phone vibrate in his left pants pocket but ignored it. When it vibrated a second time, he politely excused himself and took a quick look at who was calling. It was Maureen. Brian couldn't understand why Maureen was calling unless it was something important.

"Excuse me, I need to take this call." Brian said to the gentleman, who nodded and stepped back to give Brian some privacy.

"Hello Maureen, is something wrong?" Brian asked, turning away from the rest of the people in the conference room.

"Uncle Brian . . ." Maureen began to say, then Brian heard her sob. After a few seconds passed by, Maureen continued. "It's Mam, she's in the hospital." Brian could hear more sobbing.

"What happened?" Brian asked.

"This afternoon, Dog had made a terrible fuss at the back door of the pub, barking and scratching the door." Brian could hear Maureen trying to catch her breath. "Padraig and Jimmy went up to the house where they found Mam. The ambulance came and took her up to the hospital here in Galway. Padraig went with her. He called me and I came right over to the hospital."

"Do they know what happened?" Brian asked, trying to hide the desperation in his voice.

"No, they're going to take her soon for tests. Can you come home, please?"

"Yes, I have the next flight for Shannon. I'll be there as soon as I can. Please . . . please keep me posted." Brian said, and was about to end the call when he asked, "Is Padraig there?"

"He's downstairs with the hospital person, giving them information about Mam."

"Okay, I'll be there as soon as I can." Brian then ended the call and looked around the room for his carry-on, oblivious to the others in the conference room. Once before, he had received a similar phone call when his Clare was in the hospital. A sense of helplessness slowly crept over him.

"Is everything alright?" the older corporate-type gently asked, seeing how shaken Brian looked.

Brian briefly paused his search for his carry-on and said, "There's a medical emergency back home. In Ireland. I need to get to the airport."

The older corporate-type went over to the corner of the conference room and picked up Brian's carry-on, which had evaded Brian's searching eyes. He then took Brian's arm and escorted him out of the conference room, where he briefly paused in front of the desk of an administrative assistant and asked the person to alert his chauffeur that the chauffeur needed to take a passenger immediately over to . . . Newark Airport, he finished, after asking Brian which airport.

"Do you want me to bring the gentleman downstairs to the car?" the assistant asked, starting to get up from her chair after she called down to the chauffeur.

"No, Mary, I'll take Mr. Hansen downstairs. Thank you anyway." With that, the two of them entered an awaiting elevator.

* * *

Somewhere over the Atlantic Ocean, Brian, in the plane's aisle seat, was staring at the monitor on the back of the reclined seat directly in front of him. It showed a map that would monitor the progress of the plane's flight to Shannon Airport. On the left side of the map was the eastern part of the United States, depicting a couple of major cities: Washington, Newark, New York, and Boston. In the middle of the upper part of the map were land masses: Greenland and Iceland. On the right side were the islands of Ireland and the United Kingdom, with cities Shannon, Dublin, and London indicated. In between the United States and Ireland was the vast Atlantic Ocean. An arc was forming, with New York being the origin. Heading upward on the right, just past New York, was the image of a small plane. Brian's plane. The flight was beginning, and so was the intolerable wait. Brian's eyes would not leave the screen for the next five and a half hours, as he would watch the plane's trajectory play out until the image of the plane merged with the word Shannon.

44

MAKING HIS WAY up the sidewalk by the hospital entrance sign, Brian paused and turned to look up at the immense building in front of him. A rather dated building, he thought. The glass-enclosed entrance, however, appeared to be a newer addition. As he approached the sprawling structure, he had a sense of foreboding. He hastened his pace. He didn't know if the feeling was because of what he was about to find inside or because of what had happened the last time he entered a hospital. When he had lost his Clare.

Through the entrance doors, Brian quickly surveyed his surroundings, noticing a sign about visitors being relatives only. He saw the information desk staffed by a couple of older women. *Relatives Only*. The words played out in his head as he thought of his options. *Husband*, maybe, *brother*—no, no brogue, *brother-in-law*—that's a possibility. As it turned out, the gray-haired lady on the left merely asked who he was visiting, which he told her. The woman checked a computer screen before taking a preprinted visitors pass and wrote today's date and a room number on it and handing the pass across the table to him. She then motioned toward a bank of elevators and said the floor number that he should take the elevator to. Brian nodded and thanked the woman.

After quickly stepping into the elevator, Brian pressed the button for the upper floor and waited, willing the elevator doors to close. He was alone. He watched impatiently as the numbers above the elevator doors lit up as each successive floor was passed. The number 4 lit up above the doors as the elevator came to stop. The doors opened, and he quickly exited onto a long corridor, almost colliding with a passing nurse. Across from him was a nurse's station with a bank of computer monitors and a large whiteboard attached to a wall filled with handwritten notes. Nurses were busy moving back and forth behind the station's four-foot-high counter, which extended for about thirty feet and defined the area of the nurse's station.

He stepped aside as a nurse moved quickly past him, pushing what looked like a rather sophisticated monitoring device on top of swivel casters. Brian looked down the end of the corridor to his left and then turned toward his right. At the very far end of that corridor was a small sitting area with a couple of leather chairs and a small sofa. Through the bright light that was shining through the window at the end of the corridor he thought he recognized someone but wasn't sure. He quickly walked down toward the area, passing one room after another. As he made his way down, he peered into each room but could only make out the bottom portion of hospital beds, some occupied, some not. As he neared the sitting area, he finally saw a young man. It was Matthew, Maureen's friend. He looked like he had aged quite a bit. Matthew stood up and tried to smother a yawn.

"Maureen?" Brian asked, extending his hand out in greeting.

Matthew reciprocated with an outstretched hand and beckoned Brian to follow him.

They quickly walked back down the tiled corridor, continuing past the bank of elevators and the nurse's station, and stopped at a room three doors down from and on the same side as the elevators. Matthew stepped back from the open door. Brian cautiously approached the door opening and looked in.

The first thing Brian noticed was Maureen slumped in a chair facing the open door. Her head was tilted slightly downward, eyes closed. Brian walked into the room and saw Moira lying on the hospital bed next to where Maureen was resting. Moira was asleep. Brian paused to look at her and was immediately struck by how fragile she looked. He gently touched Maureen's arm. She stirred, raising her head up. Momentarily unaware of where she was, Maureen quickly looked to her right where her mother was asleep. She moved her head slowly away from where her mother lay. She then looked up and focused her eyes on the man standing in front of her.

"Uncle Brian," she whispered, as tears began to well up in her eyes. She pushed herself out of the chair, stood, and buried her head in Brian's chest, wrapping her arms around him. Brian gently ushered her out of the room, looking back over his shoulder to see that Moira was still asleep. They made their way back to the sitting area, where Brian indicated to Maureen and Matthew to take a seat before he sat down across from the couch where they were sitting.

"What happened?" Brian asked, looking from Maureen to Matthew.

"They, " Maureen began, "Jimmy and Padraig, they found Mam unconscious on the floor at the foot of the stairs in the house. They called for an ambulance. Padraig called me when he got to the hospital with Mam. You must have just missed him. He came up to the hospital with Mam in the ambulance. Nora came up later to bring him back home so he could rest before he comes back up later."

"Do they know what caused her to become unconscious?" Brian asked.

"They immediately ran some tests when they got her here," Maureen began. "They think it might be some kind of tumor on the brain. Apparently, she had regained consciousness when she got here, and they asked her a bunch of questions about how she had been feeling before it happened. They called the tumor glio... glio..." Maureen, exhausted looked toward Matthew for help.

"Glioblastoma," Matthew said in a soft voice, completing Maureen's sentence. Looking very uncomfortable, Matthew's eyes met Brian's, then he looked away. There was no need for Matthew to go into any further detail. Brian knew that glioblastoma was an aggressive form of brain cancer.

Brian leaned back in his chair and sighed. He looked tenderly at Maureen, seeing tears flowing down her cheeks. He turned to Matthew and said, "Why don't you take Maureen back to her room so she can rest awhile. You both look exhausted. I'll stay with your mother," Brian said, leaning forward and taking Maureen's hand in his. Seeing Maureen was about to protest, he continued, "I'll be with her the whole time. You need to get some rest—an hour or two. Please. I will not leave her side. I promise."

Matthew stood up and helped Maureen up from the couch and slowly walked her down the corridor to the elevators. Brian returned to Moira's room and stood in the doorway. While they had been down the hall talking, a nurse had entered Moira's room with one of the sophisticated monitoring devices. The nurse appeared to be finishing up taking Moira's blood pressure. She then took a handheld device and moved it across Moira's forehead. The nurse turned and saw Brian in the doorway and nodded. Brian nodded back. The nurse then went over to a computer that was mounted on the wall at the foot of the hospital bed, pulled out a tray with a keyboard, and proceeded to enter information. Finished, the nurse started to roll the portable device out of the room, where she paused in the corridor just outside the doorway.

"Is there anything I can get you?" she asked Brian.

"No, thank you," Brian said with a tired smile. "How is she?" he asked the nurse before she had a chance to move further down the corridor.

"She's resting. The doctor should be by later and will be able to tell you more." With that, the nurse headed back toward the nurse's station.

Brian returned to the opened doorway and began taking in the various sights inside the room. Above the bed where Moira was lying was a monitor with a continuous waving line moving across the top of the screen. Numbers appeared below the line, which changed every so many seconds. On the other side of the bed, a bag with liquid was suspended from a metal stand. A clear plastic line traveled from the bag downward and entered Moira's right arm above her wrist.

Her head was propped up slightly on a pillow. A white sheet covered the lower part of her prone body. On the wall across from the foot of Moira's bed was the computer that he had seen the nurse use to enter information. To his right, Brian noticed a neatly prepared hospital bed that was unoccupied. Brian crossed the room to the empty chair next to Moira's bed. He angled the chair slightly so he could see Moira's face, and he sat down. He leaned his right elbow on the bed's mattress and reached out and gently took Moira's hand in his. He leaned back in the chair and gazed upon the woman he loved—the woman he desperately didn't want to lose.

45

MOIRA KNEW SHE was in a hospital. The doctor had told her that when she woke up in the sterile white room with multiple occupied hospital beds. It was noisy. Not a loud noisy, but a busy noisy. Hospital staff were moving back and forth with purpose. The emergency room was also very bright and had a slight smell of disinfectant. Next to her bed she saw another bed with an older woman lying quietly. The woman didn't look too good, she thought. She wondered what she herself looked like to others. The doctor had asked her several questions about how she had been feeling the weeks and days before this incident. She had been told she would have several tests to help try to determine what had landed her in the hospital. She knew something was wrong. The headaches, the vomiting, and now her eyesight was blurred. She must have fallen asleep when they performed the tests.

Next thing she knew, she was no longer in the bright busy area but in a room by herself. She vaguely remembered seeing Maureen and Padraig in her room before she had fallen back asleep. They had looked very concerned. All she wanted to do was go home—with the man now holding her hand. She squeezed his hand. She could sense him stirring.

"What are you doing here?" she asked.

"I don't know," Brian replied, trying to focus his eyes before adding, "I like to visit women in hospitals. Didn't you know? My consulting trips are merely a cover. I visit various hospitals and hold women's hands," Brian finished, with a gentle smile.

Moira squeezed his hand again and said, "I thought so. Like to see the ladies in their backless gowns, do you?"

It was Brian's turn to squeeze Moira hand. They remained quiet for a couple of minutes.

"Maureen . . ." Moira began.

"I asked Matthew to take her back to her room so she could rest. That was . . ." Brian paused to look at his watch. He frowned. Two hours had slipped by. He had fallen asleep for nearly two hours. "Two hours ago," he finished. Tired from the flight and then the hour ride from the airport, he had quickly dozed off.

"No, not that. I'm worried Maureen will need a place, should I . . . go . . ." She was exhausted.

"And just where do you think you're going?" Brian asked, squeezing her hand.

"You know what I mean," Moira responded, trying to overcome her exhaustion. "I worry about her . . . her future."

"You have always provided Maureen with a home. One filled with love. And, for the last year, you and Maureen have also had your own house." Brian let that last comment sink in. "A year ago, I met with Conor and had the house placed in yours and Maureen's names, just in case something happened to me, with my travels. You and Maureen turned four walls and a roof into a home for each other and for me."

Moira sighed and shifted a little in her bed before closing her eyes.

"Thank you," Brian heard her say in a hushed voice.

"For what—the house?" Brian responded. "The house . . ." Brian fell silent as Moira slowly shook her head.

"For loving me and allowing me to love you," Moira answered.

Before he could respond, Moira continued slowly, "For oh so many years, I would see couples deeply in love. Young couples who would steal a kiss at a table before their evening meal was served in the pub. An elderly couple from the village who, every Sunday afternoon for years, would sit on the bench down at the harbor, watching the boats come and go. They wouldn't say a word to each other, but the entire time, they held each other's hand, as though they were teenagers once again. I could see these people were in love, but I couldn't feel the emotions they felt, the love they felt, for each other. I could only imagine what love might feel like. You allowed me to feel what it is like to truly love someone and what it feels like to be loved. It is something that I will forever cherish." Moira barely finished the last sentence, saying the words in a whisper.

Tears welled up in Brian eyes. He squeezed Moira's hand and she, in turn, squeezed back.

Some more time passed by before Moira had the energy to put her thoughts into words. "You know. I could have darned your socks."

Brian chuckled as tears began to roll down his cheeks.

"Moira," he began, "I would have been very disappointed if you had darned my socks."

He partially stood up from the chair, leaned over her and, with his free hand, brushed a loose strand of hair back from her forehead and then gently kissed her lips.

46

Two Weeks Later

AFTER MAKING SURE she was alright for the second time that morning, Brian told Maureen he would meet her at the church. He had to do something first. Matthew had assured Brian that he would watch over Maureen and would drive her to the church service. Brian had nodded and made his way through the front door to his car. What he had to do was be alone for a little while. He started the car up and drove. Past the pub, past the center of the village, up past the tower on the side of the mountain, and then onto the main road, heading north.

He could not escape the empty feeling that had haunted him the last couple of days. He had felt the same way when Clare had passed away. Now he wondered how he had gotten to this point. Gone were the two women whom he had loved with all his heart. Was the world cruel for taking them both from him? Or had he been blessed by allowing him to experience a life with the unconditional love of two women, while many others yearn for the love of just one person?

Perhaps, he thought, it wasn't an either/or answer; rather, the answer embodied a little bit of both feelings.

He was concerned about Maureen. She had lost her mother. But Maureen was a strong young woman, and a smart one, and very much like her mother. Brian smiled at that thought. Maureen would be alright. She had Padraig, Conor, Daniel, Nora, and a whole village to keep an eye out for her, along with Matthew. Brian checked his watch. A half hour had passed by. He should be heading to the church, he thought.

He didn't want to be late for Moira's funeral service.

* * *

As Brian pulled the car over onto the grassy area alongside the narrow lane, he looked at the line of cars parked on both sides of the lane. The cars stretched for at least a hundred yards back from the church. Apparently, not only had the entire village come out for the funeral, but also the entire county. Brian closed the car door, leaving it unlocked, and began to slowly walk. The church was up ahead on the right. He walked parallel to what seemed like an endless low stone wall. On the other side of the wall, Brian could see stone markers that stood upright in the large, neatly maintained field beyond. *The church graveyard where Moira would soon be laid to rest.* He sighed and continued walking. He checked his watch again. There was still time before the church service began.

Finally, the stone wall to his right came to an end. He arrived at a series of large flat stone slabs that made up the walkway from the lane to the church entrance. To his left was a gravel parking lot full of cars. To his right was the graveyard he had just walked past. Brian paused and looked up at the stone structure that rose up before him. It was a fairly large church, but not huge like the immense cathedral that he and Clare had visited in Galway. The church looked like it had been around for quite some time. As he looked at the large stone blocks that made up the outer walls, he marveled at how the stone masons of old built such magnificent structures without the benefits of modern equipment or technology. Mortar lines looked perfectly straight. The roof of the church was without a single missing or chipped slate; the dark green moss at the peak and along the roof's edges hinted at its age. The steeple reached upward as though seeking a place among the clouds. As he continued toward the entrance, Brian wondered how many weddings and funerals had been witnessed over the years within its walls. He nodded to some folks who lingered outside of the church, some talking in small groups while others enjoyed a last drag of nicotine before entering lung purgatory.

Brian entered the church and paused so his eyes could adjust to the dull light within. He moved over to the side so as not to block anyone coming in after him. When his eyes finally adjusted, he saw a church packed with people. Standing room only. The pews were almost completely filled, with a few remaining open seats in the very front of the church. People were standing along the side walls, two deep in a few places. He quickly moved to his right and secured an opening for himself along the very back of the church. He leaned back against the cool stone wall. The walls seemed to amplify the sound of people's conversations, resulting in a steady drone of unrecognizable noise. As he looked up at the vaulted ceiling, he could see rays of light darting down from the stained-glass windows that interrupted the masonry blocks along the side walls. Dust motes disturbed by the assemblage of people floated among the rays of light, giving the illusion of a light snowfall without the accumulation.

Brian looked back by the entrance and noticed Jimmy from the pub escorting an older couple toward the front of the church. The slightly stooped woman was holding Jimmy's arm as they slowly made their way down the aisle. Following close behind was a neatly dressed older gentleman who kept pace, occasionally giving a little wave to someone he saw in the congregation. Brian searched his memory. The man looked familiar, and then it came to him—Colm. *This is the older couple who would bring food around to villagers who were ill.* Padraig had pointed out Colm to Brian one time in the pub. Brian smiled at the thought of the two Good Samaritans.

Brian leaned back against the wall as far as he could, to allow a young couple to walk by him, momentarily blocking his view of the crowded pews in front of him. Two people over from where he was standing, he noticed a rather large, surly looking man whose fingers were engaged in a battle with a too-tight shirt collar that was buttoned at the top. The man was without a tie. He looked extremely awkward in a poor-fitting dark-gray suit. A couple days of facial-hair growth and a halfhearted comb of a mop of hair didn't help the man's appearance. The sturdy looking woman next to him kept elbowing him, trying to get him to call a truce with his shirt collar. Brian didn't think he would want to meet either one of them in a dark alley. The farmer continued to attack his shirt collar as the farmer's wife shook her head in disgust. Brian resisted the urge to place a finger down his own tight collar, although he took the opportunity to loosen his tie a bit.

He leaned back against the stone wall again to let another person pass by. The man dawdled in front of him for a minute, searching his surrounding, before taking off for a spot on the far wall. Looking over by the entrance, he noticed Jimmy again. This time Jimmy was pushing an older gentleman down the aisle in a wheelchair. *Jimmy must be the official usher*. Brian didn't recognize the older man in the wheelchair. There was no reason that Brian should have recognized Mr. Byrne, as he had been pretty much housebound since his wife had passed away. The gentleman was the beneficiary of the pub's worst-kept secret. For this was the gentleman who was the pub's official taste tester—in name only.

Another person walked by. As Brian looked straight ahead, he thought he saw Maureen at the very front of the church standing up, scanning the various pews and then looking around toward the rear of the church. Searching for someone. Standing next to her was Matthew. Both Maureen and Matthew seemed to be scanning each pew one by one, starting near them and working their way back. Then he noticed Conor standing up and looking around before he sat back down. Then Padraig stood and surveyed the gathering behind him before eventually sitting back down. Brian wondered who they were looking for. Another person passed by him in search of a place to stand without blocking the view of others. Brian followed the person's progress to his right. As he was about to turn back to look at the front of the church, he saw a button fly out in front of him and then land on the stone floor of the church, where it skidded a couple of feet. He looked to his immediate right to see the giant of man he had noticed previously give a sigh of relief. The man's finger was free of the shirt collar, which was now open. Brian couldn't help but smile, and he shook his head. His eyes traveled past the large man to the far wall, where he noticed two of the local garda dressed in what must be their parade-best uniforms, hats held in front down by their waists. They both appeared to be suspiciously eyeing a weasel of a man who stood a couple of feet to their left. The man nervously looked at the two men in uniform. Brian vaguely remembered the man. During one of their walks, Moira had pointed out Gavin and told Brian about how Nora *assisted* Gavin out of the pub. Who knows what had possessed Gavin to enter God's house? If he was seeking sanctuary, well, he picked the wrong day.

Brian turned his head back toward the front of the church and saw a very determined Maureen making her way back down the center aisle. The droning noise grew quieter and quieter and eventually stopped, as the people sitting in the pews and standing along the walls grew silent and turned their heads to watch Maureen quickly make her way toward the back of the church. Brian tilted his head, wondering where Maureen was going. He found out when she stood directly in front of him and reached out and took his left arm and proceeded to lead him back down the center aisle from which she had just come. All eyes in the church followed the pair in hushed silence.

When they arrived at the front of the church, Brian noticed that attorney Conor and two people who must have been his wife and daughter were standing in front of the pew to his right. Conor nodded to Brian. Next to them at the far side of the same pew stood estate agent Daniel and a person who must have been his wife along with two young children. Daniel also nodded to Brian. Maureen moved Brian toward the opposite front pew, where Padraig and Matthew were standing along with Nora and Jimmy. Maureen pointed to the vacant spot next to Padraig.

Brian looked down at the empty spot on the pew and frowned. He turned back to look at Maureen and said, "But Maureen, this section is reserved for family."

Maureen looked Brian directly in the eyes and, in a gentle voice, said, "You are family—you're part of our family." The occupants of the two front pews sat down, except for Brian, who was so taken back by Maureen's words that he hesitated.

Patting the empty spot next to him on the pew, Padraig uttered one word: "Sit." Brian slowly sat down alongside Padraig, Maureen next to him on his other side.

Just then, a priest arrived in front of the congregation. An older, heavyset man with a full bushy white beard, rather long white hair, and kind eyes. He cast his eyes around the church. Slowly the noise died down, to be interrupted by a young girl's voice.

"Why did everyone stop talking?" the little girl sitting in a pew a few rows back from the front asked her mother in a loud voice.

"Shhh, we need to be quiet now," the mother said, trying to silence her daughter. Smiles appeared on some of the people's faces in the immediate area.

The little girl looked around her and then spotted the priest in the front of the church. She reached behind her and grabbed the back of the pew with one hand and pulled herself upright to a standing position on the pew so she could better see the man with the white beard. The young girl's actions went unnoticed by her mother, who was trying to stop the little girl's younger brother, who was sitting on the other side of the mother, from falling headfirst onto the floor below.

The little girl's mouth fell open at the sight of the priest. She pointed at the bearded man standing before her and blurted out, in a loud voice which seemed to echo throughout the church,

"Look Mommy, its Santy!"

A slow ripple of laughter rolled out from where the little girl was standing, across the pews and along the perimeter walls. The laughter grew steadily louder until the congregation erupted and laughter could be heard from every pew and every corner of the church. The tension that had been building shattered like a piece of glass into a thousand pieces. Tears of joy flowed freely as the words of a one little girl turned a solemn occasion into a joyous one. Perhaps the loudest laughter came from the people occupying the front pews, for they knew that if Moira was sitting with them, she would have been laughing along with the rest of them.

The smiling priest made his way over to the lectern and waited for the laughter to slowly die down. He saw the little girl, whose mortified mother was trying desperately to get her to sit down while maintaining control of the little one on her other side. The priest waved to the little girl, who responded with a big smile before finally taking a seat next to her mother.

The priest began the sermon.

47

WITH MOST OF the people gone from the cemetery, Brian stood beside the open grave alone. The congregation had followed the casket out from the church to the recently unearthed site in the adjoining cemetery. The priest spoke more kind words, the casket was lowered into the ground, handfuls of earth were showered down on the casket's wooden surface, and then the service was over. Some people had loitered in the cemetery for a while. Some were trying to find grave markers of deceased relatives or friends. Others were chatting with folks they hadn't seen in a while. Slowly, however, they filtered out of the cemetery, making their way to parked cars. For many, the pub would be their destination. At the conclusion of the service inside the church, the priest had announced that the McGuires had extended an invitation to all for food and drink at the village pub.

Brian thought back upon the service itself. The priest had kept the sermon mercifully short. He had a soothing voice, one that was comforting. He spoke of Moira in a loving way and included a couple of stories of her kindness to the village locals, and a certain homeless dog. He spoke of Moira's never-ending love for her daughter. He also included examples where Moira took no guff and, in one well-known case, visited righteous pain on the deserving party. This brought chuckles to the knowing congregation, except for one individual standing in the back of the church. The farmer had looked down at his immense shoes when this story was being told. The farmer's wife was unable to stifle her laughter.

Brian let his eyes scale the heights of the church's towering steeple. He tried to think back to the last time he had been in a church of any denomination. He could neither remember when nor could he remember the occasion. *Probably a wedding or a funeral,* he thought. Although, as the years moved along, it seemed like the funerals were outpacing the weddings. Brian nodded to himself his agreement with this sad truth.

He then thought back to the church service for his Clare. Realizing that was some seven years ago, he shook his head. A loud sigh escaped him as he reflected how two people he loved and cared so deeply about had both been taken from him at such a young age. They had been taken from others also—daughters, sons, sisters, brothers, uncles and aunts, cousins, neighbors. He wasn't the only person who had lost someone, he realized. He knew he was being selfish. Brian's eyes drifted from the church steeple down to the stained-glass windows, then to the ground and the rows of flower bouquets which bordered the open grave directly in front of him.

A sheep bleating in the pasture next to the cemetery brought Brian back from his thoughts. He looked over to where he thought the bleating was coming from. Past the stone wall bordering the cemetery grounds, he saw a flock of sheep grazing in a field. The young lambs were frolicking with each other, but never far from their mothers. His gaze traveled up to the hill beyond that slowly rose upward, more green pastures bordered by a labyrinth of stone walls. As his gaze continued upward, vivid green pastures were eventually replaced by the blue sky and white puffs of clouds that floated along in the gentle breeze. He smiled to himself. Once again, he thought he had never seen a land with so much stone. Stone walls, stone cottages, stone churches, and now—stone grave markers.

The clouds passing in front of the bright sun resulted in shadows being cast on the land below. In the cemetery, the moving shadows made the stone markers look like they had come alive. Instead of feeling unsettled by the apparition, Brian felt remarkably at peace in these surroundings.

As he looked around the cemetery, he noticed a familiar person standing by a grave marker about twenty yards directly behind him, under a large tree that sheltered both the man and the stone marker in the shade offered by its branches. Padraig had a single bouquet of flowers in his right hand and stood motionless, with head tilted down toward the stone marker. Brian bent down and picked up three bouquets of flowers from among the many that adorned Moira's grave. He slowly made his way across the grassy area, passing other stone markers, and finally paused alongside Padraig. Brian looked at the inscription on the stone maker and knew this was Padraig's family—his wife and child, lost all those many years ago. Slowly, Brian bent down and placed the flowers on the ground in front of the marker. Brian turned around and, in a soft-spoken voice, said, "From Moira, Clare... and me," before slowly walking back from whence he came to return to his own vigil. Padraig gave an almost imperceptible nod.

How much time had passed by, Brian did not know. He sensed movement from behind, and then a shadow fell across the open grave in front of him. Padraig rested a hand on Brian's shoulder as he stood next to him.

"If we are fortunate enough," Padraig began, as he looked down into the open grave, "our cherished memories of loved ones will never fade away. And the joyous feelings of our love and time spent together will be forever captured in our beating hearts."

Padraig raised his head up and turned to look at Brian. "Brian, my dearest friend, it is time we both move along. They would insist our place now and for the foreseeable future is among the living." After a minute had passed by, Padraig said in a kind voice, "I'll see you at the pub—heathen."

Brian turned to look at Padraig as a smile crept across his face. It had been quite a while since he had been called a heathen by this man—his friend—standing next to him.

"Sure, I'll be along shortly. I want to stop by the house first, then I'll be there. Save me a seat."

Padraig gently patted Brian on his back before making his way through the graveyard to the church parking lot. After a few minutes, Brian heard the crunching sound of car tires on the gravel parking lot. He looked up and noticed the car's taillights light up as the car braked before entering the lane. Turning left, the car headed back toward the village. Brian nodded to himself and slowly made his way to the side of the church and walked on the stone slabs leading from the church to the lane. Walking along the lane, he saw that his distant car was the last one remaining. The only sounds he heard were the chirping of stealth birds somewhere in the trees bordering the road and the occasional piece of gravel skidding along the roadway that he absentmindedly kicked with his shoes.

* * *

As he drove through the village, he noticed it had been invaded by cars parked in every imaginable space along the road and in fields bordering the road. People spilled out from the two open doors to the pub, milling around, pint glasses in their hands. Mouths moving, heads nodding up and down, and occasional laughter interrupting conversations, were evidence of people enjoying themselves after a solemn ceremony. Men's ties were either absent or hung loosely down the front of partially unbuttoned shirts. Women's high heels were abandoned for more comfortable shoes or no shoes at all. The smokers had been considerate and congregated across from the pub by the wooden tables and benches. Empty plates and pint glasses adorned the top of the picnic tables. Brian slowly drove by, avoiding people who had turned the road into a pedestrian walkway.

As he turned up the narrow lane, he had to slow the car down to a crawl. Parked cars had lined the left side of the lane. He had to completely stop a couple of times to allow latecomers to walk down the narrow gap that was once a lane as they made their way to the pub. Nods or waves from walking passersby acknowledged Brian's courtesy.

At the house, Brian took off his suit jacket and tie and placed them on the back of a dining room chair. He undid the top shirt button as he made his way over to the back door, which he opened to greet an eagerly awaiting Dog, who approached Brian with a furiously wagging tail. Brian bent over and reached behind Dog's ear and gave him a good scratch before moving to the bench, where he sat down. Dog took up a position on the slate patio next to the bench and laid down, his head on his front legs, tail at rest. Brian looked past the stone wall bordering the patio to see the waist-high fields of golden wheat gently waving in the breeze. There was no rush to get to the pub, he thought. By the looks of it, the pub was overflowing. The vast number of parked cars bore witness to that. No, he would sit and enjoy the blue skies and passing clouds, at least for a little bit. After a while, he would take a walk down the lane and become one more among the many.

Lost in his thoughts, he hadn't heard the back door open, but he did see Dog get up with his tail wagging. Brian felt a presence, and the presence took the form of Maureen, who sat down next to him on the bench. She reached over and took his hand in hers. They sat in silence, looking at the wheat fields together. Dog resumed his position on the slate patio, head once again resting on his front legs.

While gazing straight ahead at the fields of wheat, Maureen finally said, "You know she loved you very much." She slowly turned her head to look at her Uncle Brian, waiting for a response.

Brian's eyes dropped down to the stone wall. He smiled and slowly nodded his head.

Maureen returned her gaze to the fields. After a moment, she turned toward Brian, tilting her head, and spoke again, her words more a statement, a confirmation, than a question. "You loved my mother. You loved her very much."

Brian's smile grew as his eyes moistened. His eyes drifted down to the patio in front of him before turning his head to look at Maureen, who stared at him with searching eyes. Then he said in a kind voice, "I've been fortunate to have loved and to continue to love two women in my life. You knew my Clare," Brian said, and Maureen nodded her head. "Your mother was the second person I was fortunate to have loved with all my heart."

The two resumed their gaze out toward the wheat fields, gentle tears rolling down their faces.

Dog was up once again, looking toward the house. The back door opened, and Matthew cautiously stepped out onto the patio and took a few steps toward the occupied bench. He hesitated before saying, "Maureen, Padraig called. He's looking for you and Mr. Hansen. I told him . . . I told him you were both here. He said to get a move on."

Maureen smiled and let go of Brian's hand. She stood up and turned to face Matthew and said, "We'll be along in a minute." She looked back down at Brian and said, "Conor told me about the house. What you did . . ."

"It was the right thing to do. Your mother and you turned this place into a loving home. For the two of you and for me and Dog," Brian said with a smile, nodding at Dog. He added in a more serious tone, "It was important that she knew before . . . well, before . . ." Maureen nodded her understanding.

Brian said, "You go, I'll be along in a minute or two. I think Dog and I would like to go for a short walk, then we'll come on down to the pub."

Deep in thought he added, "Best tell Padraig I'll be along in a little bit, otherwise he'll have his sentries scouring the countryside looking for me."

Maureen hesitated, then bent down and kissed her Uncle Brian on his cheek before walking over to the back door, where she paused to reflect upon the man sitting on the bench. She wiped tears from her cheeks using a handkerchief that Matthew had handed her. Then she disappeared through the open door, followed by Matthew. The door gently closed behind them.

Brian stood up. Dog was ready, head tilted to one side, waiting for instructions.

"What do you say, old boy? Shall we go for a walk?" Brian asked, pointing to the opening in the stone wall and to the fields beyond. Dog was off; he didn't need to be asked twice. Brian followed behind. Dog was quickly swallowed up by the field of wheat, parting wheat stalks moving every which way, evidence of his travels.

Brian waded out into the vast sea of wheat, slowly making his way down the field toward where the village lay. He would periodically pause to track Dog's progress before moving along. After a while, he stopped and took in the surrounding fields of wheat, which seemed to disappear into the awaiting blue waters off to his far right. He could see the sightseeing boats plying their way toward the towering Cliffs of Mohr. Turning back toward the village, his eyes drifted beyond the village and its stores and the storybook cottages up the side of the mountain, to the round stone tower that seemed to beckon to him.

He stood still, surrounded by the gently waving wheat, staring at the tower as if in a trance. Then he heard a familiar voice that he hadn't heard in a very long time:

"Some men never grow up . . ."

Brian slowly shook his head and smiled as he recalled Clare scolding him while she sorted through the ladies' undergarments in the clothes basket.

He continued to smile as another familiar voice followed the first, the tone much different:

"I don't do darning. Do you hear me? I don't do darning!"

Brian's eyes looked up past the pointed top of the tower to the incredibly vibrant blue skies above and the immense, slow-moving cumulus clouds drifting toward distant villages, where others might marvel at their splendor. His trance broken by the nearby wheat being disturbed by Dog's travels, Brian's eyes followed Dog's progress through the separating stalks of wheat, which now formed a straight path heading toward the village.

With a knowing smile, Brian slowly followed Dog to the village and the people who had embraced him and shown him immeasurable kindness.

And made him realize that there would be another tomorrow.

48

Twelve Years Later

A LIGHT-BLUE PASSENGER VAN slowly made its way over the narrow bridge onto the road where the village stores and pub were located on the right. Occasionally, the driver would pause the van, and his protruding arm would become quite animated, pointing out a particular sight.

"There, that's the store where we'd buy the delicious chocolate for the grandchildren. The chocolate that you folks would sneak from your children. Didn't think we knew about that, did you?" Brian said with accusatory tone, trying to hide his smile.

Brian's daughter Mady, sitting in the front passenger seat, smiled and looked over her shoulder at the other passengers in the back seat—fellow chocolate thieves. In unison, the three people in the back seat looked up at the ceiling of the van and gave a "Who? Me?" look that didn't go unnoticed by Brian, who chose that moment to look in the rearview mirror.

"Yeah, right," Brian said.

Mady bore a remarkable resemblance to her mother. From the position of her head leaning against the seat headrest, it was obvious that she was tall, like her mother. She was also slender and immaculately dressed. Dark-blue blouse and neatly pressed gray slacks. Her husband John, also tall and slender, was sitting directly behind her in the van's rear seat. His dark mustache would soon turn gray to match his head of hair. White golf shirt above and black slacks below. Next to John, in the middle, sat Joan, Brian's daughter-in-law. A head shorter than the two men sitting on either side of her, Joan had incredible blue eyes. Shoulder-length blond hair fell softly onto her dark-red blouse. She also wore black slacks. To her right, by the window, sat her husband Robert, brother of the woman riding shotgun. He wore a short-sleeve light-blue dress shirt and gray slacks. His eyes followed where his father's arm extended out the window, continuing to point out different places.

"There's the pub," Brian pointed out, bringing the van to another stop after first checking to make sure there were no cars behind. In a somber voice, he said, "That's where Moira worked. I wish you could have met her. You would have liked her." The passengers looked at each other, nodding, knowing he was talking about the woman that helped save the man who was driving.

Sensing he was being maudlin, Brian changed tack and said in a loud, cheerful voice, "Moira's uncle, Padraig, was the owner of the pub. What a character. To him I was a heathen, having Viking ancestors from the north who invaded Ireland all those years ago. He took to your mother, though, because of her Irish ancestry." Brian shook his head and let out a laugh. "The things we . . . I mean *he* did, well, simply amazing. The stories . . ." Brian left the sentence unfinished.

Taking his foot off the brake, Brian moved along, completing the tour of the village shops. Prior to making a right turn up the lane, he pointed ahead down the road, indicating that the harbor was located about a mile down. Slowly, Brian made his way up the lane, following it as it turned to the right. As he approached the place where the lane turned sharply to the left, he stopped the van again and pointed out an immaculately kept B and B on their right.

"That's where we'll be staying. The hostess is very nice—she'll make you feel like you're right at home. And the breakfasts—they are something! From here, you can walk to the different places in the village and down to the harbor." The passengers gazed out the windows at the quaint cottage.

Continuing, Brian followed the lane that turned once again and drove past the fields of wheat on their left. One of the advantages of the van was that the riders sat up higher than in a car. They were able to take in an incredible view of the expansive fields of golden wheat which flowed down the gently sloping land. They could also clearly see the blue ocean, which seemed to embrace the fields far off in the distance.

"What an incredible sight," Mady said to no one in particular. Her fellow passengers voiced their agreement.

The van turned left into an opening in the stone wall and noisily made its way across the cattle grate before coming to a stop on the pebbled driveway. The sound of the van's sliding doors opening and closing was replaced by the crunching sounds of people walking across the pebble driveway.

Brian noticed the curtain move behind the front window.

* * *

As they approached the house, the front door opened.

"Welcome," an older-looking Matthew said, with a broad smile. Brian had immediately recognized Matthew, even though the last time Brian had seen him was the day of Moira's funeral. Matthew reached out and clasped Brian's hand in both of his. A child was hiding behind Matthew, clinging tightly to the cloth material of his pants leg. Brian smiled at the little girl who peeked around her father's leg to look at the newcomers. Brian then bent down to take a closer look at the shy little girl with long curly hair and wearing a pretty floral dress. "And who might this pretty young lady be?" Brian asked.

"This is Moira," Matthew said, gently placing his right hand on his daughter's head. His daughter tightened her grip on her father's pants leg.

"Well, hello Moira," Brian said with a beaming smile.

"Please have a seat," Matthew said, as he ushered everyone into the living room.

Brian took this opportunity to introduce his family—his American family. As he introduced each person, Matthew nodded. The little girl's eyes zoomed in on each of the adults as they were introduced, though she still cautiously remained behind her father's leg.

Introductions completed, Brian was about to sit down on the sofa when he glanced over his shoulder and saw her—Maureen. For a second, he froze. Then a smile spread across his face. He crossed the floor to the grownup girl who quickly approached him from the kitchen. They met halfway and embraced, holding each other for a long moment.

Brian turned back to the group and said, "This is Maureen."

Maureen took a few steps toward the group and looked at the tall woman and said, "I know you're Mady. You look very much like your mother." Then they hugged. Maureen went to the other three visitors and briefly hugged each one. She turned and took a long look at Brian, then said, "Come, you folks must be hungry after your long journey. We have sandwiches that were just brought up from the pub and some iced tea or beer. Moira, do you want to help me bring the food out from the kitchen?" Moira followed her mother, looking over her shoulder at the visitors, especially the one who was older than the rest.

Brian let the others pass by him as he remained in the living room. The sight of Maureen and her family brought back fond memories of times long ago. Maureen the teenager, the time he spent helping her with her coursework at the dinner table. Maureen the college student, striding across the college campus to greet her mother while Padraig and he plotted their deception regarding the scholarship. And now a mother. He sighed as he thought of Moira not seeing her daughter all grown up and her beautiful grandchild.

Any concerns he might have had about the two families meeting for the first time quickly faded away when he saw the three women chatting away with each other as they brought the food to the dining room from the kitchen. Smiles and occasional laughter were evident as they made successive trips back and forth from the kitchen. The men were busy with conversation by the rear glass wall, heads nodding up and down and arms extended, pointing out something outside the house.

"Uncle Brian, come now, time to eat," Maureen called out to Brian in a voice that demanded attention.

Whether it was the tone of her voice or Brian thinking of times gone by or a combination of both, for just a fleeting moment, Brian imagined it was Moira calling him to the dinner table. Realizing it was Maureen who beckoned, he smiled and turned toward her as she was pointing at the dining room table. He raised his hand slightly and headed toward one of the chairs.

* * *

A few sandwiches were left on the nearly empty large metal tray at the end of the meal. The younger men preferred the beer, Brian and the women, iced tea, and for Moira, a glass of milk.

"You missed Nora and Jimmy," Maureen said to Brian as she placed her napkin next to her empty plate. "They brought the food up from the pub just before you arrived. We'll be having dinner at the pub tonight, so you'll see them there."

"Nora," Brian said to no one in particular, his thoughts drifting back in time. "She's . . ."

"The same," Maureen said, before Brian could ask. "Hasn't changed a bit. Still the pub's cook and enforcer."

Brian chuckled before saying, "Good old Nora." Looking at the others at the table, he continued, "Remind me to tell you the story about Nora."

"There are a lot of stories about Nora," Matthew interjected.

"True," Brian said. "But the one I'm thinking about is when the guy wound up in the field across from the pub." Brian shook his head and continued to chuckle.

Matthew looked across the table at Maureen, raised his arm with the wristwatch, gently tapping the glass dial with a finger before he said, "It's been two hours."

Maureen stood up and looked at her guests and said, "Excuse me for a minute, I'll be right back." She made her way around the table and walked up the stairs by the kitchen. A few minutes later she returned, cradling a bundle in her arms. Mady, who was sitting on the side of the table facing the staircase, stood up and quickly walked over to greet Maureen as she made her way down the stairs and stepped down onto the floor. The men all stood up along with Brian's daughter-in-law Joan. Moira remained seated, focused on the bowl of ice cream in front of her.

Maureen carefully moved the little blanket away from the baby's face, whose eyes searched around before settling on her mother. Mady and Joan made sure they were right up close to get a better view. The men drew near, except for Brian, who remained by the dining room table.

"I would like to introduce you to our youngest—Clare," Maureen said proudly. A chorus of *awws* filled the room as Mady and Joan nestled even closer.

Brian smiled and slowly walked over from his position at the table to take a closer look at his wife's namesake. Maureen held the bundle out so Brian could get a better look. "I hope you don't mind?" Maureen asked. "Her name."

All eyes were on Brian, to see his reaction. He let out a sigh as his smile grew even larger, eyes glistening. "Not at all. Clare would have liked that. She's a beautiful baby. Takes after her mother—and her grandmother." Maureen smiled warmly.

"Matthew, why don't you take our guests down to the pub and introduce them and get them a pint or whatever they'd like. I know the folks down there would like to meet them. Brian and I and the little ones will be along in a little bit," Maureen said, as she gently touched Moira's shoulder, now that the little girl had finally made her way over to stand next to her mother.

Matthew nodded and pointed out the various available upstairs and downstairs powder rooms to the guests. After a couple of minutes, the sound of the front door opening and closing could be heard, leaving Maureen, Brian, and the little ones by themselves.

"Let's go sit outside on the bench," Maureen said, pointing to the backdoor. Brian nodded and walked over to the door and held it open for the ladies. Once outside, Moira went off to play in a recently added sandbox, at least recently added since Brian had last been here some twelve years ago. Beyond the sandbox, Brian could see the familiar upright posts with empty clotheslines strung back and forth between the crosspieces. A host of memories came flooding back to him.

Maureen had grabbed a very light cloth on her way to the back door. The baby started fussing. Maureen and Brian crossed the patio to the bench where they sat. Maureen turned to Brian and said, "It's nursing time, I hope you don't mind," as little Clare made her presence known—rather loudly.

Brian turned to look at Maureen, understood what she meant, and discreetly turned away to give them some privacy before saying, "No, go right ahead." Wife, daughter, and daughter-in-law had all nursed their babies, so he knew the drill and cast his eyes on the field of wheat. After a moment, he heard a sucking sound as Clare began to nurse.

"I'm so glad you and your family came," Maureen said, adjusting the cloth to better protect Clare from the bright sun. "It's been too long," she chided.

Brian sighed and nodded. She was right; it *had* been too long. "I should have come to see you sooner." Brian paused before continuing. "When your mother passed on, I threw myself into my work, trying to escape the feeling of loss that once again overcame me. It wasn't fair of me. I should have done more than just the occasional phone call or text to you. I'm sorry."

Maureen reached over and patted Brian's leg. "It's alright, we both needed time to grieve in our own way. I threw myself into my schooling. I know that was important to Mam."

For a few moments, they sat quietly, gazing out at the sea of wheat beyond the low patio wall.

"Tomorrow's ceremony should be brief," Maureen said, breaking the silence, turning to look at Brian. "The new president of the university is not one to drone on. And it was important for me that you be there with Mam gone..." Maureen's voice trailed off.

"So, what will your new title be?" Brian asked.

"The full title will be Vice President and Director of Research. Rather fancy for a university title, don't you think?"

"I'm impressed," Brian said.

"My primary responsibility will be partnering the various university disciplines with corporations and government entities, improving their internal workflow processes and product development." After a brief pause, Maureen continued, "Almost didn't take the position, though," Maureen said, looking down at the slate patio.

Brian turned to face Maureen and asked, "Why?"

"They didn't want me to teach anymore. They wanted me to be strictly an administrator. I told them thanks, but no thanks. Teaching is important to me. A certain gentleman I know, quite a few years ago—at the dining room table right back there, in fact," Maureen tilted her head back toward the house, "taught me the importance of taking the time to help a person understand even the most difficult problem. Patience and perseverance can make all the difference in the world in helping someone solve what might seem unsolvable, he taught me. That to me is more important than fancy titles." Maureen reached out and took Brian's hand in hers.

"With the title comes a full professorship," Maureen added, somewhat embarrassed.

"Now I'm *really* impressed," Brian said, smiling.

"Actually, I don't know whether I should thank you or blame you for all of the notoriety," Maureen said, raising one eyebrow in mock indignation as she looked at the man sitting next to her. "Sending those corporations our way with research projects and, of course, the generous funding."

"The companies asked my advice on who I thought would be best suited to help them solve their problems. And I told them: you. And, it would appear, you proved me right," Brian said.

"Research at the university has really taken off," Maureen said, shaking her head. "I must admit that it's been good for the students, getting them involved in the research projects. Trying to solve real-life problems, working together with their professors, and interacting with corporations has helped them better understand what the textbooks are trying to convey. It has helped quite a few students land jobs after they've graduated. And, of course, the corporate funding is very much appreciated by the powers that be.

"Matthew's been very supportive of my career. He's a well-respected English professor at the university. He took time off when Moira was born and now with Clare. If it wasn't for him, none of this would have happened," Maureen said, with a smile.

Brian and Maureen sat quietly as the minutes passed by, enjoying the slow-moving clouds that paraded along. Little Clare switched positions and began nursing on the other side after Maureen adjusted her clothing. The sucking sound slowed down as it seemed sleep was next for the little one.

"I was sorry to hear about Padraig," Brian finally said, breaking the silence. "I should have been here for the funeral."

"No. It was so sudden—a heart attack. One day he was fine, then, well, Jimmy found him in the basement of the pub. An ambulance was called, and he was taken to the hospital. He was alert when I visited him there in the afternoon. He knew his time was up. The doctor had told him that he'd had a rather significant heart attack. He insisted that he didn't want a big to-do for a funeral. He just wanted to be laid to rest next to his wife and his daughter," Maureen said, looking over to where Moira continued to play in the sandbox.

"That evening I went to visit him and, well, he was gone."

Maureen chuckled as she looked down at her crossed legs. "But so much for not having a big to-do for a wake. The church service was standing room only, like Mam's. After he was put to rest under the tree next to his wife and little girl, it seemed like the entire county showed up at the pub. Nora outdid herself, putting out a nice spread of food, and Jimmy, well, he was prepared. He had ordered extra kegs of beer and cases of wine and brought in additional bartenders."

Maureen leaned over to pat Brian on his knee and laughed out loud. "And guess who showed up at the funeral and afterward at the pub?" she asked, soothing little Clare, who had been briefly disturbed by the sudden convulsion of Maureen's chest when she broke out laughing.

Brian looked at Maureen, shaking his head. He had no idea. "Who?"

"Padraig's two lady friends," Maureen replied with a big smile.

"You knew about them?" Brian asked, surprised.

Maureen nodded her head. "Everyone knew about them. How long do you think a secret like that could be kept in a village like this? Mam and I had known about them for years. We, along with the people in the village, had the good manners not to say anything to Padraig. If he was happy and the ladies were happy—so be it."

"Did the ladies know about each other?" Brian asked with a smile, thinking back to the time he and Padraig had found themselves in the lingerie section of the dress shop in Galway.

"Well, if they didn't know about each other before, they certainly did after that day. They sat together during the service. They stood next to each other at the gravesite, and they spent the afternoon and evening together at a table in a corner of the pub. The entire time, you could hear the two of them laughing. When Jimmy and Nora finally closed the pub, well into the early hours of the next day, Jimmy put the two of them in a taxi together. I can only imagine the tales they told each other," Maureen finished, trying to suppress another outbreak of laughter as she closed shop and handed the sleeping Clare to Brian to hold. Brian gently shifted Clare in his arms so the sun wouldn't be in her face, as her mother had done.

Adjusting her clothes, Maureen said in a somber voice, "We met in Conor's office for the reading of Padraig's will. Padraig had left one-fifth of the pub to Conor. Padraig thought it would be a good idea to have a lawyer involved in the pub's operation. One-fifth to Daniel. Padraig thought Daniel had a good marketing sense. The rest he left to me. What am I going to do with a pub?" Maureen said, looking at Brian. "I have enough to do at the university. So, of my three-fifths, I gave one-fifth to Nora and one-fifth to Jimmy. Those two are the ones who really run the pub, now that Padraig is gone." Maureen shrugged her shoulders as if to say that her decision was a no-brainer.

"One thing I don't understand. In his will, Padraig included a clause that if Conor were to ever be heard telling an Irish joke, he would forfeit his share of the pub. His share would go to me. That seemed very strange. I must admit I don't have a clue what Padraig was thinking," Maureen said, shaking her head.

It was Brian's turn to laugh out loud as he held the sleeping Clare away from his chest so as not to wake her. Maureen turned toward Brian with an inquisitive look. Brian tried to stifle his laughter. When he had some semblance of control, he turned to Maureen and said, "Someday I'll tell you what's behind Padraig's bequest." Brian shook his head as he looked down at the little one in his arms, who moved slightly as a smile blossomed across her tiny face.

Moira came over and stood next to her mother. She looked up at her mother, who picked her up and placed her on her lap. Moira ignored the baby but stared at the older man. After a few moments, Moira grew restless and wriggled her way down from her mother's lap.

Maureen looked at her older daughter and smiled. "Moira," Maureen said, getting her daughter's attention before continuing, "why don't you go and get *him*." Moira looked at her mother then at the back of the house. She didn't have to be told who *him* was, as she skipped across the patio over to the back door and went inside. Brian was oblivious to the mother–daughter conversation, as he was captivated by the little one who was sound asleep in his arms.

The back door opened slowly. First one front paw reached out tentatively, searching, finally finding the slate patio below. Then a second front paw reached out and joined the other front paw on the patio below. Slowly, two rear paws reluctantly made their way through the door down onto the patio. Moira closed the door behind her and followed. Then she moved ahead of the slow-moving furry animal, leading him over to where her mother was sitting. The two of them neared the bench under Maureen's watchful eyes.

Maureen reached over to take Clare from Brian's reluctant arms. Cradling the still-sleeping Clare, Maureen said, "I thought you might like to see an old friend." Brian looked at Maureen, trying to figure out who she was talking about.

Someone from the pub? The village? But he didn't see anyone behind the bench as he looked over his shoulder.

Dog had made his way to the side of the bench, with his tongue lolling from the side of his mouth. Moira urged him on past the side of the bench to the front, where numerous feet rested on the gray stone slates. Brian turned his head back from the house, not seeing anyone, and started to look at Maureen, when his eyes drifted downward. Brian and Dog locked eyes on each other. Dog's stationary tail began to wag slowly, picking up momentum, sweeping back and forth. Brian stood up and moved over to where a much older Dog was standing with a mostly gray coat of fur. Brian first kneeled and then sat down next to Dog, resting his back against the bench with his legs outstretched. He reached out and began scratching his old friend behind his ears. Slowly Dog lay down next to Brian, resting his head on Brian's thigh, eyes staring up at Brian, tail continuing to move back and forth more slowly.

"Well, old boy, would you look at us now," Brian said. Overwhelmed with emotion, tears began to roll down his cheeks. As he continued to look at his old friend, his thoughts drifted back in time and tapped his memories from long ago. The time he first met Dog under the kitchen table, Dog's endless search of the patio for dropped clothespins, the long walks he and Dog would take together. Dog being the village greeter, waiting patiently by the benches across from the pub, letting children pet him. Brian's walks with Moira and Dog. Brian brushed away some tears. Maureen handed him the cloth she had used to shield Clare from the sun.

With her head tilted to one side, Moira turned to her mother quizzically after seeing the man with tears.

Maureen smiled at her daughter and said in a soft voice, "Tears of joy."

Moira sat down on the patio on the other side of the animal and helped the kind-looking man pet Dog, whose eyes remained fixed on the older of the two humans on either side of him.

Clare had decided nap time was over and let her mother know it by wriggling in her mother's arms and letting out a short, loud cry. Sensing that something needed changing, Maureen stood up and went into the house to change the little one's diapers.

* * *

With Clare wearing a clean diaper, Maureen opened the back door and stepped down onto the patio. Moira's voice traveled back to her. Maureen had started to walk toward the bench but stopped suddenly.

"What was my Nana like?" Moira asked, looking at the man sitting across from her.

Brian looked up from Dog and peered at the little girl, smiling, before he turned his head to gaze at the fields beyond the stone wall. After a moment, Brian turned back toward the young girl, who stared at him intently. "Ah, your Nana was a very kind and loving person. She was very generous and helped those who were in need." Brian paused, then nodded at the animal resting between Moira and him. "She took Dog in, one cold and raining night when he was hungry and had no place to go."

Brian paused again, this time observing a passing cloud in the sky before he went on. “When your Nana smiled, the rain would stop, the clouds would disappear, and the sun would shine brightly. At nighttime when she smiled, the stars would come out and twinkle with delight.” Brian looked at Moira, who had a big smile on her face.

“However,” Brian paused and put on a serious face, “if she was mad at you, uh-oh, watch out!”

Moira eyes grew wide, and her smile disappeared. “Was she ever mad at you?” she asked.

“Yep.” Brian nodded his head.

“What did she do?” Moira asked, her voice rising.

“Oh, she chased after me, raising her finger, shaking it at me.” Brian raised his arm up and pointed a finger, shaking it.

“What did you do?” Moira asked, her eyes glued to the man sitting across from her.

“Well, I up and ran away from her as fast as I could,” Brian said, pumping both arms up and down like he was running.

“Did she ever catch you?” Moira asked, her voice filled with suspense.

“Nope, I ran too fast,” Brian said, still pumping his arms up and down.

“What did my Nana do then?”

“Well, I would wait until your Nana tired herself out and turned around and headed back to the house,” Brian said, no longer pumping his arms up and down. In a hushed voice, he continued, “Then I would quietly follow her, sneak up behind her, and tickle her until she started laughing,” Brian said, wiggling the fingers in both hands, pretending to tickle someone. “Then I would give her a big hug. And you and I both know that if you give someone a hug, a really big hug, they can't be mad at you anymore," Brian said, shaking his head.

Moira sighed. "I wish I'd met my Nana." Moira's voice trailed off as she continued to pet Dog.

"I wish you had met her too," Brian said wistfully. "But you know what?" he said with an upbeat voice. "I know she's up in heaven, looking down, and she has a big smile on her face because she knows that she has two beautiful granddaughters."

Moira looked up from Dog to the man sitting across from her and saw that he was serious, nodding his head up and down. In response, she slowly nodded her head up and down.

With moist eyes, Maureen made her way over to the bench. "Shall we head down to the pub?" she said to Brian and her older daughter.

Brian looked up from Dog and nodded before saying, "I think Dog and I might take a short walk, if that's alright with you." He gestured toward the field of flowing wheat. "I'll bring him back, then I'll head on down."

Hearing the word "walk," Dog struggled to his feet, tail wagging.

Brian also struggled to his feet, using one arm on the wooden bench to help hoist himself up off the patio.

Maureen nodded, then reluctantly said, "Just a short walk. There's a box of snacks on the shelf in the laundry room, when you bring him back. You'll see them. For the dog—not you," she said with a smile. With a serious look on her face, Moira looked up at her mother.

"You mean I can't have one of Dog's snacks?" Brian asked, giving a wink and a smile to Moira.

"You can have a snack at the pub when you get down there," Maureen said, admonishing the silly man.

"Boy, she is one tough lady," Brian said, looking at Moira.

Moira nodded and smiled at Brian, then looked up at her mother.

"Just like her mother," Brian pronounced in a kind voice, looking at Maureen, who gently cradled her other child in her arms.

"Come on, Dog, adventure awaits," Brian said, giving Moira another wink before he turned back to a slightly rejuvenated, if not eager, Dog. The two old companions slowly made their way across the patio, through the opening in the stone wall, and out into the high flowing wheat, where Dog immediately disappeared, leaving a narrow trail of divided wheat stalks behind him. Following Dog, Brian soon disappeared, swallowed up by a field of golden wheat that he and his Clare had first gazed upon so many years ago.

ACKNOWLEDGMENTS

MANY THANKS TO Tom Clark and Charlie Dullea, whose encouragement motivated me to carry on until the final word, of the final sentence, of the final page of this book. Thanks also to Jacquelin Cangro and Erin Willard, whose editing skills sharpened the focus of the story while providing this novice with a valuable education along the way. Also, I would like to thank the folks at AuthorImprints who provided me with valuable guidance and introduced me to the world of publishing.

This entire journey would not have been possible without the support of my wife Lynn, who tolerated the ongoing mess of papers on the dining room table and elsewhere as this story was written.

ABOUT THE AUTHOR

P.F. TORGERSEN has made trips to Norway and various parts of Great Britain in addition to numerous trips to the Emerald Isle. From Dublin to Belfast, from Waterford to Londonderry, along the Wild Atlantic Way, the author has traveled to many locations of historical significance and incredible scenic sights within Ireland. The Irish people, with their "gift of the gab," enhance the beauty of the land and provide a charming welcoming to all, inspiring the setting of *Two Tomorrows*.

www.ingramcontent.com/pod-product-compliance
Lightning Source LLC
LaVergne TN
LVHW100509110826
845146LV00002B/563